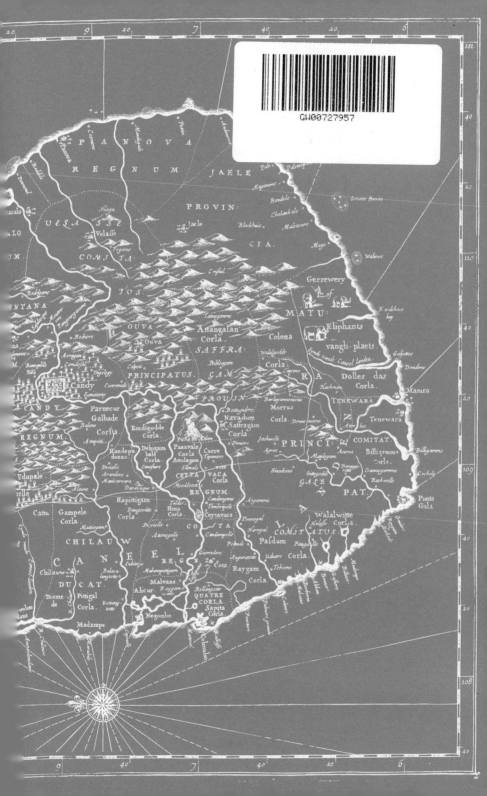

THE MAGISTRATE OF GOWER

BY THE SAME AUTHOR

The Spiral House (2013)

THE
MAGISTRATE
OF GOWER

CLAIRE ROBERTSON

UMUZI

Published in 2015 by Umuzi
an imprint of Penguin Random House South Africa (Pty) Ltd
Company Reg No 1953/000441/07
Estuaries No 4, Oxbow Crescent, Century Avenue, Century City, 7441,
South Africa
PO Box 1144, Cape Town, 8000, South Africa
umuzi@randomstruik.co.za
www.randomstruik.co.za

First edition, first printing 2015
1 3 5 7 9 8 6 4 2

ISBN 978-1-4152-0764-2 (Print)
ISBN 978-1-4152-0884-7 (ePub)
ISBN 978-1-4152-0885-4 (PDF)

Cover design by Joey Hi-Fi
Text design by Monique Cleghorn
Set in 11pt on 16pt Adobe Caslon

Printed and bound in India by Replika Press Pvt. Ltd.

To James
and
To Philip

CONTENTS

I

THE
WITHERING
LOFT

1

I N THE END, YOU COULD choose to say no more than this: that in the high summer of 1938, in a courtroom in the town of Gower in the Union of South Africa, a case of arson came to an abrupt and irregular end, confounding those who had followed the matter and prompting speculation that approached, but did not quite deliver, scandal.

Even before it ended so suddenly, the case had been variously interpreted, and to its end likewise were ascribed reasons that reflected the view of the person holding the floor far more than they did the facts of the matter. The magistrate was corrupt—. The magistrate was afraid—. He was in league with the sorry creature in the dock or at least bent on rescuing the reputation of the people that the accused, and the magistrate, could be said to belong to: the theories veered from venality to cowardice to a clannish and ignorant break with form. They agreed only in that none admitted any part for honour – but then honour was not in fashion that year.

The magistrate before whom the case was heard was only three years in his post at the time in question, a circumstance that may suggest a younger man. He was in fact well into middle age, having come late to the office, and both the lateness of the honour and its eventual conferral, like the opinions about the court case, had as much to do with the place as any lack or ability in him. The place, and the time.

His fifty-four years had straddled the turn of a century and the end of an age. Impossible as it is to imagine him as a baby, he had been born in his parents' bed in the low second room of a farmhouse by the light of oil lamps and at the hands of the cook and his own aunt, in the mature years of Victoria's reign (although she was his mother's queen, not his), a time that claimed to recognise in itself the destination of mankind. The farm was so remote and white men so sparse that the eventual magistrate had been on this earth for fully nine months before his family's wagon was inspanned for a veld communion where he could be put before a dominee to be baptised, under a white sky in a circle of thorn trees. They wet his head as Hendrik for his father's side and Buchanan for his Scots dam. He was by family Vos.

His eventual courtroom, under the portrait of Victoria's great-grandson, was the prized building of a modern town. It was lit by electric light, and among the sounds that reached it were those of telephones and motors and the wireless. There were paraffin refrigerators in some of the homes and a bioscope on Friday and Saturday nights. Many of these things were not that new to the wider world; they had come forth in the years just before or after he, among the women's strong hands, had drawn breath and bawled his toothless bawl at the reed ceiling, but most of them had only recently reached the town where he presided. A place accustomed to catching up to the world, it had, however, quickly grown used to such wonders.

By then the world, although it had delivered man (and woman, moreover) from toil, was poised at the top of another cycle of woe.

Between boyhood and now, at the previous century's end, he had ridden his horse to war, Victoria's war on his people, or theirs on her, and it is at the end of his war that his story begins, on a slope of open ground divided by train tracks, among men littering the field like standing stones, awkward without rifles or ponies to keep their hands busy, bored with the end of things and with only the clink of bridles and their low mutter breaking the new silence.

Hendrik 'Henry' Buchanan Vos, who will be old someday, who was a small boy once, is seventeen when he picks his way between the men in the field, moving from the table where he leaves his rifle and gives his name and age, to his friend who is at the far side of the rising ground.

As he passes among them, men shift and make space for him, glance at him and prepare their faces and bodies to greet him. He has his hat on, pulled low and tight on his brow, but even so he is recognised. He has worked out, in the year or so of his small fame, that this is its effect on people: when they first see him, they are confused for a moment into remembering him. The men in the field tilt their heads with a question and their hands stir to claim him as someone they know; their minds trip on the message brought by their eyes and by their memory of a representation of him in a photograph or biograph that they have seen.

The biographs, the Mutoscopes, the Living Pictures, this new arsenal of penny heroics and falsehood. *A Sneaky Boer* was the title of one such marvel of the age, its wildly popular perfidy still recalled decades later by the Africanders with disgust: in the moving picture's twitching square of light, an upright Khaki in a pale field yawns and leans on his rifle to sleep. The Odeon orchestra kettledrums signal fear and calumny, and from behind the field's lush tussocks there lope the pair of Boerish sneaks, simian in slouch hats and dark jackets slung with bandoliers, two on one, to strike him, in a crash of chords, from behind and with so criminal a weapon as a knife. The tussocky field calls itself Transvaal, but it is the Yellow Hills of Blackburn, Lancashire, and anyone with the eyes to see that no African field ever overgrew itself like that can see these are no sorts of Boer but enemy actors called out to rouse England with slurs and fancy tricks of light on this, the war's other front.

This is the root of Henry Vos's fame:

Almost ten months ago, at the start of his war, he was taken and captioned in the *Illustrated London News* as 'A Young Boer' and a few months after this – was he the only fair boy in all the two republics? – made the subject of the less-than-a-minute biograph *On Commando, A Young Boer Mounts Up*.

In the photograph he is hatless and unmounted, standing at his pony's shoulder. The pony, Samson, is taking this chance to rest his left fore-hoof. Was Samson wary of the hooded man behind the high-standing camera box? Did seeing one man hiding behind a machine make it easier for him when he later noticed the greater biograph box in front of which his master mounted him, and towards which he was then made to trot, one of them pretending to be himself, one doing as he was told? The pony would have been spared the result of all this effort, but there was nowhere for Henry to hide as, without translation – there ought to have been some moderation – he was suddenly there, the length of his body, the stretch of his thigh brought so close by the size of him on the church hall bioscope screen as he reached for the stirrup, the saddle, and was up.

Perhaps, in the way these things play out, by the time Henry Vos – or at least the grey, black and white pattering on the screen – had become him mounted on Samson, and the two of them were in motion, it was usual, no longer uncanny. Just a palsied boy waving from the saddle in this jittering light, hesitating as if thinking he ought to do something else, something more, then taking the decision to trot past the camera and off the screen.

The thigh, the size, the shocking sense of his presence, this was the experience of Adaira van Brugge, watching the biograph many years after it was made, sitting alone on a folding chair towards the middle of an otherwise empty room as the projectionist, Servaas Adler, ran it for her from his high booth at the back of the hall in the town where the magistrate held his court. Adaira blushed to imagine it being seen all those years before, between its fellow attractions on the ancient reel, proof of the actual moving world brought home: *Rt. Honourable Cecil Rhodes Riding in Hyde Park* (Sssss!), *The King and Queen of Italy*, *His Honour Paul Kruger Doffing His Hat* (Hurrah!) and, at last (painfully thrilling to her to see him up there the first time Mr Adler ran the reel, thrilling and shocking surely to Henry himself those first times in a camp tent or at a concert for the wounded), *A Young Boer Mounts Up* (the evening's loudest cheer).

The boy on the pony in the biograph was Henry Vos before Adaira was born. Before this church hall existed. Henry on Samson did not belong to her, and she watched it only that one afternoon, although Mr Adler was generous and ran it over and over, four times perhaps. Many in the town were gentler with one another for that brief week, once the shouting for the wagon procession had died to an echo and the fierce faces had calmed back down, and they were made to count their losses and perhaps recognise in themselves a diminished thing.

Henry on Samson. That was the job Adaira had set herself: inventing young Henry, and how else to begin to do so but picture him watching his mute self mount Samson and trot towards himself where he sat in the half dark among his fellows, with the men around him shoving him and reaching to touch him, his head or shoulders, and those further out craning with unguarded looks, and some of those looks asking, What is it that makes you the one among many?

But the surprise and envy give way to ownership, and by the time the war proper starts and the playacting is done with, Henry, although he is considered to have unreasonable fame for a boy of no rank or proven courage, is unshakeably a mascot, his face known in the music halls of Johannesburg, where *A Young Boer Mounts Up* is a feature of every show, and known for a split second even in Piccadilly, where it is tolerated and then taken off as the war bites hard and grows shameful there, and people's tastes swing towards the like of *Sneaky Boer*.

That much Adaira found out for herself, when at last she

took what Henry told her and what she had invented, and measured it against the record the world had made of him.

Henry Vos in the field, at the turn of the century, knowing he is known to many, pulls his hat lower on his brow and pretends to be in faraway thought as a reason not to meet any eyes as he moves among the men milling beside the railway tracks. Good for the cause, he has had a lucky war, with a score of brothers, a dozen fathers, to watch out for him in any battle, any ride through open country. Where he is now, this field that is the end of his war, are perhaps three hundred men, down from their ponies, stripped of their rifles and bandoliers, not knowing what to do with their hands but pluck at the space where their Mausers should be and look up at Henry's passing among them. They watch him with unseeing eyes that sharpen in recognition and dull again when they see the trick of fame for what it is.

Samson and the rest of the horses are corralled some distance from the men, on higher ground. They can be seen, and can be smelled when the wind shifts and brings the good stink of pony. Between the horses and their riders there are the railway tracks and a line of scowling Khakis, bayonets in position like figures on a painted backdrop. Their martial posturing disgusts the men in the field, who know it is not weapons that keep this order but the weight of their own surrender. The Boer fighters lift their hats, play the brims through their hands, replace them, shift their weight from foot to foot in the way that ponies do.

Henry finds Clem at the far edge of the field, and Clem

greets him, as he often does, with boys' mockery: 'Young Boer! For it is he!' Henry narrows his eyes, bumps shoulders with his friend.

The two of them stiffen: they hear a train, the one they have been waiting for, the one that will take the men and the boys to the next thing that will happen to them.

After a day and a night on the train Henry will see the sea for the first time. 'First everything' is what he will come to call that time, those few years between school and his return to his mother's farm, when he graduated to war: first orders from a man not his late father or elder brothers, first shot fired directly at a man, first man dying alongside him. He has yet to see a woman die. Yet to kiss someone who is not his mother or aunt, see a woman die … there must be other things he has not done, chapter-worthy things, things that when they arrive shove a boy forward an appreciable distance, but these are the few he can name. Nonetheless, Henry believes he is already rich in experience, on the train heading through the Colony.

Will this count as an absolute first, the sea towards which the train is jerking and swaying? When it arrives, he puts 'first sight of the sea' in a category lower than the things he has done and seen done by men, puts it no higher than first machine gun; the sea seems to inhabit a queasy no man's land between the industrial and the natural worlds where it rocks and slops, slicked with oil and so very far below the hard edge of the harbour wall.

The men arrive in Cape Town at dawn and spend the rest of the morning at the docks, waiting for the weather to ease –

or so Clem the good scout finds out – and for ships. Unseen ships are coming for them the way the train came.

'So here is the sea,' Henry thinks. 'Now I have seen the sea.'

But in the afternoon the Khakis shout at them and they are on their feet again – herded, because they do not march, the Boers – back to the station. They climb up into the dim narrow cars of another train and begin another journey, to a safer harbour.

The new train runs out of the city and through sparse villages and stretches of swampland, with mountains at the edge of the plain to the right, and the trees and grasses as green as summer veld. Some of the men in the rough car are dozing or wiped down by shock. Clem is asleep and leaning against the car wall. Henry stands, his forearms pressed to the planks of the wall, and looks out. Parallel to the train, a gravel-grey ridge of hills meets the coast; the train swings around and finds the last possible gap between the ridge and the water, and once it is beyond the hills, Henry crosses to the other side of the car, and is rewarded with a better sea.

Here, low-growing things at the edge meet a blinding smooth stretch of sand that slides under the water. Henry swallows, wants to shake the men around him awake to see this, wants to keep it to himself. He thinks the train might carry him away again, but after a while forgets to worry about this and breathes in the savoury air as the train holds to the coast.

The tracks run close to the sea, so close that for a while Henry is looking down onto wet rocks and the rush of foaming water. There are ungainly dark birds, red-billed, yellow-billed, and gulls with pure markings. The train cuts along a small bay, then around a headland, then reaches the start of a wider, flatter bay where the water is the colour of thick glass, of the broken edge of glass looked into from an angle. Henry first sees the bay – the slice of it he can make out between the slats of the cattle-car wall – in a lazy instant between waves, so that for a moment it is a lake, a dam, a disappointment. But here comes the next one, a swell rising the width of the bay. He holds his breath. He, standing facing the car wall, is moved sideways along the face of the wave. The wave presses towards the shore, towards the track. The shadow of the train reaches across the sand to the water, and the wave is lit by the low sun; he can see into it, into the sliding berm of it. Although he is watching between two planks, and his narrow view is broken every time they sway hard and the planks shift together, the wave fills his whole sight.

It is not his first wave, surely, but it feels as though it might be. Henry remembers to breathe, pulls a deep breath into his lungs and holds it. Now. It must be now that it breaks … but the wave holds the line, its far edges gathering more water to it, the good torture holding. The little train is midway across the blunt bay. The wave, pulling its waters from the sea to the point either of collapse or separation, must surely break now, but at the instant that it must, it turns into a close and gritty wall of scrub on white sand. Henry pulls back from his spy slats. And then they are past the dune, and the water is flat, broken, already falling back from the beach.

Some few miles along from Henry's wave the train eases to a stop at a neat town between a mountain slope and the sea.

Ahead, the tracks end at a stone wall, beyond which are blue-gums and shade.

The men, prodded off the trucks by their Khaki guards, still do not march, will never march, but they shuffle into rows of four or five abreast and make something of their roadside delivery from the end of the line, along the main road, to the naval dockyards. People – women – stop to watch them and the men notice that none of them – not Boer, not Khaki – is getting all of their approval. Three wagons follow with the wounded.

At the docks there will be time for:

– Waking the next dawn on a wide sloping quay to see a bristling steamship at anchor some way out and somehow aimed at them.

– Being called to stand, Henry and Clem, among bored men in the late morning, to make themselves known and claim a parcel apiece from the Vos farm, Craigievar, and Clem's family's farm, which shares a fence with it. There is a hiss of interest in Henry.

– Waking in the night to see the ship lit with electric lights and alive with ape shapes among the shadows. Beyond the ship, a lighthouse in the bay, another first, flashes, and he spends some moments, hunched over his knees, trying to learn its rhythm and predict it.

Before another dawn they are loaded by relays of lighters.

Word passes among men on the seaward side of the steamer and they point to a smaller ship at anchor: 'Cronje is there,' they say. The prison ship adds to Henry's store of things to explain the world: a terrible thing, isolated, visible to all, holding the general unreachably far from his men but in their sight.

There is also:

– The man Engel, of whom Clem will write in a letter and who Clem will plead with Henry not to 'become': 'Engel we saw at Simon's Town that day, Engel on the ship.'

Adaira, discovering Clem's letter, had grown alert for spoor of this hiding Angel, of what he was that Henry was not, or not yet.

Among Adaira's store of things to explain Henry there were, of course, gaps. She had filled the first of these with him on board the steamship, looking at the sea.

A Khaki who has been made peevish by his unending nausea tells them they are headed for a terrible rock – a rock island with constant wind and no water, and tents somehow pitched on it.

'Seabird and sea biscuit for your dinner,' he says, 'and seaweed for pud.'

Oh, and this, because Adaira had it from her own dominee: his, Dominee Ysel's, uncle, leading a prayer as the ship gains a pulse and pushes off into False Bay, with the sorrowing theme, 'That is the last we will see of Africa, perhaps forever' – only to find themselves mocked by half a day more of African mountains to port, a reminder that matters are never so neat as in a biograph, or a photograph captioned 'Africa, Farewell'.

Or perhaps that mistimed prayer is just another thing the defeated men believe they have fumbled.

This they also believe: that unless more of them surrender, and those who lay down their arms swear a loyal oath to the queen empress, they will end their days wherever the ship is headed.

They see dolphins. Clem sees a whale, but is uncertain about its size, colour and conduct, and concedes it might not have been.

They taste ship's biscuit and do not mind it much. Perhaps seabird will be no worse than over-brined biltong or the tinned salt-beef they are given on board.

Nothing they say out loud seems unreal, nothing quite real.

After three weeks at sea, the Khaki's barren rock could be smelled before it was seen, in wafts between the coal fug of the ship. It had a good scent, green, with an edge of the spices of a store cupboard, sharing the currents of air with a sweeter rot.

Their prison island turned out to be, in the words of the Khaki who had mocked them with the rock, 'fucking paradise, you stupid cunts', and Ceylon.

Henry made money out of this; presumably those who had bet on the rock kept quiet about it, and they and those holding slips for Australia or England itself paid up.

'Fucking paradise you stupid c—s' appeared among his things, in a crabbed hand on the blank side of a postcard: Adaira recognised it as Henry's writing, and his sense of humour. The postcard photograph was of a boy, a water buffalo, palm trees. Paradise.

He is seventeen. The ship docks.

Close by, Ceylon smelled of rubber, open drains and burning oil, at least at the docks. Worse still, among the brown-skinned men on the quay was an audience of white women and men come to watch their arrival. Some of the women were young and pretty, which caused the men at the ship railings to straighten their spines and grow stern while their guilty eyes stole looks.

A city man among the farmers on the ship forced a joke, 'Can't resist a real man, eh?', and at this even the shy greybeards eased their grim brows and the gloom of being spectated shifted, a little.

The gangplank crashed into place and the prisoners left the ship in swaying, stumbling single file. Ahead of Henry, a Boer fighter lifted his hat as he neared a pair of girls sharing a parasol. In response they brought handkerchiefs to their noses as though to block his smell; it seemed to be a rehearsed or at least collaborative insult. In a few steps Henry and Clem reached them; the girls' eyes flicked over Henry and now it was they who drew up their bodies and lifted their brows to hold themselves wide-eyed.

'Victory without a shot fired, brother,' Clem muttered to his back. Henry coloured and jabbed an elbow backwards.

At last they were through the British gauntlet and being loaded again. Henry found his chink in the wall of the goods car and braced himself to watch Ceylon open out from the crowded town. Behind him in the car one of the men was saying with disgust that 'burgher', their mark of citizenship, was an insult in Ceylon – that this was what they called the half-whites here. But the next moment men were laughing, calling others to come to the car wall to see: bearded women! Bearded women in the fields! Cingalese men with hair to their waists, and apparently in skirts, were working their way abreast across a paddy.

The little train wound its way towards the hills. A low, sea-driven storm was threatening at its back. There were valleys, more paddies. He cried out once, 'Elephant!' but it had gone by the time Clem got to his gap in the car wall. It had looked, impossibly, like a tame creature, freckled with pink on its forehead.

Many of the fellows in the car were pressed to the wood. Now the green was broken by a white tower rising from a bulbous dome, in a clearing on a hillock near the tracks. The train was straining up the incline, giving the men time to take in the scene: not a white man in sight, but many brown men with bare chests and, where their trousers should be, the hitched-up-skirt affair. The women were draped in coloured cloth. Their dark hair was loose or in a single plait down their backs; their arms were bare and from this distance there was little to choose in beauty among them, mostly slim and all gently draped as they were.

'The pink over there with the jar! Her!'

'Mine is the one next to her. Look this way, lovely!'

The women were circling the thick, low tower, placing their jars and bowls at the base and backing away. The train left the scene and Henry, standing alert for what the next bend of the track would bring, was elated by this glimpse of a new religion, by the sense of Ceylonese gods, fresh gods, reclining vastly out there.

They left the small farms and paddies at the edge of the jungle. Now entire hills were subdued by a single crop – ranks of slim trees, each with a cut across the trunk like a regimental sash, each wearing a bucket at its waist; or a spread of fat, low hedges cut through with red-earth roads, neat as a garden, and which they recognised from their wives' or mothers' painted tea tins. From time to time a house with shutters and gardens broke the fields. Here were horses, white women.

The afternoon dimmed to night as the little train moved steadily deeper into the island, through tunnels, across a viaduct spanning a gorge. Men on either side of Henry down the length of the car settled to sleep against the swaying boards.

2

T HE BRITISH OF THE ISLAND of Ceylon did not visit Diyatalawa Prisoner of War Camp, or none of them but the governor, who passed through on a tour of inspection and accepted at the end of it a stiff delegation that began by protesting this or that indignity and eventually asked only for so reasonable a concession as a readier supply of fresh fruit, which was granted. Matters of censored reading material, censored letters, the insolence of the guards and the ban on political songs – these were the province of wartime, and, even had he been inclined to rule on them, which he emphatically was not, the governor could not have ordered otherwise than the officer in charge of the camp.

If this Ridgeway and his aides were the only civilians to enter the camp, however, they were not the only ones to take an interest in it; it was the custom among the white men and women of the plantations to drive out on a Sunday afternoon and stop along the road that rose in a lazy zigzag out of the wide bowl in which the camp was set, and picnic with a view over the place where the lines of rubber trees and the dense, hunched tea plants were interrupted by this agglomeration of sheds and stamped earth.

The British picnickers were too far away for the men to make out more than that some of their number were women, women in white skirts and large hats, leaning small parasols on their shoulders. One of the men in Henry's shed, watching the Sunday-afternoon spectators, named the thing that bothered him about the scene – 'Do you see, there is not a single child!' – and this was thereafter remarked on by one or more of them every time Sunday afternoon came around, because it was known that the British sent their children for other people to raise when they were barely old enough to sit on a horse, proof that the mothers of that nation were not outdone by the iron-cold hearts of the men.

This was where they would meet their enemy now: in sentiment and name-calling.

One Sunday there were no carriages or carts on the steep road, no parasols, and the Diyatalawa men, although they congratulated one another on being left in peace, felt lonelier than ever and somewhat frightened. The next Sunday the picnickers were back and it had only been a horse race in Kandy that had drawn away their crowd. 'People may not like to be watched,' Henry told Adaira, 'but most people want to be seen.'

In the environs of the camp was a small house that had been taken over by the camp commander; it had housed the headmaster of the Diyatalawa Industrial School before the steam presses and looms were carted out and beds for the enemy combatants thrown into the deep sheds, and kitchens made where the hay store had been.

Sharing the bowl with the camp was a rubber plantation and manufactory, only just visible from Diyatalawa. The planter and his family could be seen quite often passing the camp; two women of the household, for instance, headed past the main gate most mornings on glossy little horses, provoking in the men an appetite so sharp it flooded their mouths. The planter they saw more rarely, and guessed he was taking his ease on his veranda and sending out orders for the bleeding of this or that line of trees. A rubber-tree plantation seemed to be an easy, if not very interesting, way to make a living from the land.

Diyatalawa Camp, this scattering of uneven, angular blocks lying like tea dregs on a saucer, was set out in two sections with a broad roadway between them. The men called this road Commissioner Street, and named the two sections Krugersdorp and Steynsburg.

Henry came to rely on this naming habit, its way of stopping the blur of the world.

– Rambutan
– Mango
– Water buffalo

These were What We Eat.

– Scorpion
– Toad
– Snake, red and black
– Snake, green
– Lizard
– Cockroach
– Spider

These were Found in the Shed at Night.
And Some Men of Our Table were:

- Sippion
- Sojoerd Bergh
- Welthagen
- Loots
- Clem and his brother
- Him

Loots expected to be applauded for his trumpeting farts. Welthagen pleaded in his sleep. Bergh barely said a word, and then only to Sippion. Sippion it was who led the prayer over the blue buffalo meat.

On Commissioner Street the Human brothers might be opening their shop, setting machine cigarettes in rows in front of a pen-and-ink sketch of the Queen of the Netherlands and, in a nest of leaves, lychees. Further along, a Bothma would have a pack of cards for sale, and shoelaces, and a stack of fans woven from palm leaves. Henry would remember the camp's shops as being like the tea parties and storefronts little girls arranged for their terriers and dolls; he said he could see, though, that mounting a rough and muddy shop-like show along the conventions of home was, like the naming of things, a handhold.

Clem pushed Henry and told him to stop thinking, or Henry tripped Clem and said the crudest thing he knew, and they took off down the row, sometimes with a stick in hand to rattle along the corrugated walls of the sheds and infuriate the old men; then there might be a meeting at which he and Clem were debated, defended, accused, and before which they would inevitably be called to account and given a lesson in behaving, two sons to let a dozen fathers be fathers for the afternoon. It was something to look forward to or dread, at least, and the punishment varied according to who was on the committee that day. Getting onto the committee, being asked to leave it, the factional arguments and insults and congratulations when peace was forged, these were ways to fill the early evenings.

The day's monotony could be broken by sleep, reading in the sheds, attending a debate of the Endeavour Society or a Bible reading. Sometimes the Khakis tipped a load of ebony scraps inside the front gate and the men fell on the pile to snatch pieces for carving. There was a daily parade.

Clem and Henry were not the only boys in the camp – there was a whole shed for the thirteen-, fourteen- and fifteen-year-olds – but they were among a very few youngsters living with the grown men. Clem's brother had them in his shed, under his protection, and bought their good manners with the threat of the boys' shed – the orphans' shed, in reality.

Freed into the camp proper, the two of them became known among the prisoners; their health, hair length, the cleanliness of their shirts and their spirits were freely commented on, not just by their own table or shed, but by men unknown to them in the far reaches of Krugersdorp.

Engel, dark Engel of the quay, was in Krugersdorp. Over the first months in Diyatalawa he gathered the wickedest men of the camp to him, scoffers, desecrators of the Sabbath and worse. They slipped into Engel's shed, attracted like iron filings, and took the places of men who picked up their small bundles and their cork helmets and looked for somewhere else to live. In Engel's shed, about three dozen stock thieves, fugitives and shifty-eyed city men held just over half the long room in a stand-off with the disgusted and uneasy men in the rest of it. In the camp, the thousands of men had fallen into order under table corporals, shed captains and street sergeants, but in Engel's shed he ruled alone as chief. As each day heated up and those unlucky enough to have drawn cooking duty headed for the hay-barn kitchens, Engel's crew slept on; their dinner was on its way, parcelled in leaves and tiffin tins, hot and spiced and made by women's hands, and reaching them by the same smugglers' route that carried in tobacco, better fruit, pornographic postcards and brandy.

Engel's shed was easy to avoid; it stood in Henry's mind like a compass point that he need not steer towards.

The Boers of Diyatalawa Camp, held back as they were from being able to determine most of what they lived through each day, put store by luck and the arcana of tilting chance in their favour. They must live thus – wear these clumsy cork helmets and not their own soft hats, eat this blue meat and rice, do what their enemy told them in place of doing the telling – but while they pushed back, and scowled and chafed, they still made space for courting fortune.

The men behaved well in the face of fortune when it came for one of their fellows; they did not believe in a kind of physics of good luck wherein one man's good fortune diminished that which might come to another. Instead of resenting the luck of others, they tended to seek out the fortunate man, as though luck might still be hanging about him. The man who received a letter in which his mother or wife had fooled the Diyatalawa censors with her talk of 'red locusts' cleared from the crop with barely one of the farmhands 'bitten' would have visitors, guests to sit on the steps of his shed in the evening for pipes and a share of the good fortune of being – in the larger picture of not being – the ones with a bit of power. The man whose letter told of a family burned out of their home, of a wife and old mother and young children left on a hillside with no shelter but wide lines of wire, there to nurse their surviving children and bury those who died like valueless things, like victims of a grievous murrain and unfit for meat – that man was left alone.

This was the grand scheme of luck they learned from the letters: good or terrible fortune visited on them months before the news of it reached them. The daily matter of luck that did not matter was important too, and they found ways to make it show itself – scorpion fights, bouts between bare-fisted boxers in a quarrelsome hut, games of chance. The visiting minister who travelled from the Cape complained about the gambling; the minister jailed with them, Dominee Ysel's uncle, did not mention it.

So there was great misfortune, and there were small triumphs in games of chance, but of the luck of daily circumstances, apparently not much – maybe your food was fresh and edible for the span of a week or longer. Maybe you were not caught by the measles, or if you were, you beat the odds and survived. It could be that your hut was one of those where there was good company, one good fellow or a few of them to keep things calm and easy – but such everyday matters were not remembered as belonging to the place where the men romanced fortune, perhaps because they would not allow themselves to give the name 'lucky' to anything that came down from Victoria's men to Wilhelmina's.

And now, on one unremarkable day, all these sorts of luck – something months ago and as far away as home, something of the survival drive in a particular scorpion, the way it chose its moment, and most of all, the effect of good fortune on a man's days in camp – all of these sorts of luck found Henry in Diyatalawa.

This was the months-ago part as Adaira put it together:

Months ago and far away, a cousin of the planter who managed the small rubber estate next to Diyatalawa had been loaded onto a ship by her family in England. In British Ceylon she was to help with the birth and first months of the baby her cousin's wife was carrying and then either marry and stay there or come home buffered from her family by her own household.

On the island, Cyella Oofit, the planter's cousin, had cast one look at the borrowed bungalow, its isolation and meanness, and set her heavy jaw to being taken somewhere else as often as could be managed. This would have to be by horseback, and Cyella was indeed the second rider passing the main gate in Henry's first weeks at Diyatalawa. But the planter's pregnant wife was soon no longer up to the journey, or any movement beyond her closed veranda, and the planter's salary would not run to a syce.

The British girl could not, of course, ride out alone, but she had not failed to notice that beyond the ranked trees were three thousand men at the command of her countryman the colonel, and white like her – or not quite like her, being Boers, but white enough. This Cyella, said Henry, had a way of making her wants known and insisting on them being met – the way, so went his theory in later life, of both the un- and the very greatly loved. There was a photograph of her among Henry's things, a curiosity, in which Miss Oofit and another girl recline, draped in some sort of pale cloth, posing in the classical mode as ancient Romans. Adaira read the girl's appetites in her thick jaw and in her look of contempt for the camera. But her eyes also showed how much she wanted to be found lovable, thought handsome. Adaira invented for her a small, a physically small, pair of parents sunken into a featherbed in England, fearing their daughter's return.

Cyella Oofit would have an Africander syce and he could exercise an Army horse. Her cousin and the colonel lay down before her, Henry said, and she rolled over them like a monstrous toddler.

There was a system of parole rewards in operation at Diyatalawa, but the colonel must have stopped to think about the considerable fuss that would be made if a prisoner loaned out as a civilian's escort should escape; was this why he chose Henry for the job? He had a true friend and could have been warned of the suffering that would rain on Clem's head and the head of Clem's brother should he be so much as late back from his ride. Perhaps it was just that the colonel had taken Henry's measure as an obedient boy.

Clem crowed at the incredible good fortune that had found Henry – a chance at a horseback ride. A girl. Henry made promises about what he would bring back, and to try to earn his gift he spoke about the hardship of the close company of an English person, even if it was a girl. He and Clem washed his trousers and shirt and brushed his short jacket and begged dubbin and got to work on his boots. One of the men from their table clipped his hair. Henry would be allowed to change a small amount of the camp's good-fors into rupees, he was told, so long as he spent them only on food and accounted for every cent.

Henry stood with a pair of ponies at dawn on the lawn of the planter's house. Cyella, coming down the steps in her riding skirt and sola topi, perhaps ready to ignore him, looked him over a second time – looked at him in a way that made Henry, he said, want to check the buttons on his waistcoat and trousers, or otherwise place his hands between himself and her appraising eyes.

That first morning there was a man selling sweet cakes soaked with a cinnamon-and-lime syrup. Miss Oofit did not have an opinion one way or the other when Henry stopped in front of the old man squatting at a crossroads on a mat of huge leaves, the cakes set out in rows before him. Henry pointed and opened his hands; she shrugged but did not change the bad-tempered look on her face for one of worse temper, and he swung down from the saddle, offered his cent and quarter-cent coins.

The crossroads where they had stopped was barely up to the name; the larger of the two roads that met there was red dirt and scraped smooth for its traffic of men on foot and pairs of little girls in white blouses and patterned bright cloth rucked and tucked as skirts, and the odd bullock cart. From one end to the other of what he could see of the road it was walled with jungle where the trunks of hugely tall trees pushed beyond the tangled lower growth. Trees of this size stood with the ocean in his mind, first sights and as powerfully attractive as his wave had been.

This early in the morning the air held smoky light, and the light-heavy air shifted in the deep, wide trench of the road. There was the faraway bawling of a buffalo calf, and business to do without hurry, and he at last had his cakes.

The second road was little more than a broad footpath. As Henry remounted and clicked his tongue to get moving again, he looked down this track and saw on it a person wrapped shoulder to shin in orange, walking towards the road. He was holding a bowl and lifting a fold of cloth over his shoulder as he came. Henry guided his horse after Miss Oofit's but twisted in the saddle to watch the orange figure bow to the sweet seller, who placed one of the little cakes in his bowl.

Afterwards Henry would waste a few moments working out, from the size and cost of the banana-leaf parcel on his saddle, just how badly the Cingalese traders at the camp gates were cheating the men. And he would recall this into his fifty-fourth year: the smoky green trench, the bowl and cake, the man like a child's drawing of fire.

His second ride with the planter's cousin came three days later. He again drew the self-assured, stout little horse and walked her up to the planter's house to collect the other animal and wait for Miss Oofit. When she joined him on the driveway this time she did not climb the mounting block and slip into the saddle, but, fussing with her hat, told him to follow her on foot with both horses on the lead, and walked down the driveway.

When they were almost at the gate she at last declared herself ready to mount up and with no block nearby must, naturally, do so from his cupped hands, braced with her own hand on his shoulder.

For a moment his face was among her skirts and he could smell her body, and in the telling he stuck out his lower lip to blow this away from his nostrils as he might have done at the time when, with a great shove, he got her into the saddle.

The orange man, as Henry named him to Adaira, had been in his thoughts. He was, as Henry played over and over his easy gait, his bow to the sweet seller and his bowl, a distant figure, unreal, but Henry did not doubt that he would see him again, as he had known he would see the hills around the camp when he woke that morning, and Clem in the next bed. Henry had not been close enough to make out his face, but he felt that he would recognise him anyway.

That day Cyella Oofit's business with her hat and hand-mounting delayed them slightly so that they came to the old sweet seller just as the orange man was making his bow of thanks. Henry had rupees and cents in his waistcoat pocket and a paper packet he was charged with filling.

He slid from his pony, aware that Miss Oofit was impatient with this halt although, again, ready to indulge him.

The orange man, with his cake now in his bowl, stood at the sweet seller's side, quite still and looking over the riders as if he had rights – the rights of an uncle or a son – in the matter. Henry did not look directly at him. He raised a hand in greeting to the old sweet seller and looked over the rows of cakes. He considered counting them but could see that he would probably need all there were to meet the appetites of Hut 76 and, bringing out the paper sack, tried to indicate this to the old man – all, he wanted all of his cakes. The man smiled and shook his head, and the orange man said something in the local tongue. The sweet seller replied, and sat back, tucked his chin to his neck.

The orange man turned to Henry and said to him in slow, almost sleepy, and careful English: 'Young sir, this father is saying that he cannot be selling all of his cakes to one who is coming but on seldom days, for what might be the consequence? That those who are passing by after will think he has closed his business, and tomorrow they will not be saving their coppers for his cakes but spending them sooner on some other thing.'

To listen to him, Henry must look at him, and now he saw that the monk was not much older than he was; something in the way he walked, the calm way he dealt with his folds and bowl, had given the impression of a grown man. He had brown eyes, black hair, the faintest stain of colour in his cheeks.

Without a change in his manner the young monk asked: 'You are from the prison? The prison of the Boer?' He said the word 'Boer' in a curious way, his mouth kissing the air to make a noise that was not really like speech at all – more a sound to do with air and water – but 'prison' was enough for Henry to make out and he nodded. The orange man said something to the sweet seller, who listened gravely and then, apparently enjoying himself, sliced a wavering arm towards the cakes.

'Half. The father will sell you half,' the monk said.

With that, he seemed to step out of the conversation, although he did not move at all, and tuck himself away in his orange cloth. He kept his eyes on Henry, however, and his calm smile directed towards him.

The business was concluded, the cakes in the bag and coins and notes on the sweet seller's palm, and Miss Oofit was making a noise in her throat, but Henry risked taking longer to thank his orange man and feel again that unsettling sensation when their eyes met in a direct look – 'right in my eyes the way people don't do very often, you know', he told Adaira.

They rode off. Miss Oofit was saying something and he paid her enough attention to gather that it was about the Natives. This had been all she had talked of on their first ride, too – the Natives, their clothes or not-clothes, their smell, their lesserness, offered to Henry as a matter of form, as one might bring up the topic of weather with a farmer, or the prospects of the standing crop in his fields.

Henry was back in Diyatalawa before noon; Miss Oofit rode only in the morning. For much of the prison camp, the afternoon was for sleeping or at least staying almost perfectly still, and Henry, after giving out his parole cakes and news, likewise waited out the sun in Hut 76, most days. On two afternoons a week, however, he crossed to a particular edge of Krugersdorp, navigating by the hills that ringed the camp, to the shed of a man the men spoke of as 'the Great Vierro', an elderly Italian volunteer who did not always win the complete understanding of his new comrades with his arguments about utopianism and communistic rights in the fight against imperialism, but was nonetheless shyly admired for his erudition, and as much a mascot of the commandos as Henry.

The old man had cleared one end of his hut's long room and propped back the side panels to make a platform open to the light. In the centre was a bare bed frame laid with planks, and eight or so men had set stools in a half-circle in front of this.

Henry stripped off his cork helmet and jacket, his boots, stockings and trousers, then peeled his thinning shirt off his back and stepped, in his underwear, up onto the boards laid across the frame, and fitted his feet to the chalk marks on the wood. Vierro consulted a sheet of paper and called out adjustments to the way Henry was standing, then came forward and made the final few himself, lifting Henry's chin and pressing down on his bare shoulders. This week he was perhaps *First Watch*. The portraitists would fill in the Mauser and bandolier later, from memory, and give him a shirt and waistcoat, corduroys. But this could wait until they had, as Vierro said, mastered his anatomy.

Vierro's studio was one of the quietest places in the camp, with an engaged, private silence among the men, and other noises blocked by the soft scratching of charcoal sticks on butcher's paper. Henry did not find his task remotely uncomfortable. In fact, the disinterested but still closely focused regard of the men in Vierro's class was so different to what he was used to – so different, for instance, to the way Cyella Oofit looked at him – that it was almost a relief. His face and body were, to these quiet men, their own end, and, in a way that he could not quite explain, made his good looks a shared thing.

Vierro's was the last shed in its row, and the opened-up

part of it was on the side nearest the fence. Henry looked past the triple fence of barbed wire and a strip of cleared ground into what he called jungle but admitted was just an unruly pocket of growth. After resting his gaze on the patch of green for a while he mentally straightened up and made an effort to see all there was to see. He chose a branch and followed it to its tree, then tried to track that to the ground, but it was behind too many others. Then he followed a shaft of light among the trunks and it led him to a smooth-leafed low plant no more than the height of a man's knee. One of its slim assegai leaves was moving as regularly as a machine in an uneven circle – around, across, back. Around, across, back. Henry's mind emptied as he watched it and his jaw grew slack.

Vierro said, 'Chin, my son,' and Henry lifted his head. The moment he looked away from the curious leaf he lost it, and had to flick his eyes from plant to plant, then he remembered his sunbeam and tracked it, and there it was, lost but found again, moving privately to its own interrupted rhythm, with no one to see it but Henry, around, across and back.

Two sentries were approaching along the outside of the fence. When Vierro noticed them, he called a rest for Henry and walked among the seated men to look over their work. Henry stretched and sat on the floor at the edge of the shed to wait for Vierro to tell him he was needed again.

Sitter, he thought. Brother, son, cousin. Horseman. Commando.

Sitter, rider, self-polluter.

– Sitter

– Rider

– Self-polluter

– Killer

His single kill had been so unexpected and so far away that it was less frightening than the time he shot over the heads of cattle thieves on Craigievar, although more frightening than plugging a buck.

His thoughts drifted on. Last week the older men had called Henry and Clem over to tell them that the rattling of their sticks on the corrugations of the shed walls sounded so much like the Khakis' guns as to almost stop their hearts when it woke them from a nap. One of the men had one and a half legs; his right leg ended where his knee had been. His point carried.

As though driven in by a wind, restlessness now stirred in Henry; he imagined tucking himself up like a scaly anteater and rolling down the lanes between the dozing sheds to feel his blood move in his head.

The break was over. He climbed back onto the bed and found his marks and worked to keep every part of himself still except his chest as he breathed, and his eyes.

On his way back to Hut 76 he had the lanes almost to himself, with only the odd man awake to say his name or watch him walk – not tumble like a pangolin creature – between the sides of rippled tin, or past the folded walls where the homes of men stood open to the air.

His plant was no doubt still moving, around, across, back. He decided it was a spider's web, the plant's own tension and a breeze that accounted for it.

3

ONE OF THE PRISONERS IN Steynsburg made a hood from a canvas bucket, with holes for his eyes and one for his mouth. These were stitched around the edges and sagging from being wetted with food and water, but he would not take his hood off. Henry and Clem made the journey to see him, and even he knew their names.

He was in the lane that ran past his shed cleaning his bed when they came by; he had upended the frame and was swiping at it with a handful of straw. As they stood there he lifted the frame and bumped it back down onto the packed earth to shake it free of bedbugs, scorpions, whatever had moved in. Apart from the stiff and exaggerated way he turned and tilted his head to see out of the eyeholes, the man moved like any other fellow. At last he interrupted himself pretending to be normal in his hood, stopped fussing with the bed, and said to them, in explanation of his strangeness, 'Not one who can really stand to be among a crowd of fellows, you see,' and Henry had the idea he was blushing inside his covering.

Days after the boys visited the man in the hood they heard that he had left Steynsburg, left the main camp altogether. The men said that he had taken to rubbing his hood against the skin of his face, without a break and for so long that he chafed it raw, and the stuff stuck to the weeping skin and it all turned bad in the wet heat. The man, his hood peeled from his bloodied head and a cork helmet balancing there, was led out of the gate by a pair of Khakis, one on each arm, and him with his eyes squeezed shut. They said he was bound for the smaller camp near the sea, where the madmen and the wicked were sent.

Henry's bed was separated from Clem's by a crate table knocked together by Welthagen. On the other side of his bed there was nothing but the shed wall; he had drawn the end. This meant his stuff was the first call for the young jackals that raided this part of the camp, and for shed inspections. But it also meant that at least he could turn his back on the long room and see no one at all. Hut 76, like Vierro's on the other side of Diyatalawa, was at the end of its row and with the door open he could see, if he lay with his head where his feet should be, across a patch of tough grass to the fences and ditch that made the camp boundary on this side, and beyond this to cleared land rising to the hills.

He and Clem were careful with their part of the room, aware of their luck in drawing this corner. There was a fashion in the sheds for advertisement posters, and there were dozens of these on the walls, for soap and tobacco and tonics. The boys had a pair of sunny girls looking up at a man. On the table they kept their books – a *Boy's Own Annual* donated by the British in Kandy, a Bible, a small, thick, schoolboy's Cicero in translation. This last had Clem's particular postcard tacked along one edge among the dense pages, held there so that it would not fall out when the book was turned upside down and flared by the shed inspectors to 'make them have to deal with it', Henry said.

Some of Cicero's on and on and on showed at either edge of the card. At the top could be read 'or fear they shall be forced to it, if they do not do it voluntarily; or drawn by fair promises and large' and at the bottom: 'and Liberty, after she has been chained up awhile, is always more fierce, and sets her teeth in deeper, than she'.

'Clem fell in love with her,' Henry told Adaira, 'but I ended up with her' – and he produced a postcard that was backed with a page torn from a book, with the words exactly as he'd said them. Along the lower edge of the card Adaira could make out the title, Ceylonese Girl. The photograph had been coloured by hand. The girl was looking away from the camera, and her breasts were naked; she seemed a touch shy, but Clem made up a fierce nature for her, fierce and fighting him off – 'Liberty, after she has been chained up a while, no doubt', and when Henry said this he pulled his head back in a small, quick movement as though at a nip of sadness, like the bite of a flea.

Also among the books on their table was an orange-brown, cloth-covered *Baudry's Dictionary of Etymology and Biography* 'with aids to pronunciation and numerous appendices', and Henry consulted the compact little book as often as Clem put Cicero in his pocket and headed for the privacy of the latrines or a dim corner of the woodcarving shed.

Henry, too, had particular pages in his book, near the start of the appendices, where he believed he had found a map to

Englishness, the part of being English that was worth something – not their viciousness, not the stunted and grimy whining Khakis, but the cool depths that seemed to keep a little smile on the faces of certain of the officers, those officers who kept slim books in their pockets, sometimes in other languages, and who he had decided never ran or even walked in a hurry, or raised their voices, or sweated. Henry had in the past months met a few of these supernaturally self-contained, sleek and feline men, with their exciting drawl and elegant bodies, and it had seemed to him – no, he was certain – he had got back from some of them a glance of fellow feeling, even though he was only a boy in corduroys and the worn field shoes of a Boer. He had felt it, and been confused and flattered by it. And now here it was – perhaps, in his magical thinking, by arrangement of the cool men or perhaps by accident: a key.

He had begun with Some Current Words and Phrases but it was not the Monroe doctrine or The Three Estates he wanted; it was in the next section that it lived, and he would come to know it well: Classical and Foreign Words and Phrases Occurring Frequently in English Books and Translations, from à bas (F), to vox populi, vox dei (L).

What sort of people would need to adopt a word such as blasé (F), fatigued with pleasure? He liked, too, Nemo me impune lacessit, no one assails me with impunity, although he could find no clue how to say it. He would save it for a letter.

Clem laughed at him for his new words and liked to say 'infra dignitatem' with thumping rhythm. But Henry liked the Latin insults and kept lusus naturae, freak of nature, in reserve to use against someone who would not understand what he was saying.

He collected:
– Dolce far niente
– Prima facie
– Tertium quid

The camp changed, not every day or every week, but in lurches, with the arrival of two hundred or three hundred surrendered fighters or captured men, or the sudden removal of someone to the smaller camp by the sea. There was a flurry of officiousness and temper as the new men sorted matters with the camp guards and among themselves. Matters of who had, and who must yield to, authority were the surest way to start up the shoving and the raised voices, but it was the law of the camp that there must be ranks among them; the cork helmets they must wear always when out of doors had been daubed with stripes of paint: such for hut captains, such for officers, blue for the rest, unless they were, as Henry called them, foreigners, in which case the stripe was black. No group among the black-banders fought as much as the Irish – among themselves, and as a flailing mass, and in single combat, for money, against all comers. This was also a way to make the days pass.

There was a swimming hole in the camp, and men who were not working on the road, or busy in the school, were digging a second one. Henry and Clem used it most days. Neither could swim – only a few of the men turned themselves horizontal and struck out – but they greatly liked to paddle and splash.

And then Henry had another pool, a pool of his own, dis-covered on a ride to a larger, grander plantation a few weeks into his duties as syce to Cyella Oofit.

This plantation, or prize estate, as he had heard Cyella refer to it, had acre upon acre of established tea bushes, a thick mat of plants appearing to have grown into one plant and kept cropped at the same height by women who moved in flocks among it, veiled like saints and working, as he saw when he came close, with a sort of absent piety about their mouths and swift, lifted hands. In the centre of this elevated drape of green was a group of white buildings: plain, businesslike buildings built on the summit of a low hill. There were sorting sheds, a three-storeyed loft, offices, a vast barn. A line of pickers' rooms ran down the hill from these and at the other edge of the manufactory an avenue of full trees led away to the great planter's house with its black shutters and furnished verandas.

On his first visit to the estate, Henry rode with Cyella down this avenue, as far as the front garden. He did not meet or even see the family Cyella was to join at breakfast; she seemed unsure of herself, unsure of what to do with him, and he took the decision, once she had dismounted, to receive the reins of her horse from the bedecked peon who met them, and to follow another man, also in a frogged jacket and long white skirts, to the stables. There he swung down from the pony and was brought tea and a plate, and waited. After an hour or so she sent a boy to call him.

Something must have been said: on their next visit, an English boy somewhat younger than Henry came from the house as they rode up. He looked Henry over; they were, strictly speaking, enemies, and it seemed the boy had this in mind, for he was wary of Henry, as though the prisoner might suddenly throw himself from his saddle and tackle him, or, worse, said Henry, say something that was not quite the thing. Henry stayed seated and looked down at the English boy.

'Look here. See here,' the boy began. 'Father says you're not to take your tea with the coolies. They have set something for you in the garden – there's a boy to take you. Boy!' He shouted sharply and a Cingalese man trotted towards them from the direction of the stables. After a sentence or two of imperious pidgin directed at the servant, the English boy turned to go, but Henry spoke, and at this he turned back and watched the Boer as much as he listened to him, as if – even though he had addressed Henry in English – he did not expect Henry to be comprehensible.

In English, Henry said: 'Might your boy show me the tea operation? When I am finished with breakfast?'

His courage came from the scent of an enemy close to his own age, perhaps, or from knowing himself, too, to be the son of a landowner, beneath his prisoner's skin.

The English boy pulled a face. 'Whatever for? Oh heavens, yes. It's terribly dull, but go ahead. After breakfast,' and he gestured towards the garden. The Cingalese took Cyella's horse. Henry followed, still mounted, and the two of them watered the animals and left them in the stalls. The man showed Henry to a gazebo and settled himself under a tree while Henry sat down to a meal that surely improved with his memory of it as the first good food he had enjoyed in a year or more. A small table was laid with a teapot, a warm plate under a dome, toast, marmalade. He ate everything under the cover and ate and drank almost all that was set before him, leaving only some marmalade and, out of pride, half the bowl of sugar cubes. The fact that he was alone, and in a fresh garden, and that there were birdsong and distant, intriguing, mechanical sounds, completed the pleasure he took.

When Henry at last laid down his knife and napkin, the Cingalese came over to him and led him across the lawn, out of the gates and towards the tea manufactory that was making the distant-crowd sounds of steam released and the regular thumping that had been the background to his breakfast at intervals, as though somewhere a door was being opened on a noisy room again and again.

That morning Henry saw the withering lofts for the first time. The building that housed them was a several-storeyed place from whose central hall and landings there opened the wide shed-like rooms. Henry and the man climbed past a number of these and at the top of the stairs entered the largest of them, a room that stretched the length of the building under a naked corrugated-iron roof. It was taken up with wide racks from floor to rafters, humped with curling leaves set out to dry and making a dark weave of lines that thickened and dimmed towards the centre.

It was when he and the man turned again for the planter's house that Henry found his pool. He and the Cingalese were on the red road about halfway between the works and the garden when they came abreast of a break in the thick growth that hemmed the driveway. Henry, testing the give and length of his leash, asked what the path was for; the man shrugged and took a few steps onto it. He pointed down the path but would go no further.

The path dropped quite steeply down from the road, and had been set with short, slim logs to hold back the earth and make rough steps. Henry followed it as it curved to the right and led to a busy stream that emerged from crowded growth and fed a small pool; a stout white-barked tree leaned its branches over the water, making a private cave.

After breakfast each time after that Henry came to the pool, if only for the hour Cyella spent gossiping at the house or for longer if she planned to play tennis or watch it being played, on the two or three mornings a week he followed her to the plantation.

At this time of the morning the family had no interest in the pool, and the estate coolies and peons were forbidden to touch their bodies to the water there. Henry learned that they washed themselves downstream of the estate, and worked out from the Cingalese of the plantation and from what he had seen on the road that the little river had its source not far from the estate, and that the water was used in a hierarchy of planter and family for amusement, here at the pool; then, beyond this grotto, by the planter's coolies to keep clean and clean their clothes; then by the Cingalese who were not of the plantation for their cooking water and to clean their bodies and clothes, all the way to the sea, he supposed.

The peon still met Henry and Miss Oofit whenever they arrived at the estate, but he and the man parted as soon as Henry had eaten his meal. The arrangement was not discussed with Cyella, nor her hosts, and Henry, although irritated to be regarded as a superior sort of servant, was happy to make use of whatever freedom was afforded him by being forgotten when he was not needed.

He had the idea, as he lay on his back on one of the boulders at the edge of the pool, of a fine steel net of pleasure knitted into his skin, so that when he stretched, it came alive and sounded a note. He could shift onto his stomach, feel the sharp heat of the rock on his thighs; he could cup his sex, feel the early sun warm the backs of his knees, his buttocks and shoulders, and close his eyes and hear birdsong, the manufacturing noise, the water as it left the pool over its little sill of rocks.

It was here that memories of battle, commando and skirmish began to occupy his thoughts as they did not in camp, even though among the men the talk was endlessly about this or that action, to the point of almost hypnotic boredom. In camp, there might be a day in Hut 76 that began with the jackal they'd named Kitchener causing a flurry by darting deep into the room to snatch their shoes, there might be a chase and a moment of good humour, but soon enough, as the men settled to whittle or sketch, or lay to read, one of them, like a man who will not leave off picking at a sore on his face, would say, 'That day at Slabbertsnek, who was it gave the alarm? Was it Hantam?' and the talk would begin again, tramping in a slow spiral, bearing down on a particular day. It was as though they were under a curse to say the thing over and over again, only slightly changed each time. They were polishing their history, and if it was what they must do while they were held in Diyatalawa, outside of the war itself but not at the end of the war – denied action in place of remembering, but denied also the comprehension that would allow them to move forward – if this was their lot, it also had this effect: the endless talk pushed their own memories deeper into their minds and they found themselves stuck in the unsatisfying place between the record and their own recollection.

When Henry was ten or eleven years old he had overheard his mother and her sister, those fine-skinned Scotswomen, speaking about the coming birth of the sister's first grandchild, and had heard his mother say something to the effect that if they could really remember what it felt like to give birth, women would not allow it to happen so often. He began to believe something of the sort about warfare, when, now that he was alone, they surfaced by the pool, these flashes of dull fear, or he recalled sleepless days and nights on end in the expectation of being shelled, and remembered the sound of his own thin, fast breathing.

His hour or so spent alone, two or three times a week, was the truly enviable gift of this syce duty, so valuable that he hoarded this time, told no one about it, not even Clem, who looked forward to an accounting each day of what Henry had seen and done. Henry very much liked that part of his syce days – bringing back news and sweet cakes for the fellows in the shed, and private parcels of breakfast ham, or sugar, and stories for Clem. But he did not mention his pool, or the monk his own age whom he met every time he rode out, waiting for him at the sweet seller's stand.

Clem was interested in Cyella Oofit, and Henry put effort into trying to notice, or invent, what he could about her. In service to Clem's interest in her, or the idea of her, Henry did not tell him how she appeared to him. Her heavy jaw and sulking eyes, his belief that she was, when in a position of power, a bully and, when beholden, a flatterer, her way of looking too often and too directly at him, her familiarity, as though there was no question about her being permitted to touch him, as though she expected her gloved pats on his arm and his thigh to be received as a kindness, as by a horse or a dog … these he kept from Clem, and in the way that he made the tea machines larger and more marvellous than they were, so Cyella became a sweet-smelling, slim-waisted girl with a gay laugh and skill at flirting.

'I bet you could kiss her, I bet you could,' Clem told him. Henry knew this was the case because he already had – or at least, had been kissed by her, violently, with her hands on either side of his face, one of them still holding her riding crop. He had not closed his mouth in time; hers had covered half of it until he twisted away. When she let his head go he was, he could feel, awash in a mortifying blush, and she smirked at him, an unpleasant look that told him she had not forgotten for even the length of the kiss who was the prisoner.

He would never tell Clem about that part of the ride. It was foolish to speak about menace from a girl, foolish to fear her. And what was a kiss from that menacing girl if that was the price of the ride, the breakfast, the little pool? So he pretended it had not happened and, curiously, so did she, and he thought of it so often that he wore down the sharp edges of the memory of it, and was able at last to see it as just another inexplicable moment among the many since he and Clem and Clem's brother had ridden to war.

On a morning like any other of his syce mornings, Henry drifted in the cave the tree made, then pulled himself from the water and lowered his body onto the rock and basked. After a while he shifted his face to find part of his arm that was not wet with sweat and at that moment, before he knew it enough to put into words, he knew that he was not alone, and his whole body fell with a dread-filled dropping sensation into the vigilance of the war, and he was as alert and still as if he were on second watch and had heard, amid the veld silence, the clink of metal on metal.

No matter how prepared he was, and no matter how little threat there was, his breath still caught in his throat when he opened his eyes to see, right in front of him, close enough to touch, a hem of orange cloth, brown ankles and dusty slim feet in sandals. As Henry sprang to his feet, the monk from the sweet seller's corner dropped to a crouch, so that the two of them were like puppets controlled by a single rod – one was up when the other was down, then both changed places.

This allowed them to laugh. They knew one another, after all, and the monk had sought him out. They had a language in common and, although it could be said that English was, in the case of the Boer boy and the young Cingalese, the language of the invader, both were proud to speak it as well as they did. Again they were eye to eye in their strange affinity. Here was someone to whom each could try to explain his life.

That first day Prem – Prem was the monk's name – did not

bathe in the little pool. He paced the yellow beach and the small clearing, looking back at Henry, talking of this and that and listening until a bell sounded from the veranda of the main house, to call Henry back and summon the peon with the horses. As they turned to leave, the monk did a startling thing: he took Henry's hand, not in a handshake, right hand to right hand, but with his left hand slipped into Henry's right; he held it as they walked up the rough steps of the path. Henry, astonished, allowed it. He said nothing. In his thoughts he quickly delivered the expected judgement on how embarrassing it was to hold hands with another fellow but at the same time the dry friction between the flesh of his hand and the flesh of Prem's hand, with its hollows of warmth and cooler edges, the give and resistance of that hand, and Henry's intense awareness of it – these made their counterargument.

At the top of the steps, where the little path met the avenue, Prem let go, nodded a smiled greeting to Henry and left him there. The day reclaimed him: walking, words, horse tackle and saddling up, the ride back to the camp, by which time holding hands, boy to boy, was just the way people behaved here, in Ceylon.

On drifting awake in the still small hours of the night, as he never did but did tonight, Henry brought his hands from his chest and his groin; he placed them so that his right hand lay over his left, then twisted to lie in it, palm up, the back of one hand in the palm of the other. Then one hand threaded its fingers up to the root of the other's and in this attitude he slipped back to sleep.

———

The next time Prem found him there he joined him in the pool, and on all the days after this. One day Henry brought Baudry's dictionary. They swam and Prem hung over Henry's shoulder to read along with him, and Henry picked up his intimate scent, a sea breath, and so in the small hours, back in his bed in Diyatalawa camp, he opened his shirt and held his hand above his chest and brought it slowly, supernaturally slowly, towards his skin. In the dark he could not guess the moment of contact, and lingered in the cushion of warm air between his hand and his bare chest until the prickle of the hairs on his nipples said he was near.

One day he arrived after Prem. He came quietly down the curving path and entered the clearing to see his friend at the moment he slipped off his heavy outer robe. As Henry watched, unseen, Prem cracked the cloth so that it billowed, brilliantly orange in the sun, and spread it on a rock. Henry, waiting at the edge, felt a word drop into his mind as neatly as a pebble into water. Nunc, he heard: now.

Every day that Henry could get to the estate, whoever arrived last at the pool quickly dropped his robes or sewn clothes and joined the other in the water and afterwards they baked on the rock, side by side. As Henry lay on his back one morning, listening to Prem, he spotted a slim daylight moon in the blue sky and felt keenly that between their bodies and that moon there was not a single other thing − that he and Prem were exposed on the skin of the earth − and felt how impossible it would be to curl into him with only his shut eyes to hide them from heaven—

'Adaira.' Here Henry Vos paused. He could barely frame the

question he seemed to need to ask, but at last she understood that he was trying to gauge how much innocence still shrouded her – innocence, or ignorance, she thought – and what the extra measure of affront might be in the outrage he was planning to confess. Neither of them looked directly at the other. She moved her head in a way that was at once a negation and a nod, to make the question go away, or somehow answer it without agreeing to answer. She flicked her glance upwards to meet his eyes, then down again to her lap.

He let out his breath. 'Well, like that. It was like that.'

He said, 'Very like that.'

He said, 'This matter ...'

She in fact knew very little about sex, she thought, although enough surely to have formed impressions of the male body, the hair and unlikely textures, its fearsome poignancy. Two such, finding each other? The thought of it was shocking, fierce, sad. But the aesthetics of it drew her: Henry's Scots paleness, the golden-brown hair he must have had as a boy, against the soft brown-russet of Prem (she borrowed from Ceylonese Girl for Prem, down to her smudged eyes) ... The appeal of it dulled none of her shock at the idea but somehow gave her a way to look steadily at it. She ducked her head, rolled her pen between her fingertips to signal her readiness to keep going with what they were about.

What they are about: heavy uttarasanga lifted and shed. Antaravasaka unwrapped from his hips. Trousers join boots and stockings, flannel drawers and cork hat. Henry tunnels out of his shirt and lifts it above his head. For a moment he is stretched taut, and he slim and golden, and he slim and pale, and with water for cloaking, and splashing for noise, one morning they cross when their two pairs of hips make the unmistakable sideways shift of no more than their own width, and meet.

His life split into two planes. Today he lived in the camp, moving like a ghost from shed to kitchen, or trailing Clem to the Commissioner Street shops, his senses engaged with Diyatalawa and even with Clem only enough to keep him, Henry, grunting assent, keep him from walking into buildings or other men. Tomorrow or yesterday, in the real world, on the other plane, none of this had any claim to exist, and the journey from one to the other happened in a death-calm dream state whose own claims on him – Cyella Oofit's temper on a particular day, or a particular colour meeting his eye – left him puzzled more than anything else when his attention was dragged forth to notice them.

It took him half a day to recover from being with Prem, and the impossibility of finding any privacy in which to do this left Henry feeling he had to hold the world away from him with his senses to make a space in which to bring his breathing, his body, back to normal.

Today, an outride with Cyella Oofit had coincided with one of the days for the life class. As Henry found his marks on Vierro's planks, breathed deeply and set himself in what he could remember of the pose, he wondered if there were marks on his body – a telltale flush on his chest where he had been kissed not three hours ago, or about his mouth, which had kissed in return; he felt there must be a sign of this change in him, in the way that he had felt his body change in the weeks since he and Prem had found one another.

He looked out at his patch of jungle but in his mind's eye was the orange and darker orange of Prem's robe: today he had arrived at the pool after Henry and had wet the edge of the cloth as he knelt by the water to kiss him. Later, dozing, depleted, on the rock, Henry had played with the idea of the water as a new element: liquid, then solid as glass, then, with the memory of their crucial small movements in it, liable to lose its shape and scatter into the sky. By what spell did it press against but not enter their bodies?

Henry did not have a name for what he and Prem were to each other; he doubted there was such a category, such a mix of companionship and predatory delight, of talking about the world one moment and the next reaching and insisting on being reached for.

As they lay on the rock, Henry had watched a small green beetle tilt over Prem's wet hair. When Prem became aware of it, Henry knew, he would lift it away to a leaf, might greet it as it left his hand. And why not? He, Henry, was brother to every creature, every peon, plant, gatepost, button. All the beetles there were.

Clem said his friend's smile must have to do with Cyella – Cyella who at the end of their ride still sometimes slid her body against Henry's when she dismounted. These days Henry lifted her away from him as gently as one might lift a green beetle, before he turned to loop the reins over the ears of her horse. One day, with some ceremony, she presented him with a photograph of herself taken with one of the estate daughters, mounted on stiff card. He accepted it with thanks, slid it between the pages of the orange cloth-covered encyclopaedia as she watched, forgot it before he had closed the covers.

Today, with the two boys bent over that same book, over meum et tuum, mine and thine, Prem had dropped his mouth to touch it to Henry's neck, and then turned Henry's head to him and kissed him with deliberation, making language with his kiss, a thing apart from the greed of Cyella's mouth.

On the ride back to camp, Henry had let the little mare make the pace. He rolled with her gait, his body easy in the noon heat. The kiss stayed with him, and he brought his finger to his mouth to confirm it, as he brought it to his mouth in the telling of it, but did not touch his lips, as boy or man, for fear of usurping Prem's mouth there.

By the time Henry's slim daytime moon came around again they had settled on the withering loft as a place to meet. It was not the monsoon that drove them indoors but a mixture of modesty and fright – fright arising from their near discovery.

He and Prem had been lying on the big rock, fingers loosely laced, when the sudden sound of voices on the little path only a few feet away brought them to a crouch, their eyes locked on one another's, and wide. Henry clutched his shirt to his groin, and in a strangled voice shouted that he was there – 'I am here! There's someone here!'

In answer, from the other side of the hedge they heard Cyella's wild giggle and a speculative murmur: two voices. She was capable of pressing on down the little path to see him stripped for swimming – indeed, might even be thought likely to do so, and he and Prem held themselves as still as shocked animals in expectation of her rounding the corner to find them both, only breathing again when a different voice, also that of a girl, called out, 'Oh I say, so sorry!' against a fresh burst of giggles. The laughter and chatter of the pair on the path retreated onto the road, grew fainter in the direction of the house.

But no one came to the withering loft's Level No. 3. They reached it by steep outside stairs that threaded up the back of the building, and Henry discovered again the low, immense room that was, at its heart, dim in a shady-afternoon way although it was still morning. They discovered air scented with raw tea and a space broken up by racks, motes, shadows, until the whole room was a series of private places. They found their way to where the light from the windows was blocked by the racks of leaves, and chose a place at the centre of this.

Prem was older in the half dark, and Henry also less of a boy. There was intent in place of puppyish fumbling, and in their embraces some knowledge of how to hold the other, of what was possible. There was uncanny ease in the way they acquiesced and took the lead as they met, now, with equal velocity.

Several deepening and undisturbed mornings in the withering loft were understood by Henry and Prem to mean that today, again, no one would come; they did not play the celestial odds and calculate that no one for a few mornings running meant, very likely, someone today. They told themselves that they would hear the slightest step on the stairs, but they did not.

Henry, or Prem, was knelt before his friend. Prem, or Henry, lay against the racks, his eyes rolled back in his head, mindless as a steer's, braced to the last small muscle of his body, and hearing only the roar of his own advancing pleasure until both heard a sing-song, half-British voice, exulting and aghast: 'Bloody hell! Bloody hell! What the bloody hell do you mean by this?'

Where they had not heard this man's feet on the stairs now they heard a half-dozen of his fellows who arrived holding bottles of dark stuff; it would emerge that this was a legation of tea-company clerks who had planned a drinking party in the privacy of the loft.

They pulled Prem from the tunnel in the racks, surrounded him and spoke shrilly to him as he cringed from them and cupped his sex. Their excited fury was kept for Prem, but Henry was not forgotten. Both were bullied into their clothing and brought, in procession, to the main house.

The mother of the plantation family, made brisk about such matters by having several sons, and in any event barely interested in the Africander and the Native who were brought before her, was not inclined to make overmuch of it. When she looked at Henry at all she seemed almost to pity him, but Cyella, wounded and eager to wound, insisted on his crime, making herself understood on the matter even though she had no words for it beyond 'wickedness' and 'vice' and 'shame'.

Prem was dismissed from the planter's home and borne away in a cloud of righteous chatter. The last time Henry saw Prem, he was stumbling down the drive, bending his neck under the slapping hand of a clerk.

Henry was allowed to mount his pony. In answer to Cyella's

near-hysterical demand, the father, the planter himself, rode back with the two of them, peeling off to the camp commander's house to make his report. Cyella, sounding jagged hisses through her nostrils but also, Henry thought, in tears, continued to her cousin's bungalow. Henry was put under guard and taken to the camp stables to wait.

This was the story Henry Vos told Adaira van Brugge. Barely out of girlhood herself, she could not then have said how she heard it. Was she his transcriber, his confessor, his judging friend? Young Henry flickered in high contrast before her, mute, scored by a penny orchestra, and she could only sit in the half dark and watch his story play.

4

IN THE NEW CAMP, HENRY was at first left alone. There were far fewer men there and the camp itself, smaller than Diyatalawa, was almost beautiful. Where Diyatalawa had zinc sheds and bare sloping ground, Ragama's accommodations were on platforms of cement rubbed to a sheen by bare feet; a structure of beams and pillars held up palm-thatched roofs. The walls of the buildings were made from woven screens of palm leaf and the men slept on cotton mattresses laid on the floor. This was a lowland camp, and hotter.

On his second day in the new camp – after he was processed in, found mattress territory, was fed and ordered to sleep – Henry was woken by bugle to softer light and men busy in their quiet way with bedding and shaving cups, or just stretching and letting the day come to them. As well as Africanders there were four Frenchies on his platform, a lone Swede, several Russians.

He was by at least a decade the youngest there. Some of the men had united Boer and Briton against them and been sent from Diyatalawa by a Boer camp council; some had been plucked from their ranks against the protest of the Boers. Several had been caught trying to escape, one pair notoriously while on parole in Kandy. There was a satirical portraitist who had enraged the British with a careful sketch of their queen empress wearing a crown made of Africander, Indian and Sudanese babies. One could see the crying infants on her smooth thin hair only if one looked closely; the camp commander had looked closely, wearing a shy grin of pleasure at the Boer-made Victoria until he made out the detail; within the hour the satirist had been on his way to Ragama.

At the edges of the new camp there were all manner of creeping plants and, in outcrops between rice fields, true jungle, and many colours through the wire fence beyond which a staked trench made the perimeter. A fascinating net arrangement complemented the barbed wire of the fence, a web of interlacing fine copper wires that, when broken, sent an electrical signal and an alarm to the guardhouses. The men felt obscurely complimented by its sophistication.

Several of the prisoners had bartered for or bought new shirts, white cotton shirts, and were allowed to wear these. The colours, the look of the place, the sort of men Henry was among – there was much to like at Ragama.

Best of all was the relative solitude, although even had he been back in Hut 76 with Sippion, Clem and the others, Henry would have been alone, arrested in the glare of discovery. Now, in his first days at Ragama, he drifted at peace, feeling that he was sublimely insubstantial, that he existed somehow beyond his body in a world that was so much wider than he had guessed.

He was allowed less than a week, perhaps only four days, in this state of euphoric shock and illumination before he was ordered one morning to report to the far end of the new camp where an internal fence sectioned off a sleeping platform from the rest and also enclosed a small room that served as an office for a military doctor.

Standing in one corner of this inner compound was a man whose face was dark with scabs, what little of his face could be seen; his head was held low and to the side as though to duck a beating or to illustrate a periodical's essay on shame – 'The Penitent', or 'The Guilty Party'; this was the hooded man from Diyatalawa and Henry, at his youth's apex of health, knew suddenly the place he had come to.

By then a decision must have been taken about his crime, for at dawn on the day after he was placed in the fenced-off asylum, four soldiers carried a vaulting horse in sections into the office, bent Henry over this and bared his buttocks and lower back. Three of them stood to one side, in a line and at attention. An officer entered the crowded room to tell Henry that he was to be birched as a boy, not lashed as a man, and then he nodded to the fourth soldier. This man drew back his arm and brought the cane down hard on Henry's exposed skin, then repeated this.

From the corner of his eye, Henry saw that one of the standing soldiers was counting off the cuts on his fingers; when this man had gone twice through both hands, the whipping man stopped, breathing hard. There was an air of improvisation about the punishment, about the impersonal ceremony the soldiers seemed to be trying for. Throughout, Henry was so stiff with shame at this schoolboy's ritual on his newly adult flesh that although he knew the brain-seizing pain of it, he felt the birch was landing on something more solid than his body. He saw shame on the faces of the soldiers, too; the room seemed to be thick with it.

Having beaten him and imprisoned him in an asylum yard nested within a prison yard, the soldiery seemed at a loss about how Henry should be further punished, or ostracised, or medicined. What was, after all, to be done? Keep him away from the general population. And the law? Somewhere clemency prevailed or Henry must have been judged too young, or his crime too embarrassing, to bring before a military court.

Even in the Boer camps it was known that Ceylon, civilian Ceylon, British Ceylon, was in a stew about its own General Hector MacDonald and the Cingalese boys; no one wanted the appearance of an outbreak of inversion in the military. Local beliefs in the matter of physical love had been so much discussed by the men as to be hardly worth mentioning – that those unnatural vices which had occasioned the destruction of the cities of the plain were, in fact, accepted and common practice among the Natives. Once one had expressed disgust and wielded the whip there was not much more to do without courting scandal. The passage of the war would set the length of Henry's sentence, not a tribunal.

Henry would come to believe that, in a small way, he was like this Fighting Mac, the hero of Omdurman and campaign coffee cans: each had been famous among his fellow soldiers and adopted as the face of their war. They had presented the appearance of heroes and thereby perpetrated their fraud. Henry wondered what would happen to Hector MacDonald. He wondered what would happen to him.

A military doctor with a clipboard and an unlit pipe of tobacco on which he sucked ceaselessly urged Henry to understand that loving Prem was not so devastatingly wrong because of what Henry had *done* so much as the fact that what he had done was a manifestation of what he *was*, and for that there was every prospect of rehabilitation because in this regard it mattered not what Henry *was*, but what he *did*. And what he did must not be that, did he see? The doctor was the only man who made sense in here and so to Henry this came to seem almost sensible, too. At least, if he could not penetrate the fog of reasoning, there was enough there to adopt as a doctrine.

In this caged asylum there was no avoiding glimpses of sickening rhythms – in the centre of the yard, against the corner pole of a shed: someone rocking, someone masturbating out in the open beneath a slack grin, someone snapping his own head against the trunk of a palm tree. Henry's fright at these broken minds kept his neck and shoulders bone-hard for weeks until he learned to push gently, like a man among beasts, to clear space for himself without frightening them in return.

He was not one of them. He saw now that the limitlessness of the world that he had glimpsed before must have been the cruellest illusion, but even in this smaller realm, he could not be one of the creatures he saw around him, nor the creature the doctor painted. He knew he did not belong here, and therefore he could not be him.

He turned eighteen in Ragama's asylum. Clutching for sense, Henry took where he was as a sort of metaphor for how he would be, how he must try to be, from now on: in the same way that he defended himself from too much awareness of the self-gougers and the asylum's screecher, he would, he decided in his stout way, defend himself from this thing within him that had put him there.

Every day there were flashes of dull orange passing on the road that ran along the perimeter beyond the asylum fence; Henry grew used to these reminders until they made a sort of language, like the confiding pulse of light from a lighthouse and the answering blink of noticing it. Some evenings, as a lighthouse will, they made him feel even more alone. He took to spending most of the night awake, his thoughts given play only when the muttering men were at last asleep and his companion was the sentry's yell, at intervals, 'Aaall's we-ell.'

On moonless nights, the sane men of the enclosing Ragama camp sometimes wandered over to the little asylum to talk to the boy whose crime was known to every man there. At the fence he learned in whispers from the Swede about what awaits a monk caught breaking his oath of chastity: Prem was almost certainly stripped of his robes and sent away from the monastery in disgrace. The thought of having cost him this gave Henry a tug of guilt. But it was also the case that he dwelt as much on what he could recall of the feel of Prem's body, Prem's mouth, as on what they had been made to pay for these things.

He was at the asylum for the death of the enemy queen and mourned her with the men at the fence (the satirist among them) and held in his arms one of the asylum men who cried out and set the rest to wailing.

The criminal Engel came briefly to Ragama camp on his way to a worse place and found Henry at the fence and sickened him with his foul breath and knowing laughter, his claim of fellowship, of shared criminality. He chaffed Henry through the wire: 'Hey? Hey? I knew it, you dirty bugger!'

Henry was still at the asylum when the peace came and the enfolding camp emptied. He knew from a parcel he received from Clem at Diyatalawa that the big camp was shedding its men in batches, too. Clem, as though he were making a point about what belonged on Ceylon and must not return home with him, sent the Cicero with Ceylonese Girl still hidden in its pages, and the orange dictionary, the photograph of Cyella Oofit. His covering letter was the stiff note about Engel that Adaira would one day find among Henry's papers – 'Engel we saw at Simon's Town that day, Engel on the ship' – and concluded: 'These English ways are not our ways.' Henry realised that Clem would reach Craigievar before him, and he, Henry, would be left to trail home when the homecoming was done and the list of losses had been closed. He begged in silence for Clem to invent anything, a broken limb, anything, to explain his delay.

In the event the hooded man and the slappers and weepers and self-hurters of Ragama and its lone invert were kept back until they could make up a transport with a hundred or so holdouts who refused to sign the loyalty oath, and it was almost seven months after the main body of men that Henry came home.

The rewards of war, among them the ear given to the endless dull tales of the ordinary returning men, were by then spent, not that Henry had any instinct to confide. On the ship home, among the irreconcilables and the mad, he had settled on his great project. By the time his ship docked he had done the work of sealing off his received shame from himself and everyone else.

At home, the delay in his return was kept so vaguely in the realm of politics and British spite that Henry knew briefly, sharply, before he blocked off the knowledge, that someone there had been told the truth about him.

Years after his ship docked, Henry would hear about the silver medals they were giving out to the men who fought in the Three-Year War. He would not send in his name for the Zuidafrikaanse Republiek en Oranje Vrijstaat Oorlogmedalje, nor allow it to be sent, for fear of what answer would come.

Rather sooner than that, Henry heard that his patron saint and larger shadow, Ceylon's British general in disgrace, had killed himself in a Paris hotel room.

The wonder of it was, he had had a wife and son.

II

ON LOAN

5

O N THE TELEPHONE ON A Wednesday morning in
1926 the man who will be his new colleague at Native
Affairs gives Henry Vos directions to the office: 'We're on one
of those side streets up from the Company's Garden. Flora,
Fauna and Bantu.' A small laugh.

The Garden he means is the walled green network of
avenues in the heart of Cape Town by which these brisk colo-
nialists and sons of the Union navigate among the buildings
and the rude traffic.

Halfway across the city, Henry ends the telephone call and
prepares to leave his brother attorneys and his office in the
halls of Justice for a secondment to the Department of Native
Affairs.

These days he belongs to an army of a different sort, a
cohort of modern men, tribunes of the rushing new world,
gripped with work to be done and the much they have to ac-
complish. At Native Affairs, for instance, they are consciously
and deliberately about the business of making a country, their
particular work having to do with bringing Native custom and
law in the former Boer republics and the colonies into alignment, with moulding this maddening scattering into a biddable

mass. In his new office, Henry will give legal guidance on the drafting of a mighty bill to regulate those affairs once and for all. It is work he looks forward to.

He crosses the city and finds the building. He is met by an Englishman from England who shows him to a desk in a room full of men at desks. The Englishman watches Henry settle in, gestures to his squared-off legal briefcase.

'Brought along your box of tricks? Good show.'

But as Henry sets about unbuckling the straps, the Englishman holds up an index finger and tucks his chin for an 'however'. Lying on the desk that is now Henry's is a folder. The Native Affairs man places two fingertips on this and slides it an inch towards Henry.

'Thing is, my minister needs one of you law Johnnies to wrap up a … uhm … ticklish bit of business first,' and he taps the file's Manila cover with a crooked middle finger.

'Mission chap, deepest Pondoland, somebody important's uncle, has got his teeth into how his flock go about … relations. Wants us to have a crack at it.'

Native Affairs allows an edge of his mouth to curl. He taps the folder again as if reluctant to surrender it to Henry.

'Pretty hot stuff, actually.'

Henry, it seems, will be let loose on the mighty bill only after he has given his lawyerly advice on some or other area of Native morality, one that is set out in the folder. And the nut of it is this: Is it required (in the blameless gerundive) that the law addresses, re-addresses, the ever-changing matter of who may do what with whom, and how be done unto? This the law had thought it had finished with, in a two-page bill that is an example of clarity and deals with the only aspect of the whole business worthy of the King's signature. Now this complication.

'I shall take a look right away,' Henry answers, clipped as the Briton. He leaves the folder closed on the desk, retraces his steps to the doorway, takes off his coat and finds space for it and his hat on a crowded stand, returns to the desk. In these, his early middle years, he is said by women to resemble the dear dead Tsar and the dear King. By this they mean the softness in his eyes, the reserve there. He is a tall, broad-shouldered man. His beauty has darkened and, like the King and the Tsar, he wears a close-clipped beard and full moustache.

There is an electric lamp on the desk and Henry pulls the chain to light it. There must be twenty, twenty-four desks. His is forward of the middle aisle that runs through them. He tugs the seat of his jacket, shifts the chair, smooths the corners of his mouth. He is grateful to have a task set before him, immediate and contained. He knows the law, can hold human behaviour up to it as one lays a shape against a template and holds both up to the light. He will know instantly where it bleeds outside the lines.

The letters in the folder are in a clear hand; there appear to be a dozen of them or more. As he bumps them into alignment, a line from the top letter freezes him: 'The membrum virile is rubbed along the outer thigh and even mimics penetration at the juncture of the thighs—'

Henry is reluctant to raise his head to look about him for fear this is a practical joke on him, the new man. When he does sit up and take in the room he sees only men bent at their notes, one or two conferring, a man perhaps asleep or at least in deep thought. There is a murmur of sound, a purposeful drone.

'The only restraint on the actions of the pair, the merest nod to decency, is that the membrum gains no admittance to the vas muliebre. The organs of generation do not meet,' the letter resumes.

The day has clouded over and less light reaches him from the long windows at the head of the room. On desks, lamps glow in the orderly gloom; he thinks the folder must give off a glow of its own, or he must as he reads what is there. He leans over it.

'Stimulation of the parts of shame per manus is not only allowed, it is encouraged. Boys are "taught" this filthy practice. Girls learn from a young age to manipulate their own—' Dear God in heaven, Henry has never in his life seen the next pair of Latin words together on a page (although he knows their meaning).

Henry clears his throat and sets down the folder. He widens his eyes to quell a bubble of alarmed laughter as he arranges some loose sheets of paper, his pen and ink.

In the folder he also finds a copy of the draft morality bill, the one the NA chap is so proud of. He uncaps the pen and, before he returns to the letters, looks it over to read the map of where he might be under law:

BE IT ENACTED by the King's Most Excellent Majesty, the Senate and the House of Assembly of the Union of South Africa, as follows:–

Any European male who has illicit carnal intercourse

with a Native female, and any Native male who has illicit carnal intercourse with a European female &c &c (sub clause cf Mentally Defective Women's Protection Act) shall be guilty of an offence ...

Not much use but of mild interest to note that the offending male could get five years, and any female who permits such intercourse gets no more than four. Henry considers this for a moment but can attach no meaning to it beyond noting the anomaly.

As for the Act, it is indeed a short draft and in it the King is concerned exclusively with preventing intercourse between Native and European outside of marriage. Almost absent-mindedly Henry draws a line through a tautology he finds there and inks in a suggestion for a better word. Nothing to help him with the legal problem at hand – if indeed there is a problem – concerned as his correspondent is with Natives alone, but the exercise of consulting the draft and adding his small improvement has had the effect he aimed for: he is still in the realm of known templates, and this sort of thing, apparently, can be done.

His mind hums with 'Boys are "taught"', 'Girls learn' as he consults the dates on the dozen or so letters in the file and again takes up the first. All have been sent to a member of parliament and forwarded to Native Affairs; every letter is from the same man, a Reverend Vibert St. John Vine, who writes from Lusikisiki, somewhere in the Pondoland, Fingoland, Tembuland part of the world, the sleepy, green, barely conquered kingdoms to the east. To Henry's mind come missionary communists and red-blanket women armoured in their musk and brass hoops.

He tightens his pen, breathes in until he is straining the buttons on his waistcoat, and bends to the problem of thigh sex.

He does not hear the noon gun when it cracks over the town, but is roused by the stir of the men about him and, with his mind still ruffled by the reverend's strutting and clucking, by his roosterish indignation, he fetches his hat and follows them out of the long room and back into the day, where fitful clouds are dappling the streets and Garden.

The civil service men disperse, heading for coffee houses and cafeterias. Henry walks, fast, towards the museum at the top of the Company's Garden. He will find something to eat before he returns to Flora, Fauna and Bantu, but first it matters to him to leave the department with the impression that he has business to conduct, someone waiting for him. He aims to keep and consolidate his place among the coming fellows of this new department, but does not know how to make an approach; for now he will at least not give the appearance of needing to be noticed. He will not trail them to an eating house and hang about until he is asked to join a table.

He completes a circuit of the Garden and doubles back to find a corner of a coffee room on St George's Street, where Henry listens to a silver-haired woman at a nearby table tell a silver-haired man, 'The world is, I think, changing for the better.'

Henry does not, or so he tells himself, eavesdrop, but he overhears things, notices the conversations he hears. The old man says, 'What? What's that?' The woman repeats her words and her companion agrees with weak sounds of gratitude and dependence. When Henry passes by again to collect his hat, the old man is speaking as though it is his turn to make conversation. He seems to be describing a system of tanks, something to do with wheels, gravity. It is as though each has decided what they will say, and it hardly matters that it has little bearing on what the other raises. On the basis of these two snatches Henry invents the pair of them, adds them to his categories of the habits of human connection, in the way that a naturalist might tuck a seashell into the watch pocket of his waistcoat, to study later and assign a place in his ordering of the world.

Although at first he used the museum only as a way to seem like a man with somewhere to be, in the early weeks of his secondment to Native Affairs Henry grows an acquaintance with the director of the museum library, a man likewise of middle years, known to him as Mr Hamilton. They take to sharing sandwiches in the Garden and, during rainy lunchtimes, at Mr Hamilton's desk beyond the shelves of pale boxes that line a storeroom.

The two men barely speak about Henry's work; neither wants to hear the Reverend Vine's anatomies, the slippery laterals and bilabials of his Latin words. The pair of them keep things in Mr Hamilton's world. Mr Hamilton describes the work he does as 'eternal vigilance, Mr Vos, eternal vigilance against false history' and grows hot bright spots on his cheeks at any whiff of fashion in the decisions the museum takes about what will go on display and what is kept in storage.

'We have a duty to the truth,' says Mr Hamilton, and smacks the back of his right hand into the palm of his left. His seriousness unsettles Henry, but Mr Hamilton is redeemed by the way he laughs at himself. He is, for instance, rueful about his own preference for the charmed intact china plates from shipwrecks over the slave pattens and muskets from the city's dryland history. His laughter keeps Henry coming back.

One green day Henry and Mr Hamilton walk in the Company's Garden and stop for tea at the café there. Mr Hamilton steps, cautious as a heron, through an excruciating disquisition that Henry has trouble following, until he understands at last that Mr Hamilton is explaining that he cannot invite Henry to his home for a meal. The reason is to do with the watchful elderly parent with whom Mr Hamilton shares his house and some judgement that will be made on Mr Hamilton with Henry by his side. Inviting Henry to his home is something he would dearly like to do, in fact feels he ought to do, he tells Henry, and dares to touch his hand where it lies on the table, but he cannot, he cannot.

Henry is relieved at what he sees as an escape from the parent's knowing eye, but also holds a small resentment against Mr Hamilton for this – for even this roundabout allusion that makes of their companionship a lesser bond, a poor substitution.

On another morning – on almost any fine morning – Henry leaves his room, and the house where this is, with a piece of fruit in his hand and his hat on his head. His body warms his shirt and the cloth breathes out the scent of laundry soap. His shoes crack small grit underfoot; the sun stings his cheek. By adding a city block to his route he gains oaks at the flowering of their translucent new leaves, gains squirrels when he is ready to feed them his apple core, gains the bell-ringers of the little cathedral at silent practice, pretending to haul down on the ropes in sequence, dazing themselves with concentration while one of them calls the changes. Having come out of his way to see this, he barely breaks stride as he passes their half-open door. Another block and his barber waits, ready with the touch of his scissors, comb and towels. Henry will lean into them as a cat will under a man's hand.

In the years since Diyatalawa, all the many parts of him have been conscripted to crowd against this one part and give it no air, this other self that was surely a product of being young, far from home and in the foetid climate of Ceylon. It is years since he wrote up a programme – for today, this week, this year. He is practised, now, at filling his days. He reads. He asks, always, what it is that the reasonable man would do. He has learned that it is better for him not to be too hungry before he eats, or too tired before he lies down. Moderation is his watchword. He installs habits where otherwise drives might have play. He is vigilant with himself. What is sex, after all? He is spared being made ridiculous by it. He is spared the attentions of the Reverend St. John Vine, for instance.

A decade ago, when the bellows-blast of the Great War was felt even in Cape Town, he had found the courage to visit prostitutes, women, and complete the act under cover of the busy nights and harbour swagger. He discovered that it flared an itch in him that would not be cooled by their flesh, and once the momentum of novelty no longer worked on his own body he found he noticed too much about theirs, noticed what he would rather not, and he left off. He did not enlist in that war and in fact somewhat resented it as the eclipsing horror that made of his own a practice round in the eyes of the mother countries. He took to saying that wars made more sense over there; here, human works were too sparse to bear their harvest.

He experimented with adding to his programme the despising of Prem. He said loathsome things to himself directed at the sort of person Prem must have been. He laid on him, too, the crime of leaving Henry here alone and hated him for it.

From this misery he had woken to a life where holding himself so hard within became its own category of pleasure. He has learned to find depletion in other ways: he tramps over half the hills of the Cape, all of Stellenbosch. Controlled falling, this is what his life is, and in this way he is at least carried forward.

During his first season at Native Affairs, in the new office where banks of men at desks draft laws for the Union and he plugs away at Lusikisiki's problem, Henry attends a conference of Native chiefs and Native commissioners. The department provides tea. On the first day Henry, as a dispensable Justice man among the NA fellows, is asked in a whisper to leave the conference early to tell the ladies to turn up the spirit lamps under the kettles and uncover the food.

Between ranks of cups and saucers on white tablecloths in an anteroom is a spread of crumpets, sandwiches, dark cake. Henry happens to be near the table when the first of the chiefs leaves the conference hall and approaches the food. He is a man of about Henry's age and is wearing a new and correct suit of dark cloth, and over this a royally blue blanket pinned at the shoulder. He walks the length of the table, taking high, wooden-puppet steps in apparently new shoes, shoes he is wearing without stockings. At the end of the table he picks up a plate and retraces his careful path.

He stops halfway down the table in front of a dish of butter that has been shaped by the women into cross-hatched balls and set out with the crumpets. The chief, his face set in stiff interest, plucks one of the butterballs between thumb and forefinger and brings it to his nose; he sniffs it, sniffs it again, and puts it in his mouth. His jaws move. His eyebrows lift and he gives the slightest nod, then tips the dish and slides a dozen balls onto his plate. By the time he is joined at his table by what appear to be courtiers or advisers, he has worked his way through most of the butter, daintily, ball by ball, with faith in his good manners.

Henry will not forget the butterball chief. He notices himself noticing African men in the street, particularly when he comes upon a man dressed in his best clothes and walking his careful city walk. In these men, as in the chief, Henry thinks he sees the material expression of how he, Henry, feels as he makes his way among people, as he steers his invented self among them and convinces himself he understands their ways – that he finds something there for him to enjoy.

He wonders, is there someone who watches the way he is and knows it to be at best unorthodox and at worst false? Is he, too, in his studied navigation of this world of men and laws, eating butterballs daintily, singly, with perfect manners and imperfect understanding?

Henry's work with the Reverend Mr Vine continues, in its demand for laws to meet opinions and observations, in its blunt and old-fashioned moral anthropology – almost, he thinks, a test that has been set for him, the new Afrikaner attorney, by the department. Can he work through all the permutations and stand firm and tell the missionary that what he wants can or cannot be achieved in legislation?

Henry brings back from the conference the view of the chiefs that the sex training of the young, the thigh games and so on, is a way to preserve and not demoralise the tribe; that going some of the way to cool hot blood prevents the young-sters from going all the way. The thing to prevent is unmarried motherhood, motherhood in childhood, they tell him, with its clan upheavals and disputes. It is normal for the blood of the young to run hot, but we must not let this fracture the tribe, they tell him.

This makes so much sense to Henry and so incenses Vine when he writes to him to explain, with relief and eagerness, the logic of it, that Henry is left thinking that, like the old man in the camp on Ceylon, the man who had so minded the rattling of his and Clem's sticks on the corrugations, he himself is missing half a limb – a moral half-limb that other men use to carry them about every day.

But all the department cares about is that the disporting of young Natives with other young Natives has been assayed for legislation and found to be not worth its regard. Henry finds no audience for his excellent discovery about the tribal, sensible purpose of the means of relieving the urges of young men upon, he must suppose, the thighs of young women, although among people so sensible in these matters it surely cannot matter whose thighs.

What matters to the department is that there need be no subclause on the placing of the membrum virile, where and to what end. Henry must hear a last passionless joke about the frotteurs of Fingoland from the man to whom he reports, the Englishman from England, and then he must put the matter aside.

The main work of the drafting office is to do with another act, indeed, another Act, one taking the name of Native Affairs itself, and the continued codifying of traditional ways. While Henry was busy on the side street of morality, his neighbour in the room with the desks has been reading up on succession; the man to that neighbour's left is deep in inheritance. He joins them for the rest of the year in the well-mapped territory patrolled by a bill that will begin with what sounds to Henry like a boy's tree-house boast: 'The Governor General is the Supreme Chief of all Natives ...'

But Henry's revelation about thigh sex has shifted his way of thinking in other areas. In a place whose very industry is conformity, he becomes known for the inconvenient habit of admitting several points of view. On the other hand, he says, so often as to prompt groans and rolled eyes from his colleagues, on the other hand ...

Is he ... is this Vos chappie a nigger lover? The question

begins to be asked by his superiors, men with no patience for missioner-soft allowances and sympathies.

One day, from his bench across a Garden avenue, Henry watches one of his chieflike young men – is he perhaps a houseboy on his day off? Is he a mechanic, a baker, a telegraph runner? What does he do all day? – eat a peach with fastidious care for his suit of clothes, watches him suck his fingers and groom himself when he is done, and feels he almost could speak to the fellow. He does not approach him, but he looks him over, makes himself notice everything about him, from his handsome shoes to his head. Henry admires the way an absolutely straight path has been razored into the man's hair. He admires the way the hair seems constructed, sculpted, into a dense pad, a singular thing that gives off no light, above a face that has gleaming planes and velvet-dark hollows.

He rides the Sea Point bus behind another of his chiefly men. From his seat Henry can see the man's neck, his perfect ear, the curve of his head. A tiny green leaf is caught in his hair, tilted against his head, and Henry only just stops himself from reaching to lift it away.

6

HENRY ON THE INDIAN SINGLE is thighs and
shoulders, chest and heart, a body moving at speed
through space. With thoughts like this he enriches stretches
of the day and night he spends on the road from Cape Town
to Craigievar. There is a way home by train but the motorcycle
has been his for less than a year and he wants to show it off
to the family – to the brothers whose approval he may never
earn and to their sister, who loves him better than they or
them. This is difficult, though, more difficult than a journey
on horseback; he must watch every rut and run-off and tune
his muscles to the armature of the motorcycle; it is exhausting
and then, perilously, relaxing. To dose his drifting mind with
fear, he makes himself think about flying off the Indian, cracking his good spine against a tree, tearing his skin.

A day and a night after leaving the city, after dismounting
to open the gate, after pushing the bike over the farm boundary and closing the gate behind him, he removes his leather
jacket, his close leather helmet and goggles, and proceeds in
shirtsleeves, the sweat on his head cooling as he goes. The
smells of Craigievar arrive in turn – dust, acacia, cowpat, dip,

the hot minerals of petrol as he rolls to a stop and braces for a moment over the motorcycle to kill the engine.

His sister, fizzing with excitement to see him, bursts from the house to be enfolded in his arms. She takes him by the hand to lead him to his quarters. Henry no longer has a room in the farmhouse, the bedroom at Craigievar that he once shared with his brothers having long since been filled with nephews.

The brothers come in from the fields before nightfall and the family gather for dinner and to share news of their lives. Here, too, his reasonableness in the matter of national questions introduces a new consideration; in his dealings with his brothers there is a stutter, a pause. He is growing to be unlike them in more profound ways than that they are farmers and he an attorney in the city, or that they have or will have wives and children and he has these only at one remove, or only through them. His brothers occupy the high seats of wagons and tractors and, lately, trucks; he is a two-wheeled man, nimbler and of use chiefly to himself. He is in too many ways, they think, soft. These differences about him – the more discreet mark he makes on the earth, the sense in him of agility, of lightness – draw their sister to him.

Anna, who was born in the year Henry's war ended, who matches in her life the milestones in his, one step later, is almost a generation younger than the eldest Vos brother. She, too, holds a distinct place in the family – in her case, that of a welcome nuisance, an indulgence. Eighteen years separate Henry and Anna, but they are a pair nonetheless, bright as water among their family of stony farming Voses.

At dinner, the brothers address that which they have undertaken to address, speaking for minutes at a time, setting out the matter as it is; interruptions in the way of questions or observations are met with long beats of silence before they set the blade back in its furrow and heave themselves once more against their narrative. Among themselves, the brothers signal approval with silence, and dissent with the emphatic handling of tableware; the thump of the chutney jar is the most one will dare in answer to another. Anna, alone among the women, the brothers' wives, chatters, although she is in her way as careful as her siblings about how and when to disagree. With her, this takes the form of blurted statements, often so far removed from whatever gave rise to them that she has a reputation among them for spinsterish eccentricity; no Vos cares to look too narrowly at what might cause her to inform the table one night, 'I will never have children,' and on another day, 'I will never marry.'

The day after his homecoming, in the cottage that had housed his grandparents at the end of their lives, Henry wakes at dawn to the sound of rain on the tin roof, and feels a farmer's tears prickle his sinuses, as though something in him wants to answer the rain. In his pyjama bottoms and singlet, he leaves his bed for the little stoep that runs along the front of the small house. He stares through the rain, through its dim, secretive enfolding of the hills. When the air chills on his naked shoulders he fetches a blanket and settles in a wicker chair, warm again and content. If he turns his head to the left he can see the main house through the bluegums. Lamps have been lit there. From time to time a figure appears on the veranda, as if sent out to verify again this that they have not seen for half a dozen years. The three-word farmer's prayer seems to lie on the air between the main house and his cottage stoep, and over the vlei that is becoming a vlei again, and close by, where the air of the stoep meets the veil of water: Soft, soaking rain, it says. Soft soaking rain, and between and beyond its sweeps of sound, the mutter of thunder, promising more.

At the clang of the triangle Henry dresses and crosses to the big house under a cracked oilcloth coat he finds behind the door, surely once his grandfather's. At breakfast every face is shining with congratulation. His brothers' laughter, cracked as the oilcloth, rolls among them and the younger children wear amazed faces and risk small jokes and gestures with their food: a sausage nose, a jam moustache. Rain.

Rain like this could last the day, and at last they allow themselves to believe it, and so they direct tasks to do with roofs and poultry and settle to indoors work; this is almost a holiday in its honour. Their mother, their aunt and Anna and the wives make space for the men, spread mealie sacks on the dining table for them, and they break out the farm's small armoury to strip and clean the guns. Among the hunting rifles and the scarred Mausers, Henry is handed a Webley, a mere pistol, a curiosity, but he bends to it nonetheless and listens to their talk. A neighbouring farm has earned the brothers' scorn by taking in paying guests. In city magazines it advertises its 'healthful air' and 'farmhouse cooking'. The talk drifts on. Inevitably, with what their hands are busy with, it reaches their war, and veers from it as though the subject has been banned, and nudges at it again. He supposes his presence has something to do with this. Not that there is great hardship in avoiding the war: they all four survived it, and the women came through too, and so much luck suggests an account mounting up into high numbers, one that must be presented to the family in due time. Perhaps his dishonour is accepted as going some way to meet the price. Such are Henry's thoughts among the sharp smell of gun oil, and he twists his mouth at his pagan bookkeeping. He believes that of all the women on the farm, only his mother knows his history, and so it has been held apart from them among men who will never speak of it.

But it barely matters what they speak about – the rank their second brother held, the success of the elder's commando, anything but the double imprisonment of the youngest and his disgrace; they might be held apart by his history, the never-spoken matter, but today the blessing of the rain has brought to the surface the older bond that binds them one to another and to this place. The neighbours, the war, Craigievar … the brothers break out stories of the old days, when the wagons and the plough and the oxen, down to each named beast, were characters in their Vos tale. The women stay near the men but barely speak. Even Anna, seated to one side of the men and busy with embroidering blue flowers on the collar of a blouse, is silent.

The rain lasts well into the next day, lasts beyond the congratulations they give one another for it, but eventually, in a loud silence followed by a flurry and a patter of drops on the roof like seed thrown to hens, it stops.

In the afternoon Henry and Anna find one another and set out for the vlei while the rain is so recent its last drops hang on the undersides of tiny plants. They are headed for a pair of twisted rocks that serve as a water mark, to read the bounty, but already they can tell, from the pools on the path and from the feel of the earth under their boots, that more has been sent than Craigievar can hold, that this rain has replenished the farm at a deeper level. Again, the melancholy of gratitude seems to lie over the shallow hills. At the rocks, Anna takes off her boots and stockings and holds her skirt above her knees to wade to the larger of the twisted forms and find the ancestral scratchings, most of which are just under the surface. She makes a sound of surprise at this, and wades back to collect from Henry the stone chisel and mallet he carries. He stays on dry land, watching her reflection twist apart and coalesce on the rippled water. He takes a few steps to his right to separate her reflection on the water from that of the rocks, so that now they are three distinct darknesses on the surface, and closes one eye to complete the illusion. A shadow suddenly cuts across his idle game: the sun has broken through. He steps back, and notices that although the reflections shift as he moves, the shadow stays where it is. The reflection depends on him, he thinks, and the shadow on where the sun is in the sky. He wonders what to make of that, allegorically, metaphorically.

By late that afternoon the farm has returned to its patterns: the brothers are in the fields, the wives in the house, the children banished to the caves of bougainvillea at the end of the garden, and Henry and Anna are on the small back stoep of the farmhouse, surplus to needs.

The wide room where he drew his first breath and its twin, the first rooms on Craigievar, have shrunk to a pantry and storeroom off the kitchen, and are flanked by so many other rooms they must be organised by passageways and wings. The back stoep is overlooked by this pantry, and at the pantry's slim window, their mother, her hands busy with sifting and cleaning raisins for the Christmas feast, watches them.

Anna is convulsed with stifled laughter. Henry is building her a picture of Craigievar as a sanatorium for rich city women. He assigns tasks to their ponderous brothers – towel carrier, masseur. 'This way, madam,' Henry says, hunched to be heavy, but floating his hands, 'this way to your ...'

'Your slenderiser mud ...'

'Your dust bath ...'

In the dim pantry, their mother bites back a disloyal snuffle. She presses her mouth into a lipless line and considers the problem of her two youngest children. No matter the gulf in their ages, they belong together in her mind, apart from their siblings, not of the farm in the way that the sons and wives are of it. But she knows it is her work to keep all of them tethered, on however long a chain, and she has furthermore set herself to heading off this fatal lightness in Henry, this restlessness in Anna. There is a change in the air beyond Craigievar, as palpable as a shift in the wind, and although she cannot name the nature of the unease she feels, she has to prepare a defence against it.

She notices the sorting that her fingers are busy with and it comes to her that this inessential work with the fruit is all that is left in this hour of the day to hands that once smoothed the clay, dung and blood of the very floor of this room. Her strong pale legs and feet, bared to the thigh, had tramped and mixed the mud for this room's bricks. The food her children ate, and the clothes they wore, and the letters they learned to recognise, and the shelter over their heads, all had come at least in part, and often in large part, from her, but in the course of her lifetime this great round of work, the labour that had placed her at the core of her family, has been shared out to a hundred or more men, men she will never know, whose goods arrive in trucks in the town to be fetched by the farm – butchered beef and ground meal and packaged coffee, milled soap, loomed cloth, sewn shirts, machined boots and stamped tin. In her imagination the factories radiate from her home, busy as they are on her behalf (and that of a thousand thousand other women) with the tasks she once did.

And at the core of this system of energy and product are not her body and capable mind, not the skills, from honing a needle to building a house, that live in her, but the cashbox in the farm safe. The flimsy pounds, the coins and half coins, these are at the centre now, and where is she? And if she, a woman on a working farm, knows her labour to have been usurped – sees her daughter and daughters-in-law cast about for occupation, for value in their days, sees the mothers among them turn from their own lives to fold themselves around their children and draw from them more meaning than motherhood can bear – how much less valued must be the women of the cities?

And yet it is to a city that her daughter longs to go.

She recalls Anna, at fifteen, a small figure walking the boundary fence of the farm's home camp, then slumping at the kitchen table to ask her mother in tones too full of despair to discipline for their insolence and ingratitude: 'Is this all there is?'

She sees Henry at the same age, the year before he rides to war, laughing to himself over what he has written in his day book.

The idea comes to her to ballast Henry with Anna, and liberate Anna with him. Her hands grow still as she turns it over in her mind, the symmetry of it.

In a matter of days she has made her plan and trade: Henry, on his return to town this time, will be followed shortly by his sister. Without a word written down about it, just a series of grunts at the desk in the farm office from the first-born son, Henry's patrimony will be cashed in early; Craigievar will buy the last children a house in the city. Henry will wrap his new Indian in greasy cloths and accede to a neat Chevrolet. Anna will make good her escape from Craigievar, and for Henry there will be a home, a sister to keep it for him, a woman to hold him in place in the respectable world where, their mother is grateful to acknowledge, he has at least decided to make his life.

It is understood that he will not seek his portion of the family's several farms when the day comes but that he will, when the day comes, have a piece of ground in the small, fenced plot behind the main house, among his brothers.

Back in Cape Town, in his room in the boarding house where he has gone to ground for years, Henry gathers his phonograph records, his clothes and shoes and books. Although he has been earning and spending for years, he owns no furniture apart from his Victrola, and even this seems to belong in a category apart from furniture, a category that must be invented. A boy comes to help him pack. He brings a deep tea chest and Henry leans into this to settle a book in a corner of the tin-lined box. The sudden scent of tea puts him in the withering loft and he thinks he will swoon. That night he has Prem in his dreams, and on waking in the new house stretches and yawns, baring his teeth in lazy delight at the memory.

He can feel an engine within him coughing to life. Between Ceylon and here there had been … what? A decade, two decades that he cannot truly recall, could not describe. To give an accounting of those years, he would have to search his papers for matters archived by the material world – graduation, promotion and, recently, his first motorcycle, his first motor car. Can one really lose a whole passage of life like this?

Now everything will be different, in a home of his own, beginning with waking to almost silence and these uncovered windows – no hawking or coughing or moaning pipes as men stir in their several-storeyed house. Just him, putting Prem from him and standing up to meet the day and wander, in his pyjamas, into other rooms, and riddle the stove he had lit last night, scratch his belly as water heats for tea. Later that day there is Anna, directing a couple of men, in the confident way of a farm girl, to unload wicker crates of preserved and dried food from the cart that brought her from the station. There is too much of it, in jars and crocks and muslin, enough for their needs and extra to bribe their mother's gods. There is furniture: a pair of easy chairs, Anna's bedstead and chest. From a corner of the cart bed she unties a young dog sent from Craigievar to complete their household. Henry takes the silken, loose-skinned animal in his arms and kneels to set it on the city pavement.

The house is lemon yellow, lacy with cast iron, shaded by a tree. Spread below them, thrilling in its uncountable buildings, its electric lights and juddering motor cars, is the small city that calls itself a town. Anna stands on their high veranda, facing the bowl of buildings, and hugs her own arms in delight. Henry thinks, This may work.

Anna is twenty-four years old. Henry is forty-two. On that first afternoon she takes his arm like a bride to head down their steep street to shop for their supper. She looks about the grocer's, wanting it to be more interesting than it can ever be, and chooses packets by their attractiveness, not their price or familiarity or even, he thinks, their contents. She is so confident that this will be a place of wonder that he finds himself setting back his own shoulders to meet the welcoming city. He will learn it over again with her open pleasure in it, in their home, in the modern world of coffee houses and bioscopes, French cleaners and newsstands.

They wear their Sunday clothes to visit a grand crammed department store so vast and open they can barely see its far wall. They arrive before the usual time, early enough to send uniformed women scrambling to take their positions behind counters of glass and brass as Henry and Anna enter the gleaming place. She has her hand in his arm; he presses it to slow her to a stroll, and he can feel the tremble that shivers through her body as she turns her head this way and that and draws the courage to stop at a counter to admire a tree of gloves. She summons from somewhere the instinct that makes her head tilt to judge the goods, and her other hand reach to touch them. When at last they speak to one of the women who, in their dark uniforms and bristling carriage, combine the airs of being maids and madams at the same time, it is in their careful Cape English, fluting and round in the vowels and formal in cadence and address. Anna's chin is thrust forward and she grows stiff with offence when her question about pigskin is met by a suggestion of calf. Henry at last plants their flag and buys something – it is a set of three handkerchiefs arranged in a slim golden-lidded box. He has a fairground light in his eyes as the transaction begins: this is what he wanted her to see: brass-clad pneumatic tubes run like exposed arteries through the long room, bunching every so often and poking together through to the floor above. At the terminus of one of these, where the handkerchiefs wait on the counter, a man in a suit takes Henry's shillings and places these and the invoice he has written out into a little metal charger, seals it with a twist and slots it like a rifle shell into an opening in the tube. Too fast to be seen it is sucked out of sight. In a while, with a knock and a clatter, back come Henry's change and the invoice stamped PAID. It is a sort of magic but Anna knows she must not comment on it or show her amazement. She presses her lips together to keep from grinning.

Anna buys a bar of scented soap; he watches as she dares to fuss with her glove when the performance of the capsule and tube gets under way. She has grown brave.

Their lemon-yellow house has neighbours. One of these, Dianna, becomes a friend. She and Anna shop together for harem pants and they wear them to lounge on the veranda of the Vos home, crossing their legs like boys, tipping their heads back to laugh at Henry's jokes. Anna glances at the street to check for passers-by before she stands to go indoors. When they are alone Dianna looks directly at Henry. She is the daughter of the house next door, and is of the city. She is tilting her head and hunching her shoulders and he names it, her coquetry, to himself. Why ever not.

Now they are three, Henry with a girl on each arm, Henry at the bioscope, Henry tramping over Lion's Head. The girls adopt a waiting air. They seem to be watching for a change in his behaviour, a reaction from him now that Dianna is so often on his arm, or holding his hand on her arm, or bumping her upper arm against his in chummy fondness. They watch him as though it is inevitable that his own arms will begin this reaching, stroking, bumping business. He has been shown Dianna, and the expectation is that he will, with decorum and wit, seize her. Henry pats her and makes himself touch her as she precedes him into rooms. She backs into his touch, pressing closer each time he slides by.

He contrives to be alone with her less often but he is no match for the girls, and one summer evening he finds himself leaning over her to kiss her. He smells her body, her breath dark with coffee, the talc scent of her hair. He is aware of their relative sizes; he is too large next to her, and her body as blandly uninteresting to him as that of a doll, but he has kissed her and so is obliged to do so again, on successive nights, and when he next heads out to take in a film he is somehow made a gift of by Anna; she stays home, and he steps down the hill with the neighbour's daughter, an undoubted couple, and his thoughts divide into two streams: he can think of nothing but how to drop her hand from his arm, even while he notices the new way he is regarded by men they pass on the street – the fact that he is regarded at all.

At work, Henry makes a discovery among a new batch of law reports. He reads:

– 'to wit, did insert his penis between the thighs of the said T and move it backwards and forwards until he, the said N, had an emission of semen'

He returns to the case many times, after elaborate detours to hide what he is looking at. He reads:

– 'seeks to satisfy his unclean inclinations in another way than it ought to happen according to the ordained order of nature'

– 'The Criminal Ordinance of the Emperor Charles V – if a human being behaves unchastely (unheusch treiben) with an animal, or male with male, or woman with woman, they have forfeited their lives, and they shall, according to the usual custom, be condemned to be burned to death'

– 'qui perversam venerem in vas non debitum rexerunt, ore, mammis, natibus abutendo' (Henry recognises 'perverse sexual use made of an improper vessel, lips, breasts, buttocks'; it is an emperor-wide net spread here, too)

And three months' hard labour for each transgressive embrace and indefinite imprisonment for a repeat embracer.

These are named crimes now. The case is labelled *Rex* v. *Narroway*; he thinks of it as Narroway and the Unnatural

Offence. To see such matters written down, recorded, is as potent as poison. It works as a numbing agent on Henry's mind.

There is the crime of Vaseline in a man's dressing table; there is 'sexual gratification by friction against the hand of another' and 'skylarking' in a bed. The judge confides that even masturbation is 'a disgusting act' and at this Henry thinks, 'Now I know something about *your* private life, Gardiner J' and keeps an eye out for the judge, or mention of him, hoping to look at him in the knowledge of this small lie, this small shame that must be in him. There is in fact every chance he will see the judge some day: the appeal was denied only last year and Henry, by his profession, moves in Justice circles.

He reads: 'There has been no change in public opinion that would cause such conduct to be regarded as otherwise than abhorrent' and wonders, What sort of law is this, giving legal weight to a guess at a poll of opinion of conduct? And realises that he has found here a law in bud: the judge is not merely trying a man in terms of the law, he is making law in terms of his opinion. Did he take even as much care with it as the dozing man in the long room at Native Affairs, he whose clause on deceased estates grew slow as a crystal in a salt solution, neglected and inelegant?

The judge expands on his masturbatory track:

'One of the reasons given for punishing carnal acts contrary to the order of nature was that by such an act a possible procreation of children was defeated. Hence the severity with which the offence of onanism was punished. An example of this is given in Leyser, *Meditat. ad Pandect.* (Spec 589). There a married man was charged with adultery, an offence punishable by a fine only. He admitted the deed. However, his counsel set up the defence that the connection had not been completed, but that the accused had followed the example of Onan. The result of this defence was that instead of being fined, the accused was flogged and banished, some of the judges first thinking that the death penalty should be inflicted.

'This affords me a convenient opportunity of saying that the accused in the present case is not in so unfortunate a position, for the advocate appointed by the Court to argue on his behalf has certainly been of assistance to him, and by his researches has been of great help to us.'

Long after the moving backwards and forwards of the penis has been dulled by over-reading, this gentlemanly aside still provokes a reaction in Henry. He cannot get past the space it claims for levity, the sense it gives of overhearing banter between officers of the opposing side before a battle, the distance it forces between the bench on one side and the lesser man – Narroway, Henry himself, perhaps Mr Hamilton – on the other.

He grows certain on repeated readings that the judge is laughing up his sleeve, making a schoolboy pun with his tortuous 'the conclusion come to is that even where there has been no emission the act is punishable'.

If it truly is a crime, why is there sniggering? It seems that dislike, more than sanction, is being expressed here. Most of all he chafes with anger that this, this smirking essay, is the record. His secret anger burns so hot it is almost not anger any more, but a sort of world above this world where, in his mind, he can only stare rudely, can only gape in schoolboy insult.

At home, Dianna presses him for more. She does this with serene assurance.

There is a warrior in Dianna, a crusading spirit that pits her against the world. She gives Henry to understand that he has her strong mind and certainties to thank for her determination to join with him in spite of his age (she is five or so years older than Anna, thus more than a decade younger than him). His age will not be allowed to matter as she conducts them towards the bargain she is determined they will strike.

He is scrupulous with her, and kind, and fond. He truly does admire her, and this is their undoing.

Dianna is a working woman, a teacher at a grand girls' school in the suburbs. She speaks often of her day, of her fellow teachers. One evening, Dianna is addressing Anna as Henry joins them in the sitting room. 'Oh, they're always dead keen to get their hands on our girls,' she is saying. Dianna glances at him for his reaction. By 'our girls' she means the teachers of her school, who are in demand by sister schools throughout the Union. Headmistresses are imported from England, but the teachers are mainly Union girls and part of a busy trade between Grahamstown, Houghton, Bloemfontein.

This trade of theirs, his and hers, that he does not understand – or, rather, that he refuses to acknowledge – is surely almost upon them. He has held her at bay with the appearance of perfect enjoyment of her company and, when he cannot avoid it, the kisses she seeks. But she has pressed on, and has taken to engineering kisses and then pulling away herself to draw him on.

Now she says, crossing her legs and twitching the pleats of her skirt into alignment: 'They have asked me to take on head of department at St Michael's. It's a huge promotion. I'd have to up sticks, though. Bye-bye Cape Town, hello Bloem.'

The response he ought to give lies before him. Anna's face, anticipating it, has adopted the o and eyebrows of woe. But Henry falters. Had he liked Dianna less he might have remembered the form, remembered to be selfish and flatter her with his loss, but instead he blurts with delight, 'How wonderful! You must take it, of course!' and she stiffens and draws back and for one awful moment is unable to leave her chair.

'When are you off?' he continues to her face blank with hurt.

She is freed by a noise that Anna makes to fill the soundlessness, and blunders from the room, knocking over and catching a vase on a table by the door, spinning to set it down, breathless with apology.

Henry is dismayed, relieved. Anna rushes to comfort him. She turns against their new friend to do so, and in the bluster and fuss of her exoneration there is no opportunity to explain himself, not that he is certain how he would do this.

Dianna takes the job and soon the memory of her pales until she is just another part of the business of setting up their new life.

But Dianna is not the last of them. Every so often he draws

another decent woman to him. They seem to find brotherliness in him, and from that, lacking any other language for what they want to say, progress to the rituals and words of wooing, or inviting wooing, until he exhales and slips backwards, away from them. Extraction always hurts – hurts the women, who know it is a lack in them. Henry minds being taken for a dishonourable man, a trifler, but the prickle of it works on him, accustoms his palate to it, and he becomes adept at telling tales, polished anecdotes to hold them rapt. He does not turn aside the attentions of the girls until he has won their interest. Anna waits them out. He watches her pat her hair in the mirror after he leaves another, wounded.

Their home in the city outlasts the young dog and a new puppy is fetched from Craigievar. In their habits and in the way they appear to the world, Henry and Anna grow towards one another until they are a pair. Sometimes she mock scolds him as Mr Vos, and he answers, slurring her title, Mizz Vos, slurring mevrouw, mejuffvrouw to remind themselves of their coupledom, to play with the idea of it. If a bioscope usher or a shop girl takes them for married, as sometimes happens, they are strict with themselves about denying this out loud and hiding their small happiness. He and Anna have Mr Hamilton to a feast of a supper in their home, triumphant, seeking an audience for the better way they have found for people to be.

The same habituated falling and correcting muscles keep Henry stepping in place.

———

One by one Henry's colleagues at Native Affairs, and even Justice men like him on endless loan, cast off for field posts, leaving to set up as their own man in distant red-earth districts, keen as hounds for the hardships and entertainments of that life – termites in the armchairs, mongooses on the stoep, the womanless, shirtsleeves romance of it. Henry is not tapped to be a Native commissioner. His soft ways with his chiefly men must keep him fenced off from them. He could press for his own advancement, but he fears that reaching would expose him, cuff and wrist; Henry, though he has his diplomas and papers, his degrees and letters, nurses the pride and sore spots of a self-made man. He keeps busy enough with the theoretical end of things, bound to the grey building near the Gardens.

He is fully fifty years old when the call comes from his old department: Justice wants him for a magistrate, in the small central town of Gower.

Magistrates administer another set of laws; Natives come under their rule, it is true, but mainly town Natives, city Natives. And besides, as well as being known as a good man, a good worker, Henry Vos can be said to be an Afrikaner – a thing lately useful in this age of quotas: thus the arguments on his behalf before, midway through the year 1935, Justice delivers him to a title of respect, another chance at small renown.

He brings the news home to Anna, unsure of himself. He sounds like a boy when he stands, filling the doorway, to ask his sister, 'You will, will you, come to Gower? Will we go on as before, there?'

She frowns at him, tucks her chin to make an Old Testament face: '"Whither thou goest, I will go; and where thou lodgest, I will lodge: thy people shall be my people", ' and they laugh.

His life clicks forward a notch:
  – Young Boer
  – Long loan from Justice
  – The Magistrate of Gower

III

GOWER

7

IT IS ACCEPTED IN GOWER that it was the British who wanted them, Gower and towns like it, spaced across the flat lands of the interior as though with giant callipers, with one built at those intervals wherever the nearest fold of earth had, in its crease, a river. Each is so like the next, its components might have been ordered from a seed catalogue: a froth of pepper trees, the shard of a church steeple, then lesser flat planes and red roofs and streets set wide enough to take the full turn of a wagon, the town at its building having been intended for all time to be the end of the road. But another would be built, north or northwest of this one, and named like its noble brother – Carnarvon, Worcester, Sutherland, Gower – and over time be fitted with a steeple, trees, a main street whose shops faced one another across a street almost too wide for hailing. They must run out somewhere, these towns, but from here it seems as though they repeat like a pattern on a vast bolt of cloth, all the way to the Vaal.

Gower has a railway, church, school and court, and municipal electrical light. It has twenty-nine street lamps, not quite enough to reach the furthest streets where trees track slim water channels.

And yes, Gower is laid out according to the British manner, the product – at some point in its brief history since it was a tent by a brook where a smous overwintered one season – of men with theodolites, pegs, line.

Henry feels the fresh air of this place, feels a mental hitching of trousers and settling of shoulders as he and Anna step towards their new life. The people of the town appear to him at a fond remove, as if he is back among his own people but is no longer truly of them. It is an engaging sensation to report on them to himself, to notice the stilted rituals of courtesy and commerce, and discount them as he might the mad tilting mannequins in a museum diorama or their sedate cousins in the window of a department store on Adderley Street.

This, everyone knows, is how people live now. People who have sold their farms to strangers and moved to town. Some among them speak of it as a choice, as the building of a new nation. The nation must change if it is to prevail for, although as a people they would always be said to be of the farm, this new nation will be built in the towns. In this becoming time, they angle to join a kudu hunt in the winter, or a drive for smaller game when a pair of days can be found among the days of the week – a hunt on the lands of the one in twenty of them who has kept and grown what he was given, or took. In town, some of the men have gardens, and some have workshops. Not one of them follows the occupation, trade or profession of his father.

There is electrical light in many of the houses, and no excuse not to be busy. The men who break the pattern – who keep, for instance, exotic animals in breeding cages and spend what they have come to call their free time on feeding, cleaning, clipping and admiring these – are known for it, and treated as harmless obsessives. Their hobby is made into part of their name – Bunny Conyn, Kiep Theron – and a thin layer of fame attaches to them; it is agreed that they resemble whatever small mammal, fish or bird is their pride.

This breeding habit is one of the ways in which Henry does not completely reconcile himself to Gower. It is neither city nor farm in its nature, this habit – much like the town itself.

He wonders, in his first months in the little town, whether he has not bought his title too dearly.

He and Anna were not unrespectable people in their city life, but there are aspects of that life that do not survive the move to Gower, and respectability is part of the reason – Gower's respectability. There is, for instance, no café society in Gower; the lone tearoom is understood to be for people passing through or stopping in town for a few days for a case in Henry's court, and it closes at five o'clock. Respectable Gower drinks coffee in its own home, and not usually after dark.

Another immediate change is the lack of a daily newspaper: Gower is served by two biweekly papers that, perversely, arrive from other towns on the same two days every week. There is a twice-weekly, not a nightly, bioscope in a room attached to the church that serves also for bazaars, committee meetings, evening lectures and, for one brief season that is winding down by the time Henry and Anna arrive, a Women's League of Health and Beauty exercise class, introduced to the town by the chemist's wife on her return from a steamship visit to England. This is a town of flaring enthusiasms.

Without a word about it, Henry and Anna adjust their dress: he does not step into the street without a hat on his head and is never outdoors in shirtsleeves. She folds away her harem pants and quickly picks up the code of when and when not to wear gloves. In several ways they button up for Gower.

Henry turns out to own one of only a handful of private motor cars in the town and its finest suits. He has his phonograph records of Mario Lanza and his American magazines. He is familiar with the latest technology, and surely familiarity with technology is one of the measures of a man. He and Anna join the round of professional men and their wives – stopping to speak to them after church (they pick up the habit of church), standing with them at town gatherings. In a way that they had not been in the city, Henry and Anna are joined in being different from their neighbours. They become aware of the habits the town adopts towards them, the flickers of deference, and recognise that they have been banished to the town's corral of first citizens.

Henry has looked forward to malfeasance in his court, and the exercise of justice, but what he finds rather more of is drudgery. The small crimes of Gower are dulled by statute by the time they reach him; a night pirate who whistles another man's cattle through a moonlit kloof and relies on the honour of men to spirit them along a chain of friendly kraals is, in his court, just an illiterate in broken shoes to be sent down for stock theft. Most of the crimes that come before him can be grouped, with stock theft, under the heading of scavenging, the scavenging, as Henry sees it, of hungry men: among unguarded flocks and herds, among women, among the old.

In his court he tries to switch places in a dispute, or tries to imagine doing so, and to substitute parts of any argument for other factors. He presses his mind to follow the reasoning – and the reasons he guesses at – of the man in the dock before him; he believes he is able to go further into the thickets of wickedness than ought to be the case for a magistrate, but he can follow, and without much effort imagine, the hunger, the separate compulsions. When he imagines the dreadfulness of discovery, however, the awful backwash of adrenalin, he can only wonder at the criminal courage of those who steal or swindle or do whatever the deed in actuality.

Henry is darkly amused to learn that one of his magisterial duties is to abet many lies on the part of Natives. For instance, Natives who wish to buy brandy must first apply to him for written permission to make the transaction. They must convince him that a relative is perishing of a fever that only herbed brandy can lift; they have the herbs, they have the symptoms down pat, they have relatives and shillings in their pockets. All they need from him is the 'paper'. But, although he laughs at the idea of it, when he has the man before him, hat in hand, Henry has no appetite for either the lies or the law and signs without meeting the man's eyes. The small reward it gives him in the matter of discretion – where the morality of a man's being free to take a drink can surface in this only slightly bent exercise of the law – is fine, he thinks, but wishes it had been in service of a more elevated matter. Nonetheless.

Nonetheless, it is no small thing to be a magistrate. 'Magistrate' means something, and if that something is less than it might have been even twenty years before, and if the diminished stature of the post is at least part of the reason it is now his … These are not thoughts he allows any play.

Natives who have exhausted the permission of the court and are thus denied legal brandy from the hotel off-sales must take their chances at the Hole in the Wall, where the stuff is several times the price and the transaction risks more than just the court orderly cursing them to their faces. A necessary dark sump in Gower, a place to collect the men's loose energy and keep the women and children and the earning and spending part of the town clear, the Hole in the Wall is on a corner at the end of the mechanics' road at the edge of town. During the day it is closed up tight with grilles on the windows and a padlock and chain on the door, looking like a storeroom if it looks like anything. But at night the grille comes down and the doors stand open, and the Hole draws the men they call sherry boys for brandy and whisky, draws off their shillings.

In his first year in Gower, Henry learns, during a case in his court, that the Hole is where Engel has gone to ground – Engel of the quayside, of Diyatalawa and Ragama, the man who thinks he knows Henry's criminal heart. The magistrate curses the smallness of his tribe that makes such a thing possible: Engel, here. He must be almost seventy years old and still he has this power, dark Engel who keeps to the dim inner office of the Hole and calls the furtive world to him.

In the fine house he and Anna have found on a treed street in Gower proper, Henry feels a tug from the mechanics' road: taking his ease on the veranda with Anna, talking over the day, at night, or as he walks the perimeter of his home before turning in: whichever way he turns, he knows which way Engel lies.

These are Gower's cardinal directions: courthouse, church and Hole, and every Wednesday and Friday a train, bringing the newspapers that serve the town, bringing the weekly parcel post, bringing, in their season, hostel boarders home for the holidays.

On a Wednesday in May, in the winter of 1938, at the start of the third year that Henry and Anna Vos expect to spend here, it brings Adaira van Brugge, the Adaira of his confession.

8

THE ENGINE SEETHES AND SETTLES and she has a clear half minute to take in her hosts before they see her. They stand, father and daughter, a coach length up the platform, facing the wheezing engine; something must be happening there, or perhaps they expected her to travel first class. Whatever their reason for not noticing her, Adaira has time, before collecting her coat and cases, to catalogue a middling sort of man and a heavy girl of about thirteen, budding. The girl speaks to the man; he answers with a twitch of his mouth and she bends at the waist, holds her hands to her stomach to laugh.

Adaira breathes to calm herself and stands still (as a jackal, as a gecko, as grass) to allow them to notice her, in the few moments she has until it begins. The similes are hers. At the coach door Adaira gathers into words everything she sees and hears, and every small sensation: the seam of her glove where her hand grips the rail by the door. The cat's-tongue rasp of one stocking top against the other. The changed air on her cheek, the sense of cinders heating the dawn breeze. The way her hat fits her head like a helmet and makes her braver.

The man, Mr Theron, is in front of her. He reaches up to help her down the steps. His hand is warm, thick, male.

'Nantie's mother has breakfast waiting for us,' he says. His breath condenses in the cold. A boy takes Adaira's things on a barrow and the three of them follow him, out of the railway station and on to Gower's main road, father and daughter Theron holding hands. Adaira walks alongside and slightly behind them.

The street is being woken by men in aprons, men in overalls, men with brooms, awning poles, buckets of water. Men in suits stand in the doors of offices, watching the morning unfurl. There are a few motors at either side of the wide road, but none of them obliges Adaira by moving in the short time the little party is on Church Street.

They leave the road for an unpaved lane and turn in at the gate of a house, and mount a few broad steps to a stoep under a red tin roof. Mrs Theron comes from the house with a careful smile.

'Your new home,' says Mr Theron. 'In you go.'

Inside, the daughter Nantie is given charge of her. 'This is the sitting room and this is the dining room. This is my room. The bathroom is down there. It is inside the house,' she says with heavy emphasis.

'This' – she makes a sweep of her hand – 'is your room.' Nantie is keyed up, officious, perhaps even scornful. Is that possible? Adaira knows she is old enough by several years to be amused by this, but feels the pinch of it nonetheless. She enters her room. Her cases are by the bed. There are daisies in water on a table.

Nantie calls her back to the wall by the door. She points to a small, flat box with two buttons. She makes a great show of pressing one of these; a light mounted on the wall above it glows. She presses the other and the light goes out. The girl widens her eyes at Adaira to make it clear that she, Adaira, is a moron, and at this Adaira can at last see in her something so young that she stops being provoked by her, and merely twists her mouth and waits for the girl to quit the room.

When she is alone, however, she finds her hairbrush in her smaller case and presses the electrical light button with the brush handle held at the end of a rigid arm, blinking and holding her breath. Of course the light lights up for her, too, and she is unharmed by it. Who is she acting this for? There has been an electrical lead into the house at the mission station for months now, even if Father claimed the right to be the only one to operate it – not his daughter, not the servant – and it came from a tame room behind the workshop, not from the town. This is not her first electrical light, no matter what (she supposes from Nantie's tour) must have been discussed by the Therons about the lacks and backwardness of where Adaira comes from.

Lacks, yes. Backwardness, yes. Who could deny it. Her home is deep in the bundu, in the gramadoelas, doorengone – a mission station built so flat and low to the earth it could not be seen by one looking back from even a few miles away, and only inferred from the sharp angle where a low escarpment met the plain, as though it would fold flat to the ground and cease to be until it rose again to meet those returning to it.

As a girl Adaira had endured a passage of annual trips from

the dwindling station and back home after almost a year each time, but she has been done with school and late girlhood for almost a decade now. When she came home from school as a matriculant she had been greeted as an equal, a companion who would end her mother's isolation and take up her share of the burden of their husband and father. But she had also been met as child to be told to her face when she failed in this. During those blank and drifting years, slipping from girlhood to womanhood and back, she had barely left the station.

Her mother, though, had left, waning like the light and leaving Adaira with so unsatisfactory a reason for her death as 'a weak heart'. Hearts *were* weak, Adaira thought; it was no excuse.

Adaira sets aside a case of clothes and shoes and opens the trunk that is more than half filled with books. There ought to have been more, she thinks, as she sets about unpacking them.

After almost two years of somehow culpatory legal letters and at last a bank draught, a bequest from her mother had delivered to Adaira a share of an adult's estate. Adaira had read in the tremendous surprise of the money the promise, or the hope on her mother's part, of escape, but she had not been able to imagine a life away from the station, not yet, and so to start with the money had gone only on books, delivered three times a year by arrangement with a bookseller in Bloemfontein. Adaira had reasoned that, with money in the bank and a home within reach, if only barely, of the Union Post Office, she could start a library.

The remoteness of her home and the sparse mail service had meant Adaira and the bookseller did not correspond each time on what the shipment should include; she could only mark most of her purchases in review, after they had been delivered. 'Something old, something new' had been her fine careless brief when she first wrote to arrange the matter. She had set fiction as her only absolute, and had hoped vaguely that there would ensue an elegant and rewarding transaction in which he intuited her taste and worked to ensure her delight and she, in enjoying his selection, somehow was in conversation with him – a slow conversation across hundreds of miles and with weeks between responses in her mind, in his.

Instead, she had grown uncomfortably aware of the nature of the man – it was surely a man, if not the man she had hoped for – who was making the choice for her: there were indications of instruction in many of the books, of childish, hollow worthiness among the pleasure and diversion. Indeed, in some of the choices she thought she was being chided – for having money, she supposed, or for wanting novels, for her unserious mind that had lit on something so feminine and jocular as a bridal superstition for her criteria.

She had waited him out, helped by the few books that, when she reached the end of the story, stayed in her hands as she turned back to the start to read the New Zealand address of the British publisher, the Berlin office's thrilling -strasse, the author's dedication, just to postpone letting them go. These few score she had brought with her to Gower.

In the end, Adaira had pushed herself to look for a different use for the money, an escape of another sort. Like the books, this had not been something that could be managed right away, or even in a matter of months. Chief among the delays had been that Adaira needed first to replace herself: she had to find, and train, a woman to care for her father. In her year of preparation for her year in Gower, of narrowing down to the town she would move to, the people with whom she would board, of ordering three frocks and a hat by post – 'something suitable for town, for fair colouring; I am unmarried, twenty-six and have quiet tastes; I enclose my measurements as per your advice': so she had written to Fichardt's in the same city as the bookseller – of spending unaccustomed moments look-ing at her own face in the station's only mirror, trying to guess what would be seen in her now that she was to be seen, of writing out for the girl Meisie who would succeed her, in pic-tographs, a minutely considered manual of care for her father: eggs thus, warm milk thus, hot water and collars and shaving kit thus – in the depths of this work that asked of her that she set down that which had been a matter of her unthinking daily round, Adaira surprised herself by concluding that her father was two people, or needed to be two people, or took up the space of, the energy of, the milk and bread and time of, two people. Whereas she took up the space of her own self, he moved through the world as himself and the necessary woman who must accompany, clothe, feed, warm or cool the house of, manage the schedule of, him. Was this to do with the sort of man he was – otherworldly, lost in his Greek and religious fever or sunk so deep in his grey moods as to seem to slip towards an animal state – or just with being a man, who does not ques-tion that, in the way of the world, he must make provision for himself and one other? She had no way of knowing, because he was the only man she knew, outside of books and imagined booksellers.

She thought she would not be missed. What use was she on the other side of the study door as he negotiated with God in shouts and whimpers? Very soon her absence would cease to be a phenomenon in the station, and its milk and daily round would be delivered without her.

And here she is: once more, in the presence of women, of people, slipping between selves. She has come to Gower as a child clutching a talisman, come with a woman's judging eye, come with her adolescent prickles erect, and as open as a girl. Living almost all her life in the place of her childhood, with her status unchanged, has kept her succeeding selves, her changing ages, fresh in her.

She would design herself in successive layers if she could, not this kaleidoscope.

At breakfast Mrs Theron passes a key along the table to Adaira: 'For your room,' she says, and Adaira slides it into the palm of her hand, drops her hand to her thigh and holds it there for a moment before she stows it in her pocket. She nods her thanks, not meeting Mrs Theron's eye. The key, her room, these are the end of a journey that had taken Gower as its goal for no more sensible a reason than that Adaira's mother had once had a girlhood friend here, a friend whose letters over the years she had received as cruel treats for their descriptions of shops and shaded streets. The friend was long gone from the town, but she had at least left in Gower the promise of a familiar ghost.

At the Theron house, Adaira grows aware in the course of the day that her hosts are as shy as she is. She tells herself, in small revenge for the lessons about indoor plumbing and electricity, that if there is a part of Gower that offers the life she intends to encounter, it will be outside this house.

Mrs Theron has planned a way for her to spend the day after her arrival in Gower. With Mr Theron at court, where he is chief clerk to the magistrate of the town, and Nantie at school, she produces *De Huisgenoot* with a recipe for a complicated cake. They could bake. Would she like that? Mrs Theron keeps a mild smile on her face and holds her words close and Adaira guesses that her presence is pressing on Mrs Theron – just a touch, but that on a bruised instinct for solitude.

They must visit the shops to find the exotics in their recipe – coconut or preserved cherries or some such. They gather their hats and walk the way Adaira came yesterday, into the town that lies between the station and a ripple of hills, its central street bannered with shop awnings, the streets flanking it under bluegums and plane trees.

They have not walked a dozen steps on Church Street when a woman comes at them.

Mrs Theron keeps both arms pulled in close to her body, with her handbag between her and the woman's accusations: 'Mrs Sara Theron! And what do we have here?' The woman has her eyes on them but her head is tilted slightly away as she speaks, as though she is commenting on them to another, invisible, party. She is utterly different from Mrs Theron: how firm and upright and solid her body is against the gentler form of the younger woman; how definite are her colours:

Mrs Theron and the other Gower women Adaira has seen this morning wear veld and forest colours – fawn, most of all, fawn with a print of pale small flowers or dim inorganic shapes, and shoes of brown leather, neat buttons. Adaira has been relieved, until now, to see that her own dress is wholly unremarkable among them. This woman, though, is in black with blocks of smacking bright yellow and chemical green, bold as a chevron. Adaira feels the woman fill her gaze.

Mrs Theron has not said a word since she introduced Adaira to this Mrs Vena Cordier, who had already, it seems, known her name. She has not stopped talking – 'don't think you will have her all to yourself, Mrs Theron, no, no' and, to Adaira, 'an uncle of mine studied with your father at Leiden you know' – all the while ranging her gaze over the two of them and off to the invisible audience. There is something she wants from them but she will not have it from Mrs Theron, who has pulled her lips back from her teeth in a stiff, repulsing smile. Adaira has barely said a word. Vena Cordier at last lets go of them, moving in a way that makes them step aside for her, and leaving Adaira and Mrs Theron with the impression that they have fallen short of her expectations.

Mrs Theron breathes deeply and they go on their way. They do not speak until she notices they are past the shop she wants and turns them back, and they find their way to the cherries and so on.

On their way home, Mrs Theron notices that the girl by her side walks like a boy, with a musical, swinging step, the step of someone alone on a street in conversation with herself. She knows something of Adaira's life of isolation with the somewhat venerated, somewhat despaired-of churchman who is her father, and wonders how, with all her books, Adaira will find the vocabulary to be understood by Gower.

That afternoon a note comes to the house. Adaira rubs buttery flour from her fingers to open it and finds Mrs Cordier's invitation to Miss A. van Brugge to attend a meeting of the Women's Federation in the church hall. She shows it to Mrs Theron.

Mrs Theron says, 'I don't go to the Federation. But you go, you go. It will be something for you to do,' and Adaira, although she convicts herself of fraud in the matter of the 'women' in the title, sets out alone into the town the next day.

At the hall Mrs Cordier waves her into a room full of members in conversation. She silences them and introduces Adaira as 'our new recruit' and says a few words about Adaira's father. As she walks Adaira to a seat she finds out from her that she kept the records at the station and can type, and names her on the spot secretary to her Committee for Social Welfare, and announces this to the room in her opening remarks to a frantically dull afternoon of resolutions and presentations, almost everything either led by Vena Cordier or interrupted by her to be corrected. The only point of interest comes during a demonstration from one of the older women of the correct way of measuring a head for a Voortrekker cloth bonnet. She has brought a deep, dark example of the old-fashioned headdress along to show the meeting. She puts it on and her face disappears. Its ribbons reach almost to her knees. She has a pattern they may copy, she says, and there is a way of quilting the edges … as the meeting ends the women cluster about her.

Somewhere in there Adaira has signed up for the committee. The committee work will be something to do, as Mrs Theron said. Adaira had thought she might find a job in Gower – had hoped to, as a means of building a tether to a different sort of life, and perhaps a reason to stay beyond the year she has set as her term here – but there is little to appeal to her in the town's range of work. She had learned from the Therons last night that Gower's only factory is a small taxidermy operation on the edge of town; it takes in girls, although probably not of Adaira's sort; in the offices among the shops on Church Street there is typing, telephony and other small work, all of which seems to settle women at tables to coax and tend machines. She thinks she sees in this work, this committee work that does not pay, at least some of the rewards of employment.

Besides, even if she is saying yes to everything that comes her way, cakes and committee work, these are still decisions, and with every decision she takes she feels that deciding muscle, that ability, strengthen. For all her brave lifted chin, Adaira is still in a truer sense inhabiting fright. She does not put into words what she risks among them, the people of Gower, the women of Gower, but it is, of course, ridicule. Every small gesture or choice is a matter of conscious reflection. Is this acting? Almost acting, yes.

She thinks, too, that she may have to become stupider. Her senses have grown used to the small range of the station's sounds; all of Gower will finish them off. She must put aside her solitary poetic habits and try to see the world in prose, to report on it to herself until she can adjust to the roar and range of it.

At the supper table that night Mr Theron does not laugh at her employment, and although his eyebrows lift and he makes a gentle joke about 'our little committee woman', he holds something back.

'Vena Cordier will have Miss van Brugge in Happy Valley every day if she doesn't watch out,' he says, the lightest warning in his voice, but whether it is about her or the place they call Happy Valley is not clear to Adaira.

Mr Theron says he has a theory about Mrs Cordier's committee and the other committees that constitute and re-constitute themselves among the proper women of Gower: this election just past was the women's second go at voting for the prime minister, he says. Having the vote is old hat already and it has given the ladies a taste for power. They want offices of their own, he says, and so they make them up.

Mrs Theron clears her throat. She says to Adaira, 'We may as well speak about the leiwater if Mr Theron wants to speak about a taste for power.'

He laughs, but Nantie glowers at Adaira as though she has brought news of her recruitment to an enemy camp.

This is Happy Valley: down by the swampy ground two streets behind Church Street, behind the street with the diesel workshop and the seed-and-feed warehouse, the town is grow-ing a tin town. Mr Theron says, 'You see them trail into Gower, new ones every week, looking at the motors and the properly dressed people.'

Something about Gower draws them – its railway halt, its

central situation in the country (although how can such scale have meaning to them?) or perhaps the fact that, with some having settled, there is now a place for others to settle, rather than pass through. Jamestown, Gower's nearest neighbour, has them too, though, the poor whites.

Vena Cordier invites Adaira to coffee at her home to explain how things work. She shows Adaira to the sitting room and kneels on the carpet there to set up an electrical heater, the first Adaira has ever seen; behind her, a wizened blonde girl enters with a trembling tray of coffee and small cakes and is directed with a flapping, impatient hand to set it on a low table.

At last Mrs Cordier pats the squat green machine and gets to her feet. She directs Adaira to sit, sit, and settles into a chair herself with a bright look. A smell of burnt dust rises from the heater.

Their conversation is a halting business, at least at first. Mrs Cordier asks about Adaira's father, and Adaira, who knows her father so well she could draw him from memory, cannot relay one simple fact about him. How to say any true thing about this troubled priest who is, at the same time, a father, a widower? How to choose which of his selves to present to Mrs Cordier?

Mrs Cordier, on the other hand, is so certain of her subject as to be able to bind and label it and hand it across in solid parcels:

There is a Committee for Education that keeps an eye on the set works taught to the children. It is in triumph after summoning the senior schoolteacher, Mr Borgaard, to question him about the teaching of *Ampie* and leaving him pleading that it was not his decision, that it was the department, the department. There is a Committee for Hygiene that alternates between circular debates about the bucket system and escaping from the hall to lead girls on hikes in the hills.

The Committee for Social Welfare, Mrs Cordier's committee, corresponds with its peers in other towns and has recently been copied on a letter from the Synod. The Purified National Party regional office also wrote to it once under the powder-horn symbol; Mrs Cordier has laid out this letter on a side table. She hands it to Adaira, who, not knowing what to make of it, takes in the Purified way, the proper way, of setting out the address and greeting.

And of course there is the general work of the Federation, Mrs Cordier says with a dismissive wave. Its focus this year is the Second Trek, but that is work everyone enjoys.

The energy of the six women who sit on Social Welfare, not counting Adaira, plus the Thursday-afternoon efforts of a half-dozen more from the congregation, are concentrated on one small part of Gower, the size of three blocks of the town perhaps, although Happy Valley does not obey anything so orderly as blocks. Vena Cordier speaks about the many failures of its shifting lot in matters of respectability, literacy, industry, hygiene. Hygiene most of all.

It used to be that they came straight off the farm, where the odd one or two had once even owned land – mostly they were squatters or tenant farmers – but now they come from nowhere, she says. They come from another blikkiesdorp, or from Johannesburg even, using up a place and moving to the next. Some of them barely have the newspaper to swaddle a newborn, and every week there comes another wretched lot, a woman with a snaggled string of small ones or a pair of old folks, and no-good, dirty youngsters.

It is a long afternoon, and towards the end, when Adaira cannot take into her brain another fact about the problem and the programme, Mr Cordier arrives home. He sets down the box he is carrying; something clanks inside it. He stands in the doorway of the sitting room. Mrs Cordier introduces Adaira to him as her father's daughter. He does not leave, but stays standing, not entering the room, not offering with words or by his actions any reason for being there. He looks Adaira over, then looks into the far corner of the room, and while he does this he slides his jaw way over to the side and nods, in the grip of a thought or eluded by one, paying them no mind. The idea comes to Adaira that he objects to not having been consulted about her presence in his front room, on his chairs.

Mrs Cordier says, low and through closed teeth, 'Was there something Papa wanted?' and he sharpens at her tone and looks at her. He does not answer her, though, but only crosses to the heating machine and reaches behind it to adjust the setting, and leaves the room without a word.

Adaira is thoroughly tired out when she leaves the Cordier home at dusk, and tiredly excited by the glamour of what she glimpsed in what Mrs Cordier described, its weight – the primacy of being invited to direct the lives of other people, of prevailing and earning their thanks. There is so much she can do: acts of rescue, improvement. There is the promise of being a necessary part of the town that the work seems to offer; she feels the draw of that, too.

On the pavement, head down, unseeing, gloved hands in her coat pockets and with a face formed into a frown by her thoughts, Adaira has not taken four steps when, a moment before she walks into a man, her head snaps up. By the spread of his hands and his smile, he anticipates an actual collision but she stops short of that at least.

He lifts his hat from his head, looks at the Cordier house, looks at her, then he catches hold of and broadens his smile, and greets her as 'surely the theological daughter, the guest of the Therons, hello!'.

At her wary silence, he offers: 'Theron is my chief clerk. He told me all about you. Not a lot of new faces, in this part of town at least, so I guessed you. May I say, welcome to Gower?'

Is he laughing at her? Laughing at something? It is hard to make out the details of his face against the fading light. She feels an answering smile tug at her mouth.

He says: 'And you have been discovered by Mrs Cordier. May we look forward to good works among the deserving poor?' He slows his speech to high Victorian for this question and surely is laughing, and perhaps at her.

She has not spoken a coherent word in his presence, yet it feels to her like a conversation. He is at least a head taller than she is, his face above his beard ruddy in the evening chill.

He says, 'Henry Vos,' with a formal nod of his head, and then he stops talking. Adaira gets her name out in response, but she is not good for much more than that and says something about being expected at the Therons, and moves away from him down the street.

She takes a dozen steps and collects herself. She worries about her manners and looks back. The magistrate has replaced his hat but has not resumed his walk. He is looking at the Cordier house and nodding in thought, no longer smiling.

Beyond the reach of the street lights, on the same side of town as the Happy Valley blikkiesdorp – on the swell of a hill rising from Happy Valley's damp lowlands, in fact – is the part of Gower known, with an unfriendly mix of precision and abstraction, as the Location.

It has a real name, used by the people who live there and sometimes by the police sergeant and the clerk of the court: Kleinbult, small hill. The hill is the lesser part of a minor range that supports several streams. These have been directed to run past the Location into Gower to fill a reservoir and wait upon a system of sluices and channels that shadow every street in the town proper.

At set times in the day and well into the evening Gower people – the people in Gower proper, not the Location or Happy Valley – lift one small gate and close another to direct the water into their gardens, to fill tanks of their own or let it run in homemade earthen channels to roses, potatoes, small stands of mealies, to plump farms in miniature that are so neat and fruitful, so subject to a man's control and liberated from rainfall and drought that they are like a dream of farming.

The leiwater system that makes all this possible, the mild dry-Africa practice of the men's ancestral Dutch sea-taming, is the core and cause of jealous battles over a few stolen minutes here or there, the site of stones lodged under sluice gates to steal a trickle, and other midnight water banditry. Men with pocket watches – men with no stake in the water on this side of Church Street, even – make a point of strolling by the gardens of those whom they suspect of stealing water; at noon these enthusiasts freeze when the courthouse clock strikes the hour and they fumble to turn their watch wheels into concord.

This is what Mrs Theron meant by power and the leiwater. It is Gower's favourite sport but no one jokes about it, or speaks of it at all – at least, the men do not; if they notice that someone is watching them watch the water, they rumble their greeting, lift hats, gesture to the day and walk on.

Adaira, after a fortnight in Gower, thinks that, if she were to choose between the men and women, she would say it was the women who had the keener instinct for town life, and that the town repaid them with gifts beyond antimacassars and a better audience for their clear melon jams and crochet work. A man's occasional weekend hunt or barter might result in the back stoep of a woman's house being strung with dark shreds, and the mesh doors closed tight to keep blowflies from the kudu ripped and hung to dry; the scent of blood may fill the house and the house dogs look guilty with their hunger for it. At odd moments a man might clap both hands on the place where his chest meets his stomach and say 'Oh yes' and 'One shot'. Tonight he and she may sleep with meat in the house and plenty to sack up when it has grown light as wet driftwood – and this good country feeling of plenty has surely always been worth something – but the women know they can summon the same feeling with the tame Ball jars and tins in their pantries, and bled meat from the butcher. The product matters more than the process, and in this they are towns-women.

Their houses have, as their mothers' did not have, a warren of small rooms off the kitchen – pantry, scullery, laundry room. Although they do no more than oversee the work that goes on in these rooms, they take pleasure in each one of them, in the delineation of one room from the next by its purpose, the extravagance of rooms standing ready, unused for stretches of the day, waiting for a word from them. Order lives in these rooms. The hunt, the women remind themselves as they settle for sleep – well, tomorrow the men will be back in the office and the hunt will be patted down to the size of a story, and in their domain the cupboards will barely be fuller or have been much emptied because of it.

In her first weeks in Gower, moving through the homes of women, Adaira notices herself noticing these things or invent-ing them, and hears her mother's complaint: Don't talk about the biltong and blood, Adaira – what about the pictures on the walls? The curtains and the crockery, the flowers and the flowered cloth?

As Adaira had boarded the train for Gower, as the engine took on splashing water, Father had folded his tall body into the coupe among her cases and addressed a print of Table Mountain screwed to the compartment wall. He had wanted to remind her of a childhood story, the only one about her he ever recalled, the one he brought out on birthdays, as though he had surfaced once, seen what he had seen, and fixed her in his mind:

Five years old, Adaira sings to herself as she winds her way around the tree in the station garden. She has been tied to it by a short rope that has two loops – one for her waist, one for the trunk. This is to keep her out of the sun while also keeping her out of the house and her mother's hair. 'This will keep you out of my hair,' her mother had said under her breath as she struggled with the sliding knot on the rope. Bending to tie Adaira to the tree brought her mother's hair close to Adaira's face as she said this, and the girl looked at, and then into, the whorls and waves of it. The rope is snug on Adaira's waist, but the loop on the trunk is left loose so that she can ride the rope, leaning against it as she sways around the tree in a sort of horizontal swing.

'Who killed Cock Robin?' she drones as she treads a circle into the ground. 'Who killed Cock Robin?' Relentless and bloody, 'Cock Robin' is the only nursery rhyme Adaira will recite. From the window comes her mother's voice, overbright (because it is she who cannot leave Adaira alone, who cannot stay out of her daughter's thin curls): 'Ring a ring of rosies? Adaira? Baa baa black sheep?' Adaira is said to have screwed up her eyes and yelled in fury: 'WHO killed Cock Robin? WHO killed Cock Robin? I saw him DIE SAYS A FLY.' Her father laughs his rusty laugh when he tells the story. 'Five years old and already at the end of her tether,' he always says at this point, pleased with his play on words.

There was more: her father had set himself, in their last moments before the train moved off, to warn her about people.

He had warned her that a wrong word at the start would damn relations for all time. There was no forgiveness in the human world, he told her, his face beginning to flush. No latitude, and a man must set up his convictions early and not waver from whatever he finds for only this will keep him safe and hold on to his place among them. A man or a woman. As she listened to his creaking, careful, frightened words, Adaira saw something she had never guessed about him: how he was among men. His silences, his intense privacy and the rages against his own spirit that would sweep through the station like a dust storm, sending Adaira and her mother running to close every opening to protect themselves, had been in her eyes no less than how he was designed to be as a desert mystic – marks of honour and suffering – and his wife, her mother, a foolish twittering distraction. Now she had an unwelcome insight: she could see there was more of fear than of courage, and she had a glimpse of the underworld where he lived, and saw her mother as a golden bird fluttering at the tunnel mouth, she who had kept him with her as long as he could hear her flutings about the world of things.

9

I N THE SATURDAY EVENING HOUR after supper, Church Street is lit with its share of Gower's twenty-nine street lamps. Someone has got the municipal boys to water the road; the surface is dark and wet enough to offer their reflection in streaks and haloes. A few of the town dogs are out, grinning their grins. Some people, those who live behind their shops or in the two or three houses that meet the street directly, have dragged chairs onto the pavement to watch their neighbours drift towards the far end where the church and its hall stand among other important buildings: the hotel, the police station, the courthouse.

Nantie walks with her father, and Adaira has Mrs Theron and her quiet notes.

'That is Magistrate Vos,' she says. He is arm in arm with his sister, with whom, she says, he shares a house on Hamer Street, Gower's best street.

Adaira studies him and his sister. He is in dark tweed, she in a dotted dress and a coat against the chill, hanging on his arm, tugging it to bring him news about the scene. They look rich and unknowable, although no one in Gower is rich. On this, her second sighting of him, Adaira notices more about his smile. His mouth is in fact turned down at the corners, but – set between deep side dimples, above a bearded chin – it smiles. His hair is thick and dark; at the sides it is short, and silver.

A half-dozen Natives have come down from the Location; they gather at the edge of a street light at the end of the road, dense as bears in their greatcoats and knitted caps. When they laugh, their breath clouds about their heads and blunted shapes.

The Theron party is on the raised pavement of a row of three shops between the bank and the post office. Mr Theron and the magistrate lift hats to one another across the width of the street.

Mr Theron says, softly, 'Your Honour.'

Tonight there will be an entertainment. It is Gower's bad luck that the Saturday bioscope has had to make way for an elderly senator with theories. In the church hall this Hunter Halgryn is waiting, packed into his suit, martial and tanned as a dachshund. Word has spread about what will go on in 'Predetermined Evolution', and the ladies of the Women's Federation Education Committee are at the door to turn away boys and girls younger than twenty-one; Nantie scowls as she leaves her parents and Adaira for the children in their pyjamas wheeling under the lights.

The adults settle in their rows of chairs. Five chairs are set out behind the senator, looking back at the room. Mrs Cordier has taken one of these, the magistrate another. Between them are the mayor, the doctor and the dominee. Only the dominee is clean-shaven; the doctor and the mayor grin and stretch their bristling chins above their collars and scratch them. Trek beards, they must be.

At the end of the room furthest from Senator Halgryn, five or six young men stand along the wall, arms folded. They are bored and watchful, in the manner of frontier guards. In a row near the front, Adaira is sitting with the Therons and Anna Vos, the magistrate's sister, to whom she is introduced just before the men rise to their feet and the audience prays. The senator takes the podium and sets out his programme: tonight, he will disprove the theory of evolution and prove the existence of God. People shift on their chairs and remind themselves that this is the only thing there is to do in Gower this evening.

Mr Theron, however, is relaxed in his chair as if to hear good music, and as the senator rolls out his arguments he nods and smiles at the string of must-haves and impossible-to-imagines to do with gibbons and horses, angiosperms and mammalian breasts; Adaira is puzzled that anyone could be enjoying this. Anna Vos catches something in her look and leans closer to tell her in a crisp murmur that, really, Mr Theron would listen to a man read out a merino stud book as long as it was in pure Afrikaans; Afrikaans oratory is his meat, she says.

The magistrate, facing into the room, has stretched his face into a mask of dispassion. He is holding very still. Adaira studies him minutely; she is certain she sees a twitch at the corner of his mouth.

By now, the senator is losing most of them. After going on for a bit more he stops, swipes his face with his handkerchief, takes a drink of water and stays silent until they are all looking at him, wondering whether they may start the clapping and the anthem that will release them—

'sex!' he barks, his hands spread wide. The magistrate clamps his hand over his mouth, his eyes above it shocked with delight. Into the burnt air the word leaves, the senator drops his phrases, his rhythms slow as a dominee's: 'If a man should ask me … what is the foolproof argument … for the existence of the Creator … my immediate reply … would be just one word … sex!'

Do they appreciate the 'perfection of the mechanism, the mightiness of the urge that drove all creation – the perfect fit!'?

'Was there ever such a machine so perfectly made as the human body, as the male and the female parts?'

Do they know, for example, that 'in one orgasm' (a gasp from behind the Theron row) 'or ejaculation' (a female noise of distress from further back in the room), 'one hundred and eighty thousand spermatozoa are thrown out and immediately start rowing like boats with their little tails as oars into the womb' (Ag no, man! – a man's voice) 'in search of the female cell or egg'?

At the back of the room the fellows leaning on the wall are listening as keenly as dogs, looking over the audience's heads to the senator as though they have a part to play in the evening. For the rest, people have their hands on or near their faces, or are seated on their hands to keep them still.

The magistrate has folded his arms one over the other. His legs are twisted ankle to ankle and his eyes held strictly on the pattern at the edge of the linoleum near his shoes. His mouth is clamped tight.

At the breakfast table the next morning, before church, Nantie begs to know what they heard, but Mother and Father Theron only share a look, and Mr Theron says: 'I'm not sure we learned anything much that was new from old Hunter Halgryn, my girl.'

Adaira smiles at her lap. Nantie tests her spoon against the milk pooling on top of her porridge. Mr Theron sips his coffee. He says, 'Oh yes, I meant to say, we are getting a Jew. A Jew for Gower.'

He does not say if this is a good thing. In fact he has kept his voice in the studiedly neutral tone of a man who is, while he speaks, also tapping a barometer, but he nods at Mrs Theron, and she widens her eyes and nods back at him, and smiles a downturned smile that seems to say, There's a thing.

He says in English to echo the expression on her face, 'There's a thing. A Jew for Gower.' And now he smiles.

'What's Achoo?' says Nantie. Her mother, her mouth dealing with toast, makes a face and crooks her finger over her nose, then straightens it and holds it to her temple. Clever, her eyes say.

Adaira says, 'A Jew. A. Jew,' but she does not know much more than Nantie. These days Jews are interesting, a thing apart from any Jewish family one might have known of until now. She has seen a picture of an overseas one in *The Advertiser* just this week, although the point of the photograph seemed more his pale armband than the man himself. He had had on a striped suit and a dark tie and the armband, and had been looking out of the picture, blank as an antelope, on a page next to a story about the Princess Elizabeth.

Their Jew, their new Jew, has taken over Hamer's Haberdashers, Mr Theron says, and as he says that Adaira knows
with a small shock that she has already met him, or at least
looked into his eyes.

'I—'

She gets as far as making a sound before she decides that
she will not tell this at the breakfast table. Nantie hears her
and makes an ape face. 'Uh,' echoes Nantie, her face turned
towards her plate. It is a monkey goading noise. 'Uh uh uh.'

'Nantie girl,' says Mr Theron, between a plea and a warning.

Last night, on the way to the lecture, Mr Theron had said,
softly, to himself, 'Your Honour,' and Adaira had waited to hear
whether he would say more than this, and in the meantime
she turned from the lights of Church Street to look into the
shop window at her back.

On the glass it said Hamer's Haberdashers, the two words
sharing a big H and written in a way that kept them apart from
it so that it read amer's aberdashers, a sign by Dickens. On the
other side of the glass, on a low display shelf in the window,
was a wheel made of smaller cardboard wheels of coloured
pins, and cloth hanging limp as dough from tall hook stands.

Adaira had been looking between the drapings into a man's
eyes for a long moment before she realised they were eyes,
black eyes under black brows. A man was standing in the dark
shop, behind the window display, watching the lit and peopled
street. A man in his thirties, perhaps younger than that, his
hair in a side part and lying across his forehead and the colour
of the dark room behind him. No one but Adaira knew he
was there, she could tell from the way, on the street behind

her, Mr Theron had started on a story to do with the magistrate, and Mrs Theron was making listening sounds.

Adaira's astonishment kept her steady; she did not look away. She made a movement with her head but still did not break the contact between them. In the dark window the man brought one hand into the fall of light that showed part of his face. He smiled. He widened his eyes and held a finger to his mouth to ask her to keep their secret, and stepped backwards into the dark.

She had turned around to rejoin the street. It must have been him.

This morning her instinct, borrowed from his, is to keep quiet about his clandestine survey of his new town. His discovery feels like the first thing she has undertaken in Gower by herself, and as the family gathers its outer clothing, bags and books for the day, she lets it build in her and does not share it.

Adaira is drawn to Vena Cordier. The force of her tires Adaira's blood, but she wants this feeling. She has encountered in Mrs Cordier someone utterly different from anyone she has known until now, but also weirdly familiar: that force in her is known to Adaira. She wants to defend herself from it and, at the same time, to experience it. She learns not to say 'Mrs Theron says', or 'Mr Theron says', when she is talking to Mrs Cordier, but no one at her Theron home seems to mind when she quotes her.

Today she travels with Mrs Cordier and the committee on an outing to the next town. She has joined them just in time for the official photograph, says Mrs Cordier. The women make the journey to the studio in Jamestown in her motor and that of another committee woman, Mrs Co-op Drukker. They are dressed according to instructions: closed shoes, plain frocks – by which is meant smart frocks, but no patterned cloth – hats, gloves. Adaira has on one of her Fichardt's dresses, and over it a brown cloth coat that had belonged to her mother. They have scraped their hair up and back, off their faces and necks. There was talk of including something that would tell their story, stand as a symbol, but there was nothing to hand or that came to mind but a food parcel or a bottle of lye, and these, they agreed, could not be said to capture the spirit of the Committee for Social Welfare.

The photographer has set a vase of imitation flowers on a plinth, and chairs to one side of this; they are only seven to be pictured. But at Mrs Cordier's word the flowers move aside, four chairs make a row, and the youngest three move to stand behind these. At the last moment Mrs Cordier decides they will take off their hats.

'Don't let me catch you with a smile on your face,' she says, and they brace for the powder flash, grim with charity.

Five of their number leave for home in Co-op's motor. Mrs Cordier keeps Adaira back for a formal portrait, something, she says, she should have had done years before.

Adaira negotiates with the photographer for three poses, and Mrs Cordier directs her this way and that – to lift her chin, to look out, out, imagine a horizon, a superb future. She fusses with Adaira's hair and pinches her cheeks, and pins something to her lapel. Adaira reaches up to feel its outline, and when the photographer turns from them to tend to his machine, lifts her collar to see what it is she is wearing. It is an enamelled Party badge, as big as a penny, with a powder-horn symbol where the King's head or the Dromedaris would be.

Mrs Cordier holds up a hand as if to forestall a protest at her generosity. 'Keep it,' she says. 'A little present.'

Adaira is, Mrs Cordier tells her, the picture of right-thinking young womanhood. From this and other remarks Mrs Cordier has made, Adaira accepts that she celebrates her for her wifely potential, her potential as a mother, even though, as she has known since she was a girl, her body must never be acknowledged in the context that follows or precedes bridehood and babies.

The photographer says Adaira's colouring will show up well in black and white. Her fine skin and eyes will make a picture good enough to give to the newspaper, he says, and they are suddenly ambitious for this. It will be good to have the right picture to hand, says Vena Cordier. Adaira will be a credit to Gower and to the committee if something comes up and they can send in the picture. The three of them, the photographer, Adaira, Mrs Cordier, are pleased with their morning's work.

On the journey home, Mrs Cordier speaks about the men to whom she will introduce Adaira. While she steers the motor along the Gower road she lists them, who their families are. She makes it clear that Adaira is wasted on the irresolute Therons. She says, 'Shame, Adaira,' and shakes her head; Adaira knows she is supposed to be impressed by the knowledge Mrs Cordier is withholding for her own good, about the Therons, perhaps their softness, Mrs Theron's city origins. She would be a better friend to Adaira than Mrs Theron. She would know how to dress her. She would line up a month of Sunday teas for her to meet young farmers and maybe even a few of the professional men of the town, those who were right-thinking men.

Adaira accepts this vigorous interest in herself. It is restful to be carried along like this, a passenger; restful to be shown the future that will catch her up with life and make her a plausible woman.

When Adaira comes into the kitchen the next morning, Mr and Mrs Theron are conspiring about something. She can make out from how they stand and their few closing words that it is about her. Nothing more is said about it while the houseboy Enoch dishes up soft porridge and Mr Theron drinks his coffee, and Nantie comes to join the family and they eat.

When they are done, Mrs Theron is left to broach it with Adaira. It is, it emerges, an offer to make Adaira a dress, the sort of dress Mrs Theron calls 'something nice' and Adaira gathers is to be, or is imagined as, something younger, and finer, than the plain buttoned cotton dresses she has brought to Gower. Mrs Theron has dressmaking in her past, her pre-Theron past. She was thinking, something in blue? Adaira can see that this is a difficult offer for Mrs Theron to make; she is reading Adaira's response for any hint that she has given offence.

Adaira wonders at the Therons' adoption of her. She is a paying guest, but from the first they have decided that she must be absorbed into the family; she, with her determination to order matters her way this time, after the disappointment of the books, wonders: does she appear in need of help? Is this the parental impulse to straighten the dress of, flatten the cowlick of, correct the grammar of, a child, or is it some new category of kindness? Adaira can, however, recognise that the offer from Mrs Theron is indefinably, but undoubtedly, different from the suggestions Mrs Cordier has for her. And although she cannot yet name all of its parts, Mrs Theron's offer has caught her behind her eyes with a sharp feeling, and she blushes as she dips her head to accept.

'Something nice' means a visit to Church Street. The two gather their hats and coats and gloves and walk down the Theron lane and into the commercial part of the town with no baskets in their hands, no groceries to buy.

A man is busy at the window of H amer's aberdashery, scraping the name from the glass. In the shop proper, Adaira's dark-eyed man from the other night is lifting a cardboard box of cotton reels onto the counter. There are breakfast smells and soap in the air, and Adaira and Mrs Theron are the first of the day.

His name is Ira Gevint. Mrs Theron and Mr Gevint greet one another formally, taking the measure of the other, with him managing the English in an interesting accent and Mrs Theron seeming somehow prettier than when she speaks to her family. Adaira is almost silent through this.

They begin their business; this is to be a smart day dress. They are here for Adaira to buy the cloth and fixings for one that Mrs Theron will make at home, Mrs Theron tells him as she pulls off a glove and taps her fingers over silk and crêpe. Ira Gevint does not look at Adaira, or at least not to meet eye to eye, but keeps himself pointed towards Mrs Theron as the customer and expert.

Adaira nurses the feeling that she would have liked to introduce him, to present him. Then she wonders if he even recognises her. After a while she notices no one is speaking and both of them are looking at her with the air of people waiting for an answer. He is holding up two bolts of pale blue cloth, side by side. With Mrs Theron and Ira Gevint looking in the same direction, with the privacy this gives them, he at last meets Adaira's eyes and she sees the spark of laughter and complicity that he has kept shuttered in front of Mrs Theron, and almost makes a sound at the surprise of it, the tickle of fright she feels.

He gets them through the business of buying the cloth and leaving the shop and Adaira does not look at him again, not straight on.

Mrs Theron has found out all about Mr Gevint even with his few English and no Afrikaans words, and at supper she tells Mr Theron that he is thirty-one years old and married and from a town near Frankfurt, and his wife, who came out on the same ship, is refusing to leave her Cape Town cousins for the interior but that her father is on his way to Gower to join him. Adaira welcomes this news, although she is not entirely sure why; perhaps it is her sense that the more of him shows above the surface, the better their secret, his and hers, will be kept. She assumes a secret on no better evidence than his having hidden in the dark to take the measure of his new town that first night, and her having been the only one to see him there.

Adaira notices that as Ira Gevint with a shop on Church Street, the new haberdasher nods to and is nodded to by the men of the town when he takes an evening walk. That when he says his name it is with a hard G and a high, thin −int, Kgeveent, and when they say it, they make it sound almost like the word for found, gevind, soft at all its edges and lower, unless they are mocking him, in which case they pronounce it as he does. Kgeveent or Gevind, it is not confused for one of their names.

Mrs Cordier keeps Adaira back after a committee meeting to teach her the Women's Federation song. She picks it out slowly on the upright piano in the church hall, and recites, the tendons in her neck standing proud:

There's work, there's work, my sisters,
For women devout
and free and strong!
O Lord, guide her,
In service of her nation,
In honour of her God,
Guide her Yourself,
The woman,
O Lord.

10

ON A STILL, COLD AFTERNOON in late June, Magistrate Henry Vos arrives at the home of his chief clerk. He calls out from the path below the steps leading to the stoep and the front door: 'Hello, the house!' He has his hands in his jacket pockets, pulling them and the hem of the jacket out from his body as a boy would. His hat is tipped towards the back of his head and he looks ready to laugh, or to say something that will make everyone laugh. Mrs Theron comes onto the stoep, pressing her hair back in among its pins, and extends a hand to bring him in, saying something about Mr Theron and the chicken cages.

The magistrate says, 'They hatched then?'

'Every single one. Bit of a handful for the old girl.'

Nantie crosses the sitting room in a blur, crowing, 'Oom! Oom!'

He releases his laugh into the room, catches her hands and spins her in an open embrace. He looks past her to meet Adaira's eye and tips his head to greet her. Mrs Theron takes his hat. Mr Theron comes from the back of the house, wiping his hands on his handkerchief and straightening his pullover. His shirtsleeves are rolled above his elbows but at a look from

Mrs Theron he has them down and cufflinks from his pocket, his jersey off and jacket on.

A footfall in the hall. Anna Vos.

'Just in time,' says Henry.

She comes into the room in her own whirl of greeting, nods once to her brother, who turns immediately to Mrs Theron and raises an eyebrow to signal something to her, and she grins back. She calls them to the dining table, and tea; Nantie and Adaira detour to the hall; on the table there, Anna Vos has left a square parcel the size of a small dog.

Over flan and cake Anna darts into the conversation from time to time to finish Henry's sentences. He laughs a lot, and Mr and Mrs Theron watch the Vos pair with round eyes and loose, open smiles, like children listening to interesting adults. Henry every so often invites Mr Theron to comment: 'Eh, Theron?' He addresses Mr Theron as Theron; Mr Theron calls him Magistrate and sometimes, as a half-joke, Your Honour.

At last Nantie is allowed to bring the parcel from the hall. She lowers it, with ceremony, onto the table at Mr Theron's place. Mrs Theron is on her feet across from him, drawing her mouth tight to contain her pleasure. Mr Theron looks around at his family, his guests.

'Everyone is in on it, eh? Well, let's see what you have been up to,' and he has it out of its paper and revealed as a shiny brown and enviable, unnaturally smooth and partly sinister box. Mr Theron looks as if he will choke with astonishment; Mrs Theron has a hand to her mouth to hold down her smile.

The magistrate says, 'The radio set is from your loving family, Theron, and these' – he takes a small package from his pocket – 'are from me and Anna. Don't bother to open them now. Spare valves. You are about to learn, my dear fellow, how quickly they run out.'

Tea is forgotten while the men set up the radio; it needs no kit work, and the aerial is, to their great satisfaction, attached; within moments Mr Theron has the radio set turned on and is tuning it; the seashell noises give way to words they can make out. They listen with slack faces. Someone on the radio is making a speech. Nantie says, 'What is she saying, that old lady?' and the magistrate says through his laughter, 'That's no lady, that's General Smuts.'

They still splutter in their tea when, half an hour later, one or other of them says, 'That's no lady …'

Anna arrived at the party later than her brother because she had stayed behind to take delivery of the radio set, delivered to their home by a cousin of Mr Theron; he had picked it up in the city on his way back to his farm and brought it to Anna, who he found waiting for him. Something about the encounter lingers with her through the afternoon, absenting her from her brother and the Therons for long moments before she returns to them, intently humorous, somewhat loud. She looks, so Henry thinks as he notices her high colour, really quite delighted to be at the modest birthday tea of his clerk.

A day or so later Adaira is out in the town in the late afternoon, her committee work done, and dawdling with the idea of Ira Gevint's shop in her mind, when Anna Vos finds her on the street and takes her to her brother. Adaira has the sense Anna was sent to get her, that she has been discussed by them.

The magistrate is in a cane chair on the veranda. He stands up and moves to the top of the broad steps as they come down the path. Anna hands Adaira on to him, presenting her as 'another reader'.

'You two can talk about books, books, books,' she says, and rolls her eyes to laugh at them. Adaira already knows that her trunk of novels has been noted by the town. The magistrate looks at Adaira, smiles his downward smile, says, 'Perhaps we can.' Anna leaves to see about tea and the magistrate brings Adaira to his study where he has shelves of this and that, mainly law books and history books, and for fiction men's stories and the Langenhovens everyone has, but among them one or two that are new to her. Something, at least, that she has not read. Most are in English, some are in Dutch, a few in Afrikaans.

After some moments spent dipping her head to read out titles or authors' names and flatter his taste with approving murmurs, she follows him back to the veranda to wait for their tea. Anna is still inside the house. Adaira takes a seat and manages a few words about the household's large dog, which has settled next to her chair, and then there is silence. The magistrate is watching her. He is carefully dressed, in flannels and a jacket. His hair shows the pathway of a recent comb. After a moment he nods to himself, clears his throat and begins to talk.

He does not want to know about her committee work. He does not ask how she finds Gower. He does not mention her father. He leans back in his chair and says, 'Imagine a tree.'

He pauses, as if for her reaction, but Adaira only blinks at him in surprise.

He says again: 'Imagine a tree. A wild fig. Near a stream, let's say, a tree so tall that transport riders and trekkers and the explorer sons of English clergymen use it as a beacon. One day, a trader named Hamer stops under it to make a camp.'

He is speaking in a way that sounds to Adaira like something you might hear on a radio programme – an unreal, distant, storytelling way.

The magistrate's hands are held up and apart, as if to cup the scene between them.

'Can you picture it, Miss van Brugge?'

He means she should, in fact, picture it. He is laying down her duties as the audience.

He says: 'First, a tree.'

He waits for her to say something. She nods and swallows but does not speak. She is keeping very still to hear what he will say next.

He looks past her. He says, 'Next, let's see, it's the turn of the smaller trees. He chops them down, each with its creatures. He makes a clearing around the fig and he offloads canvas, poles, buckets. He has – what does he have? A chest, a metal chest.' He describes this with his hands, too.

'What does he do all day?' The magistrate opens his hands to ask the question, keeps them open as he answers it. 'He hunts for his supper. He beats his servant – there is a servant. What else?'

This time the question seems to be for her, and Adaira risks speaking. 'He is a trader,' she says carefully, believing she will be judged on her reply. 'If anyone comes through the bush he calls to them and sells them, uhm, small things: string and knives and tea. Weak knives and sour tea.' There was a smous at the station from time to time; this is what he sold.

The magistrate smacks his knee and laughs. He says, 'Sour tea! Yes!' He is applauding her answer. He says: 'The tree is probably already three hundred years old. It had changed so slowly until then – growing a little higher, a little wider. Maybe it lost a branch to an elephant.'

Her instinct for conversation – he is, after all, in the chair across from hers, however like someone on a stage he is behaving – makes Adaira want to react to his words, but there is no time for her; he is in spate.

'Things move fast after the clearing and the tin trunk,' says the magistrate. He rushes through a skittish trade in cloudy stones – raw diamonds, she is left to guess as he pushes on – and the arrival of another man and a copper still and a wagon chiming with empty bottles. The wagon leaves with bottles clacking dully and corked, and now there is traffic from a new direction, and in time a crossroads. At 'crossroads' he catches his breath and then seems to run out of energy. He says, with a gesture that she reads as a weary 'voila!': 'Gower.'

Under cover of his words she has scrambled for what she will say in reaction – what she can ask, or add, but as he winds down, she says nothing at all. His words and his delivery have left her feeling as a radio programme might, pleasantly indifferent – or perhaps as though, were this a meal the magistrate had laid out, she had tasted its flavours but not had any nourishment from it. She thinks she will remember almost nothing of what he said. Could this sort of display be what is meant by charm? She gives him the slimmest of smiles, and transfers her regard to the dog.

Just in time, Anna comes to call them. Adaira and Henry follow her inside to drink tea and talk of everyday Gower things. The strange hollow storytelling of the magistrate is at the front of her thoughts on the way home. He is like the sort of man you would encounter in a book, not on the veranda of a house in Gower, she thinks – unless this is indeed how some men are.

A few days later the cousin, the radio-set-delivery cousin, returns to Gower to bring a sack of quinces to Anna Vos, pretending the fruit is a favour she can show him, a late glut that must be dispersed or rot in the orchard, from an old hedge that is the particular pride of his garden, she will have never tasted the like. He heaps on the reasons.

Anna finds Adaira again. She says, 'I want you for me this time,' and puts her to work by her side to preserve this Johan's first gift.

They leave half the hard yellow fruit in the oven to bake while they tackle the rest, which is bound for jelly. Adaira's fingertips roll up the skin's downy fur to find the smooth layer beneath.

The magistrate is in court. Anna wants to talk about him. She wants to tell their story.

'I was born two months before Henry came home from the war,' she says. 'Home from his camp in Ceylon. And he was only eighteen himself.'

She means their war at the turn of the century, not the war since then, the Delville Wood and Windhoek war.

'Three years earlier and I could have been Lily Eileen,' she says. 'Lily Eileen or Rose or Catherine.' She sighs. 'But no. Anna Philomena Gertruida Vos. At least they got the order right. Imagine *Gertruida*.

'We were all of us coming home from camps,' she shrugs. 'Although of course I don't remember mine, and as for Henry, he won't talk about his at all. He never has, even though it has been his big project since we got here.'

At 'big project' Anna waves a hand in the direction of the passageway that leads to the private rooms of Anna and Henry's house. Adaira does not know what she means by this, but does not know how to ask. She is happier just listening, and watching Anna.

Yellow and white, the blocks of quince tumble from their hands into the water. Anna chops ginger roots, eases mace from a small bottle. Their people were farmers – 'big farmers', she says – but Henry would not farm.

He left for his long law studies; when he came home to the brand-new Union, ready to make his mark, he stayed on the farm only long enough to be his little sister's first love, Anna says, laughing. He promised that one day he would come for her.

And more than a decade ago, she was sent to join him in the city.

'We made it our business to reinvent the world,' she says. 'We were so modern!' She widens her smile to mock him, her.

Two tall pots of sugar, water and fruit are heating on the

stove. Anna wipes her hands and tells the boy Ephraim to keep an eye on them.

'I knew there had to be more in the world,' she says. Adaira thinks Anna's restlessness drums in her even as she speaks about her restless girlhood self.

Three years ago, this preferment.

'He had to go to Pretoria for magistrate lessons, months of lessons, and then we got Gower.'

They prepare to leave the house to buy more sugar for the syrup. Adaira waits in the hallway beside Anna as she pulls on her hat before the mirror. Anna turns her head from side to side, her eyes inspecting her face. She slips the lid off a tube of lipstick and twists it to work the expensive swivel-up stick, dabs colour on her lips. While her right hand is busy with this, her left has found and is holding her gloves. Rather than bring the greasepaint towards the pale cotton to perform the little manoeuvre of closing the stick, she shocks Adaira by inserting the golden tube with its projecting red nub into her mouth to grip it with her bared teeth while she twists it closed, a split-second barbarian queen, casual, sexual and bold.

When Adaira takes her turn at the mirror she cannot quite find herself there. She thinks that she looks like someone who has bought all that she is wearing in the course of one after-noon, from one shop, or ordered it from a catalogue, and to someone else's taste. These are the clothes of an older woman, wifely clothes. She touches her collar and thinks of the blue dress that is taking shape in Mrs Theron's sewing corner. She looks again at Anna, and back at her own reflection, and seizes on an image of herself as a lake and Anna as someone subject to the pull of tides.

It is a trip of perhaps four blocks. They must drive, Anna says, because the bags will be heavy, but Adaira suspects that restless Anna will find any reason to take the motor out.

Hendrik arrived here with a story in *The Advertiser* announcing him as the first Afrikaans magistrate in the district, says Anna. Even then the craze for counting the first Afrikaans this or that was sustaining itself on things no one could know for sure, such as first Afrikaner put in charge of a railway station, or farm matters like first Afrikaner to win best of show at the Royal Natal (this Afrikaner was a hump-backed bull). These days, *The Advertiser* hedges its bets with 'one of the first'. The business of counting Afrikaners still goes on in the newspaper, though, and in particular counting when there is no Afrikaans such and such, or only one where the prime minister had promised there would be hundreds.

Anyway, Anna continues, Henry 'arrived with me on his arm. They were polite, so polite – until they found out I was only his sister, and then you should have seen the smiles and the fuss!' Anna arches an eyebrow in judgement of Gower's women.

Anna parks the motor and they cross the street. Outside the general store she points out a young woman pushing a high black baby carriage towards them, says her name as though it is a mild insult, 'Huh, Dolly Nel.' Dolly Nel is one of those who ran after Henry when they came to Gower, says Anna. Adaira watches her; she has noticed the magistrate's sister, Adaira thinks, but will not look at her. There is hurt in Dolly Nel's set mouth and tight shoulders.

She is still on the pavement when Anna and Adaira leave the store. They watch as she leans in to the knitted layers that round upwards from the pram as though the warm baby is rising to fill the carriage. Her whole hand, palm and fingers, touches lightly on the blanket and her winter-yellow face loses its hurt look. It is clear to anyone who sees her that Dolly Nel has been taken on by love. Anna shifts the sugar in her arms. Her voice thins. She says, 'He still sits out with one or the other when he feels like it.' She hands the sugar to Adaira. 'But it never lasts.'

Adaira already knows the magistrate is spoken of in circles of Gower's matrons and widows, each small fact of him, each new thing, brought out like a prize and rolled about as though it is a shiny pebble and they the water, an eddy in a river.

Anna and Adaira load the sugar into the motor. As they pass Gevint's, Anna stops talking in a way that Adaira notices.

By now all of Gower knows that Gevint's father-in-law is on his way. Twice the number of Jews the town already has, and with more implied in their relation to one another: if a father-in-law, then a wife. Children, in time. For the moment the prospect of two men. Not quite something new, just a doubling of what the town has thus far accepted as civilised people and believes it is being duped, having its goodwill abused, into doubling. As a lone man, an extension of his shop – a man of use, even, to the town – that is one thing. As a father, husband, a man with facets, with roles beyond shopkeeper … this is a new proposition.

In Gower you can hear a faint but certain echo of what you read is happening in the cities. A boatload or two – yes, a credit to us when England said no, America said no, and Jews are white besides, or white enough, but there are Purified petitions already to say there must not be more.

Adaira and Mrs Theron have settled on Monday afternoons to work on the dress. Adaira has little to do except stand in her slip and hand pins to Mrs Theron as she lays cloth this way and that, folds and tucks it, touching her body in a way it has not been touched since she was a child. This Monday afternoon leaves Adaira tender with the sensation of those light hands moving over her, chalk pressing the cloth against her skin.

When they are done for the day she pulls on an ordinary dress and makes her way to Gevint's. It is a good day outside in the waning afternoon, and slow within. She curls on a seat at a small table near the window, looking through a pattern book while he pulls bolts from the upper shelves to dust and restack. The door is open to the covered pavement. They speak from time to time and then do not speak, but they are aware of where the other is in the shop, and align, one to the other, as though still in conversation.

In come Magriet Meurs and one of the Burggraaff boys with his excess of consonants, his heavy name, his exhausting air of strain and menace. Something is going on between them; Magriet smirks and giggles as though they have just kissed or said something secret. They go up to the counter; they do not see Adaira behind them, where the light cutting in from the window makes a private space of her corner.

Adaira closes her book to watch Wyville Burggraaff bend his arm in a secretive way and extend a finger to poke Magriet in the back as if to prompt her. Magriet clears her throat and giggles at Gevint, who is on the shop ladder, a roll of cloth in his arms. He would be swiftly down for one of the town ladies, but these are youngsters and have the air of being there to ask directions or something else, something not to do with buying cloth, buttons, braces.

Magriet asks, in her piping English, an unnatural question about types of waistlines, or maybe it is collars, and Ira pushes the cloth he is holding into the shelf and comes down a step, still above them, and reaches with his hands for the right words. He is still on the 'How do you say' of his answer—

Burggraaff barks, 'What?'

Ira frowns, smiles and frowns in a friendly way, looks at Burggraaff, looks back at Magriet and with one hand describes below his own shirt collar the arc of a neckline—

'What?'

This time Ira waits a moment. Then he begins again, speaks only a word or two—

'What? We can't understand you. Say it right, man!'

Magriet squirms at this, and Burggraaff steadies her with his hand on the small of her back, and she dips her head to look at something in her hands – she is carrying notes? Adaira thinks – and asks another question, as though Gevint, having been marked down on that one, must try again. Some technical dressmaking matter again, to do with darts this time, and again, with a puzzled and almost friendly look at both of them, Ira begins to answer her, and this time speaks over the What so that Burggraaff grows angrier and is almost shouting when he braces both hands on the counter and leans across it towards

Ira to say, slowly, loudly, in words heavy with insult, 'You. Don't. Even. Speak. English.'

So a line is crossed and no one is pretending to be doing something else, to be in a different conversation. Ira keeps silent for a moment, then answers Burggraaff in German. He pauses, speaks some sentences in French, directed at Magriet, and then, his body changing for this language, says a handful of phrases in what he will later tell Adaira is Yiddish. This Yiddish makes his shoulders move, and his eyebrows rise – his mouth tugs down as if he is debating Burggraaff with himself: maybe this, perhaps that – and laughing at him, with Burggraaff standing like an idiot while he is spoken to and about in a language he can barely catch one word of.

Burggraaff mutters something to Magriet, whose back has gone slack at Gevint's display, her hands in their brown gloves hanging, then tells Ira, in a voice that is sullen and weak, that he is not welcome here. He says it in Afrikaans, but to one who speaks German and the bit of English Ira has, its meaning is unmistakable – Jy is nie welkom hier nie.

It sounds resentful and sulky, not threatening; Ira is, after all, the elder of the two, and they are separated by the shop counter, and neither has clear authority over the other. Burggraaff pushes Magriet out of the shop, guiding her by her shoulders in front of him. Several fellows come to meet them as they reach the street, gathering about them. Some of them are the wolfish boys from the old senator's Sex talk.

Inside Gevint's, Ira is at last down from the ladder and standing behind the counter, his hands in his trouser pockets, his head bowed, lost to his thoughts. Adaira pushes back her chair and stands and at the noise she makes he returns to himself and rubs a hand across his face. He picks up a box of bobbins; his hands are shaking.

Adaira's outrage burns off her reserve. Her hands are in fists at her sides, her cheeks reddened. She tells him: 'Those Burggraaffs are pigs. Don't listen to him.'

She watches him. She can't tell if he has heard her. On the face of it this was just a rude prank, but the newspaper world of men in armbands and German regulations that are so baldly offensive as to be barely credible, these are the context of Magriet and Burggraaff's clumsy playlet; the larger offence there makes of this puzzling small offence a larger thing. Somewhere in the world men have stepped forward and declared a breach in what had been the furthest boundaries of human behaviour; in the grip of vertigo, the likes of Burggraaff are being tugged to follow them to this new edge. Adaira is flushed with how near she has stood to the naked electrical spite of it. Some appetite in her scrambles to remember and experience again certain moments of it, moments when all of them in the shop seemed to have broken through to the new realm. There had been an almost physical shock to it, to the lawlessness of open hostility, and a terrible pull to it, to the sort of impulse that kindles in the eyes above a wild creature's trembling snarl.

By now Adaira believes she has learned the town, and the undertown. It is mapped in her – the attraction of Gevint's, of Mr Vos's house, of her Theron home, the committee hall that she approaches with a sense that her last few steps before reaching it are spent shrugging into a smart new coat whose edges she has to tug to get them to meet over her breasts. Happy Valley, where she has been many times but never alone.

A family stands out in Happy Valley, a nest of them, known by the committee as a bad lot. These are the Poleys, a clan of babies, girls and grown boys, then a gap where one would expect their parents to be, then their grandmother, the family's only Mrs Poley. Mrs Poley is the magneto of her family and she harnesses its push and pull to make its power, but even so, if they can, members detach themselves from the clan to drop onto whatever passes and offers food.

Surviving in Gower this winter are more Poley grandchildren than the committee can keep track of, even though the members spend time each meeting, at Vena Cordier's prompting, working out which ones are which to stop them getting away with more than is their due. Mrs Cordier is convinced that, through the Poleys, Happy Valley mealie meal is ending up in the Location – that Mrs Poley or her grandsons are selling food parcels, the committee's food parcels, and probably for less than they are worth, otherwise why would the Natives not just buy the stuff at the general dealer like everyone else? Although it is free and charity and all that, they are giving this food for a reason, and the reason is not so the Poleys can end up with money. They are supposed to boil it and feed it to their children, not sell it and use the money to set up a business buying brandy to sell to Natives and then buy something else themselves, something they would rather eat.

It is the yellow jersey that closes it down, this rogue traffic in donated goods.

The jersey is an unlovely, indestructible article that had

belonged to the Drukker family, whose several children each in turn had use of it. After passing, over the course of many winters, from Drukker sons to Drukker daughters, it ended up this winter on the poor table, to be carried off by an evil-eyed Poley girl. She tried it on and walked away still wearing it, back to her grandmother's midden of corrugated zinc, the terrible colour of it easy to see right until she turned the corner.

But the next thing the yellow jersey turns up in the Location and Mrs Drukker's houseboy, who has washed it often, recognises it and runs to tell his madam.

Mrs Drukker reports this to the committee. She says, with a flinch, a recoiling of her chin towards her collarbone that looks like heartburn, that she cannot actually even look towards Location Hill without thinking she sees her children's jersey moving between the shacks on the back of a Bantu.

That same afternoon Co-op rolls his eyes and sends one of his boys to get the thing back; as for how it travelled from the Poley girl to the Location, the next morning Vena Cordier goes herself to the tent and shacks of Mrs Poley to get to the bottom of this once and for all. She takes Adaira with her as a threat that what happens will be recorded.

They have to knock, and the wide tin door leaning against the gap in the tin wall makes a noise that sounds more like a gust of wind than an attempt to get the attention of those within. In any event it produces no reaction, and Adaira and Mrs Cordier stand there in the winter sunlight, wondering if they should lift the door or push it. Then a boy arrives and barely slows down, just hefts the corrugated sheet aside and enters, calling out, 'Ouma! Committee's outside!' in one long insolence, proving by this that they have a name in this household.

They follow the boy inside. The room is a kitchen, bedroom, sitting room, and very dark. Adaira can just make out a huge chest, a wagon chest, against one wall. There is a colourless carpet of many layers of newspaper on the ground, and sand is coming up through it in patches. Needles of light cut across the gloom from holes in the walls and show how thick with matter is the air.

Mrs Poley comes through an opening in the side of the room and walks right up to Adaira and Vena Cordier, and so they step backwards, but she keeps coming, and of course she is chasing them, at walking pace, from her home. Once they are back outside she drags the door panel closed behind her, folds her arms under her loose bosom and regards Mrs Cordier with a dead-level look.

'Mevrouw,' Mrs Cordier begins, in a thin, cracked voice, and she has to stop and clear her throat and start again. She says something about being there on the matter of such and such, but Mrs Poley just looks and does not say a word, and Mrs Cordier's voice goes high again.

At one point she turns to Adaira and says, 'Miss van Brugge, write this down!' but at last she runs down and they can only stand there in the humid silence Mrs Poley has made.

Adaira listens to Mrs Cordier breathing and to the Happy Valley sounds: children and dogs. She thinks that Mrs Poley has the same buzz of power about her that Mrs Cordier has. She feels an ache of tension across her temples. At last Mrs Poley shakes her head, swivels it in its cushion of chins, as though to say that all she has heard about this Vena Cordier is apparently, regrettably, true.

And then she turns around and goes back into her home, lifting the leaning door closed behind her. Power leaves Adaira and Mrs Cordier like a sudden hollowing of their chests and they must breathe hard to fill them again.

The committee has learned nothing from Mrs Poley, but the jersey in the Location is nonetheless taken as proof of a trade in food parcels and charity clothes; after this there are no more food tables set up on the roadside between Happy Valley and the mechanics' workshop. The following week the committee women pack the parcels into Mrs Cordier and Mr Drukker's motors and drive to Happy Valley as usual but do not stop; they carry on along the track that leads between the shacks, as far as a motor car can go. Even then, with every child in the place smacking the side of the motor and hanging off the running boards, the women do not invite them or their big sisters to help themselves to a parcel. One of the women stays to guard the food, and the rest set out in pairs to deliver one parcel to each family, at their doors or, if the women or elder daughters there are not quick enough in coming out to meet them, inside their homes.

'You must try to talk to them,' Vena told them back at the hall. 'Not for such a long time that you are delayed, but long enough to get a proper idea of what is going on.

'Use your eyes,' she told them. 'Use your noses.'

When every shack has its mealie meal and its tins of pilchards, the committee women, dog tired and with mud drying on their ankles and headaches from the noise and the awkwardness of it, reconvene. They give their reports of what they saw and Adaira, their scribe, writes it down in dun exercise books, the ennobled gossip and disinterested spite. As she makes her notes she feels she is wandering into a new world, one whose signs she cannot quite decipher.

The poor table, likewise, must be treated with extra vigilance. The six women and Adaira go by motor to the street that marks the boundary between Gower proper and Happy Valley and there they set up the table with old clothes for Happy Valley families to pick through.

In the course of the afternoon Adaira recognises one of the Cloete children from the family next door to the Therons, a proper Gower family. She is holding up a shirt against her brother's chest.

Mrs Cordier's briefing before they left the church hall today included a reminder of the rules: clothes for the poor of Happy Valley, according to their needs. Not too many for one, and like for like: no men's trousers to that forward pair of sisters; baby clothes for babies, boys' pants for boys.

Adaira, thinking she has spotted another category in the breach – a child from the town, here, at the Happy Valley table – leans across the table and says to the Cloete girl, 'This is not for you. Go on, off you go.'

But the dominee's wife, sorting through a bundle alongside Adaira, touches her arm and says quietly, 'It doesn't matter, Miss van Brugge, if they need it.'

The Cloete girl stops looking shamefaced and gives Adaira a look of triumph. Her elder brother, though, he who she has set out to clothe, holds his head twisted almost over his shoulder to look away from where he is. Mrs Dominee Ysel, at Adaira's side, passes another shirt to the girl with a murmur.

Adaira is struck silent by this exchange – by the force of the revelation in the gentle words of Mrs Ysel. As her hands sort and fold the stale and musty clothes, she reasons it out: it is as though she has discovered herself following a new set of rules without questioning whether she ought to. And almost worse was that such a thorough departure from kindness could be immediately made apparent and set to rights by such a gentle nudge. She had been unkind by reflex, without conviction.

The Cloetes have fallen on hard times, Mrs Ysel says when the girl and her brother have quit the table. This puts them above and apart from the Happy Valley shanty families, who are marked down as being immutably poor. Shanty people have No Visible Means of Support. The implication is that they are teetering on the very edge of a fall. It feels to Adaira as though the committee women are making this judgement on the No Visibles from a distance – that the poor families are at the crumbling lip of a donga on whose opposite, firmer bank the proper women of the town stand and from where they cast them a quick look, reading them in a flicker.

Thus, the work of the committee.

11

THE RADIO COUSIN BRINGS OTHER gifts. He woos Anna Vos through July, into the first days of August. It is bitterest winter, but the rainless nights allow the two of them to sit out together on the veranda in the early evening and observe the rituals of courting. Some Saturday evenings Anna walks with both men, Henry and Johan, and sometimes the magistrate falls back and follows them. He watches them, amused that his sister has attracted a suitor. Good for her.

Johan's suit is of only mild interest to the magistrate; he knows it must end in bafflement and rebuff for the Therons' kinsman. He does not notice that Anna is unsettled by it. She takes to pacing before the window of the front room. Her unquiet irritates her body and she comforts it, holding her hips in her hands, stroking her arms.

On a Saturday morning, Henry stands at the window of his study, looking out at the street. It is empty now, taking its Saturday rest. Earlier this morning there had been light traffic in voluntary constables on the far side of the street; none will pass now until early evening, when the water roster takes in houses to Henry's left, ending at the house before his and staying dry until it starts again on Monday at Henry's home.

In the few years he has lived here, Henry has taken to waiting in the shadows of the veranda on a Saturday night, and every Saturday night at the stroke of nine o'clock has been gratified by the clunk and scrape of the sluice and faint clicking sounds of running water: nine o'clock on a Saturday night is the turn of Albertus Meurs, Henry's neighbour, and he never misses it. On Saturday nights Henry, on his veranda, tilts his wristwatch to catch the light from the front room, holds his other hand in readiness. He brings this hand down to mark the moment and makes a small sound of amusement as Meurs, to the minute, starts the process, predictable as a punch line. If the sluice noises begin slightly before or after nine o'clock by Henry's watch, he adjusts the watch, equally satisfied.

That Henry's house should mark the start of the new week does not sit easily with him; in all matters he would prefer to be unremarkable among his neighbours, to be a Thursday or a Wednesday man.

Anna knocks at the open study door, holding out to Henry his hat and jacket, and the two of them leave their home among its spreading trees, head out in their motor car. As soon as they are beyond the town limits he pulls over and they get out and change places. She enjoys driving but prefers not to do so in town if he is also in the motor – some complicated decorum of hers, some response to Gower. He takes his seat and smiles to see her so upright, alert as a meerkat, gloved hands placed just so on the wheel, her head in its small hat held just so.

Changing down at a crossroads, she grates the gears and makes a small sound against herself. She says: 'If only there were a machine ...'

'... like the human body,' he completes the thought, and they smile the same smile.

The shared joke, so mildly at Gower's expense, comes of course from the evening lecture of the old senator. Henry had listened less to the lecture than to how it was received by Gower's people. From his seat behind the speaker he had watched them look about to seek their neighbours' opinions on whether to stay and listen or rise as one and knock the fellow down. He had seen them cling to the fact that this was science, science moreover in the service of the Creator, and he had known that only this and their natural courtesy kept them seated against the ovaries and oarsmen. That night Henry had felt a quick fondness for the town, its competing vanities, its grace under this provocation.

Even in the face of his misgivings, he knows that it has come to matter to both of them to be part of the town's life. Their life, this life of comfort and position, is the vessel into which they have agreed to pour themselves. Henry thinks, as they travel the lifting road across the wide berms of the hills, heading for the horizon, that this is perhaps, after all, where he belongs. Certainly, by her side. The thought rises to the surface for a moment and then blows away, leaving his mind clear.

It is their habit to drive out on a Saturday. Farm children as they once were, but masters these days of no large animals, they grow uneasy about the Chevrolet if they are prevented in a certain week from exercising it. There is also this: without a break from the close horizons of Gower, Henry and Anna grow irritable. Today they are headed, as they have taken to heading on recent Saturdays, for the farm of Johan Leibbrandt, the radio cousin, the quince suitor.

In another half-hour they are there. As she hauls on the steering wheel to guide the motor through the gates of the farm, Anna shifts in her seat and the moment she has a hand free, fusses with her hair, her hat. Henry is curious about this busyness and becomes aware, now that he looks properly at her, that she is dressed carefully, almost formally. Has he forgotten an occasion? Are they on their way to something he does not know about?

Now she is grimacing, either from tension or to stretch tension out of her mouth, and although it has been miles since she spoke, there is a new quality to her silence, and a distracted, bloodless quality to her smile as he waves her through the last of the gates, as though she is not thinking about him at all; he is reminded suddenly of his mother's smile. Anna charges the engine as she waits for him to take his seat.

He is upright beside her and scans the farmhouse now in sight. Something is up, he grows more sure of it. He almost asks her outright but cannot frame the question less childishly, less fearfully, than 'Is something happening?'

Johan is on the stoep to greet them. Rising from her seat in the depths of the veranda is a woman. She holds a black hat at her stomach like a supplicant.

Henry takes notice of everything. Johan is his usual self, shaking his hand – is he smiling more broadly, too broadly? – making them welcome as he always does. The thought arrives:

the woman is Johan's 'intended'. It is an explanation, and Henry holds it ready while at the same time sickening himself with such weak subterfuge against what he fears is coming.

He takes a seat. The woman takes a seat, smiles at him. She was introduced to him seconds ago but he cannot imagine what her name might be. He nods to her. Her careful questions about their journey, her stiff smile, these do not come without effort, he guesses. She is accustomed to silence.

Johan has not taken a seat. In fact only Henry and the woman are sitting down, looking up at Johan and Anna. Johan clears his throat. Here it comes, Henry tells himself. Johan looks at the red floor some small distance in front of his feet. He is speaking about a farm – another farm, not this one – the land abutting his, from the sweep of his arm and the way he looks up for a moment to turn his head in that direction. He has for years admired it, for its spring, its steady boreholes. He has this week offered for it and been accepted.

'Mrs Klaasens has accepted my offer,' he says, and for a moment Henry allows himself to believe that Johan is, in fact, announcing his betrothal to his neighbour, but he knows it is a diversion. He knows what is coming, a catastrophe he must meet with loving good cheer. In the way of the place and the species, Johan will add to his abundant land a wife. And who but Anna, who has not sat down, who stands by Johan's side, her hands open as if she is holding the arm of a ghost Johan alongside the real man as he tells the red stoep floor that she, too, has accepted his offer.

Henry shouts, desperately, loud enough to startle himself, 'Ah! Yes! Terrific!'

Johan, with Anna's hands now on his sleeve, rubs the back of his neck, looks stricken and proud. Mrs Klaasens is congratulating him, Henry, on this, the decimation of his happiness. He feels his face twist into a lopsided grin-like shape and he rises to shake Johan's hand and berate Anna with mock umbrage that she will know is real: 'You kept your secret pretty well, I'd say! Who knows about this? Do they know at Craigievar?'

'It is hardly any distance down the road,' she says, to salve the wound she knows she has made in him. 'We will visit often' – and 'We' flies past him like a knife.

It becomes clear, as they move into the house, that Mrs Klaasens has been invited for his sake. Anna points out to the magistrate and the widow facts about the other. Henry believes of Mrs Klaasens that she welcomes this no more than he does – then he notices her swiftly pinching her cheeks to bring colour to them as they take their places at table. He feels sympathy at this; she, catching his gentle tone and taking this for pity, stiffens against him and goes about her meal in near silence.

At last Anna prompts the neighbour through a description of her profitable venom operation. It is as bizarre and as dull as a recounted dream, the Widow Klaasens' laboured sentences about her cages of female white mice (the males, she says, go to the university) and the safest way, the least dangerous way, to milk an adder.

Henry pushes the Chevrolet to its limit on the run for home. Anna is not beside him to lighten his foot; he imagines her sounds and locks his leg, almost standing on the pedal. The boxy motor sways when it corners, its weight off the two outside wheels. He does not slow by much until he reaches Gower, and even then he hurls the machine with a kind of light-hearted fury down the streets, jerking the gears and at a corner imagining himself driving into the blameless house there.

Night has long since fallen by the time Johan brings her back to him, and Henry is almost drunk. In his mind he has punished her with sneers about middle-aged romance and desperation in a wedding veil, but he does not say such things as she stands before him, her happiness blocking him out, and asks to be understood in the matter of the suddenness, the secrecy.

She cannot apologise for leaving him, for breaking a pact that has held for more than a decade. It had meant everything to the two of them – at least, he knew it meant that to him, and had believed it of her – but he knows too that in the way of human society, human family, one may choose to act by the code of such private and never-spoken pacts or turn from them without a moment's shame and declare oneself to be living by different rules, by the rules of the world, to have in fact been so living all along.

The unspoken bond had been to be each other's person, to make a fit where there was no fit to be found out there, but the world had known this to be a permanently temporary arrangement, a contingency that would hold only until one of them rubbed the sleep from his or her eyes and joined the prescribed march. He has no stomach for her reasons, which would no doubt include, somewhere among them, the unanswerable case of biology.

Anna has unpinned her hat from her head and peeled off her gloves; their pale shapes in the dim light of the entrance hall put him in mind of the widow's mice. Henry watches her hands and feels afraid and hears, like a sad joke, coming to him through the open door at his sister's back, the clunk and scrape of the sluice as his neighbour claims his share.

Word about the magistrate's new state spreads fast as air.

Anna is buffeted by congratulations but at the same time there is a flutter of concern about the magistrate. This is directed not so much towards the collapse of his domestic arrangement, his sibling coupledom, because Gower has been with the world in failing to find much value in it. He may feel it as a divorce, but to Gower it is only the playing out of the inevitable, if somewhat delayed, marriage of his sister. No, the flutter is for the fact that he is womanless. Henry alone is an unstable variable in the tribal round of Gower. Adaira, a frequent visitor to the Vos home in the weeks before and during Anna's romance, feels a tightening of attention from the women of Gower in the wake of Anna's news, feels it settle into watchfulness.

Anna leaves within the week for Craigievar where, it seems, she must be prepared for marriage – heaped with linens, measured for new dresses by the woman who has, for Anna and the brothers' wives' generation at least, always come to the farm to perform this service. In Gower, a town not given to evening visits, there springs up a round of these to fill Henry's empty hours. Vena Cordier is known to disapprove of the magistrate's politics and humour; therefore, some of these evenings of talk and coffee are clandestine, or at least not spoken of in the committee before they start, when they settle their things and share their news. But the visits go on, even at the homes of the committee women.

Henry escapes to the home of his chief clerk, and Adaira and the Therons work together to welcome him in their small way.

The magistrate throws himself into their after-supper craze for the Monopoly game, and Mrs Theron is happy to give her place at the board to him and take to her easy chair under the lamp to read or knit while they play at being rich. He is the top hat. No one has chosen it as their piece before he joins the game.

When he is not in the house he has two places in the Theron home: the early evening one of 'Is Mr Vos here yet?', 'When is Mr Vos coming, I want to show him something', 'Wait, Nantie, don't bring it out until the magistrate gets here', and the break-fast-table one where Mr Theron mutters to Mrs Theron about how he seems, about good days and bad days, about how Mr Theron just doesn't know.

Mr and Mrs Theron discuss him in code. Adaira and Nantie understand effortlessly. When he comes home for lunch, Mr Theron reports on the magistrate's condition like a doctor with a patient, telling Mrs Theron 'No better' or 'Worse than yesterday'.

They manage to keep him close for less than a fortnight – held there, it seems, only by the tin top hat and Mrs Theron in her pool of light. Soon the magistrate is slipping away from them, too, barely clinging on. He joins the family on fewer nights for supper and a game. When he does, Adaira watches him closely. What she sees is a man with red-rimmed eyes whose smile, when he smiles, is weak as water. Adaira thinks that if she did not know that these were the result of drink, she would worry that he was ill and want to help him. Nantie hands him things to watch his hand shake as he takes them, and does this until Adaira hisses at her to stop.

As he worsens, the magistrate holds her interest in a way he has not before. The tug as he slackens and falls back awakens something in her. Almost by reflex, she tries to hold more tightly to him as he slips away.

This change in her is lost on no one in the Theron household. Henry stops by one afternoon after court, and on his way out he and Adaira speak for long moments at the garden gate. As Adaira says goodbye to him, she places a hand on his arm. When she turns back towards the house she sees the Therons' boy, Enoch, stopped on the path, wheelbarrow lifted, stifling a grin, and knows that Nantie will have a report of her arm and the magistrate's sleeve within the hour; Nantie and the boy enjoy a conspiracy that amazes her parents, an exchange of gossip that somehow gets through the membrane that separates town from Location.

The next day at breakfast Nantie says, 'Daira and Henry sitting in a tree, kay eye ess ess eye en gee,' and Mrs Theron and Mr Theron share a look.

'First comes love, then comes marri—'

Adaira says, 'Nantie!' She wonders why she has never had

the girl's respect; how is it that she believes she can speak to Adaira like this?

Nantie makes kissing sounds and chants, 'Daira loves the magistrate, Daira loves the magistrate.'

Adaira colours. Mr Theron, looking down at his plate, says, 'I trust that's not the case.' She cannot read his meaning exactly.

Nantie hugs herself and says the magistrate's Christian name out loud without coupling it with the honorary, respectful Uncle, something more or less forbidden a child in the case of a white adult: 'Oooh Henry.' Both her parents tell her to stop, and give Adaira worried looks. No, not worried looks; puzzled looks. Puzzling looks, Adaira thinks: looks that are puzzling in themselves.

Nantie leaves for school. Adaira is headed in the same direction, to the part of Church Street that is a block from Nantie's school, but she waits a moment so that she will have the walk to herself. She has given herself half an hour to get to the church hall where the committee will gather to pack food parcels.

Being on a town street is still a matter of active enjoyment for her. Passing house after house to be greeted from the garden or the veranda, or just to look over hedges and fences at the lives of other people, the story she guesses of other lives, absorbs all of her attention. She likes, too, the crunch of the rough pavement under her shoes, and the shade, and the perspective down the street, the idea she has that the houses are waiting for something, waiting perhaps for men and children to return to them, and are meanwhile busy with themselves and the women who tend them. In place of 'tend' she tries out 'groom', and with her solitary ability to say things out loud to herself, tells the Gower morning, 'Groom.'

As she nears the house of the magistrate, he is closing his garden gate behind him. He greets her, and she him, and he says, 'Shall we go on together?' He is subdued but also has about him an air of purpose, the air of a man who is trying to take himself in hand. He brings a naartjie from his jacket pocket and strips it of its peel in three movements, splits the fruit and hands half to her as they go.

His glance snags on the badge that she has kept pinned to the lapel of her brown coat but he does not say anything about the powder horn and its circle of words. They barely speak at all. When he is done eating his half of the fruit, he toys with the peel, pressing it to break out the scent. From time to time he makes a small sound to indicate a direction they should take. Adaira does not know the town as well as he, but she can tell that they are not using the most direct route to the part of Church Street she wants or the court building further along the main road.

They turn down a side street. The magistrate is looking about him for something – in fact, testing the air for it, and he brings them across the road to a garden where a shaggy jasmine plant on a trellis is massed with blossoms. He slows, and so she slows, but they do not stop. It seems the aim is not to visit the garden, but rather to arrange things so that jasmine scents their walk for these half-dozen steps.

From the jasmine, they turn more or less in the right direction, this time along a street where the trees are uniform and full. After a while Adaira notices that the magistrate is moving in erratic rushes, out of balance, as though the street has tilted, slowly, steeply one way, then righted itself and tilted the other. Adaira wants to take hold of his arm and slow him down.

Once, Henry squats to look at something in a leiwater gutter. When Adaira bends down to see what it is, it is only a weed, moving regularly in the flow: around, across and back, around, across and back.

They meet Church Street and, although there is no apparent need to cross the road, they cross it, to a showroom where a salesman is polishing a red tractor, and they pass this with the red reflected in their eyes. From now on they keep to a more logical path on the main road, crossing back only once, and still are met every short while by something good – a smooth face, an arresting colour, a sweet smell from the seed store.

The magistrate stops at Gevint's Haberdashers. Ira Gevint comes from the shop and the men speak in shorthand about the news from Germany, but soon the magistrate lifts his hat and leaves Adaira there, his eyes already busy for the next thing, the thing he is apparently using to bring himself along the street to where he must go, or take his thoughts away from where he is. He seems to need to touch whatever he can – touch it, smell it.

Adaira and Ira enter his shop, where she has only ten minutes before she must leave for the committee hall. By now she seeks no pretext for being there, and only seats herself on the high stool at the counter and opens herself to what he has to say today.

12

O N THE FIRST SATURDAY IN September, Miss Mostert of the hygiene committee will lead her girls into the hills around Gower for their spring hike, and they will set out each Saturday from then until the end of autumn. But this year Miss Mostert and her girls are not the ones to wake the kloofs. Ira Gevint, who has travelled for half a year to find himself a stranger in Gower, can feel this, his second spring of 1938, approaching: in the odd warm breeze at dawn, in the way the town dogs mouth one another in play with spread jaws and gurgling mock growls, in the frisking of girls. Without the Palmengarten, nor any public garten in this town, nor Taunus mountains, nor any mountains, he eyes Gower's hills.

On a Sunday morning in late August he watches the church hubbub of motors and people passing. Then, having dressed himself in proper boots, and buried his trousers deep in stockings, and with oranges in his rucksack, he strikes out for Gower's far edges. He quits the town's paved streets, and even the dirt lanes at last, but still spends far longer among people than he expects to. He skirts Happy Valley, its warrens chill with shadow in these damp lowlands. In a patch of sun at the edge of the settlement a small girl watches him pass. She is tilted back against the weight of the baby in her arms; at her feet, a toddler chews wetly on a stick. Ira, tugged past her by momentum, regrets not sharing his oranges, at least until he is out of her sight. By then he has crossed the stream buried in growth in the crease of the little valley – crossed it in one spread step; it is barely there – and is making his way up the first slight rise to the lip of the Location.

Here the shanties are spaced further apart, as if in answer to the nakedness of the hill, although some five of them in a row lean on one another, each shack's rusted, lacy corrugations lapping the next like scales; by instinct, Ira marks these as the homes of men without women. In front of these and other, more substantial, shacks, thin heat from outdoor fires ripples the air. Pig-iron pots are tucked among the coals.

Two boys caper on a cross-lane at the edge of the Location, keeping pace with Ira and miming his hands at the rucksack straps. At the end of the lane they stop and watch him go. Their orange earth roadway is barely distinguished from the orange earth across which it lies, but is a border to the boys and they do not cross it to come nearer.

Ira's walk has not yet left people behind, but already it is bringing him the sort of thinking he wants, about this place, about permission, about anything but his new trade of cloth and buttons, or what might have become of his marriage.

That first Sunday, Ira finds a pretty kloof, its defile blocked by a fall of massive boulders. Trees have settled here and he uses their roots and branches to haul himself among the rocks. At the top, beyond the trees, he reaches a trickling fall of water and a pool, and here he rests. After his fill of birdsong and water sounds and fruit, he heads back down and, travelling through its layers, reaches Gower by the same path.

He is out again the Sunday following, seven days deeper into the season, and this time nods to children at the edge of Happy Valley and waves and calls, 'Hello!' to his boys, or different boys, as he passes the Location.

He knows that between that Sunday and this the hygiene girls have been here, and it is this knowledge or his new isolation or his senses that perfume the trail through the boulders and to the pool with female. He is alone at the pool as before, but also among them, among it, the idea of the girls.

Ira strips off his boots, his stockings and corduroy trousers, his shirt and sleeveless pullover and German hat. He takes off every stitch by the pool and stretches in the warming morning, shows his body to the naked air. His skin is silvery pale, grained with black hair in flowing symmetry on his chest and belly, converging at his groin or, if his loins are the source, blooming upwards from there, in stem past his navel and flowering at his chest. He tilts his head back, reaches for himself, shows his throat to the sun.

With the arrival of spring, Henry leaves to watch his sister wed at Craigievar. On the day he comes back to Gower he invites Adaira to tea. Outside his study, as she gathers her books to leave, Henry leans the side of his big body – his arm – against hers. She welcomes him. She presses back, easy with the feel of his jacket against her. His height relative to hers makes the embrace fatherly, brotherly, she thinks, but it fills her thoughts on her way home.

A night or so later he calls at the Theron home, his first visit in a week or more. He drinks coffee with them, then stands up from his chair and says he would like to take a walk, to go for a walk. Will she, Adaira, come with him? Around the block. Stretch their legs. Get some air. Look at the stars. She is already on her feet – they do what he wants, all of them – but still he comes up with more reasons for this simple thing, this walk.

In her pool of light, Mrs Theron is not looking their way, but has tilted her head to hear. Her hands are unmoving among the wool and needles. Mr Theron is tamping the bowl of his pipe and patting his waistcoat for matches and looking away from them, and there is embarrassment in the front room of the Theron house, as real as a colour. Even Nantie is all hands and has no eyes for Adaira or Henry as she sorts the Monopoly good-fors into piles. Everyone in the room knows what the magistrate is asking; what he wants is a matter of unease to the elder Therons and satisfaction and interest to the younger.

There is nothing to be done but for Adaira to take her cardigan from the back of her chair and go with him.

As they close the garden gate behind them she draws a deep breath, concentrating on keeping the air in or its release quiet. She must not sigh at this, whatever it might be, although the thought of what it must be grips her and of course she has guessed it, the outline of it at least. Her hands pester the buttons at her waist.

Henry's language-bearing fore-mind has put something into words, has made a theory or a plan, and now they are seven steps along the road, moving towards the lights of Church Street, and he is lifting his hand to touch hers, to make her stop. He turns to her, turns her to him, swallows loudly.

He says, 'Adaira, you are … very dear to me.'

His eyes are hidden in the shadow cast by his hat and the street light. Adaira can only look towards him, and then turn her head to the side as though to brace for an unkind word. He puts his hands on her shoulders, guides his body to hers: she, stiff with alarm, he stiff with not wanting this.

By the meeting of her chest to his, Adaira's head is tilted up, and now he has an arm around her and is pressing a dry kiss onto her mouth. It is over in a moment and she is ducking her head, pulling her lips through her teeth to remove the feel of him. She catches a shocking glimpse: his face is contorted. He has the back of his hand almost at his mouth before he stops himself and brings his hand to his hat instead.

He says something or she does and they hurry to get away from that kiss and walk on in misery. When they return at last to the Theron house the family are still up, even Nantie, and the clock points out that not even twenty minutes have passed. Adaira hurries through the front room, head down, before Nantie can say something. She closes and locks her bedroom door and sits on the edge of her bed.

To see him that way was as truly sad as … she cannot make an analogy. Quick scenes snap to mind, to do with his reaching for her, leaning for that kiss, to do with animals made to dress up, animals brought into human play-acting – the shame humans feel when they see an animal compromised in its dignity. She bites back a frightened laugh that threatens to turn into a wail: for God's sake, she does not see Magistrate Vos as a tea-party chimp; but she knows that there was an assault on his dignity under way, and that deep in his eyes – as she has seen in the eyes of a newsreel chimpanzee dressed in frills and making with its rictus of dislike a human's smile – he had known this. Could this be the man she is supposed to love? Even unspoken, the suggestion is one she wants to brush from her skin and for a moment Adaira raises her open palms and tenses in a writhe of refusal.

The town reads this change, their shame. There are whispers, a susurrus of Vissanter, Visagie. The hiss of interest warns her off as surely as a gander's; she stays away from him, and what between Henry and Adaira might have been freed by the next exchange of books or a street greeting is left to brew with unease. She practises stronger feelings about his kiss than had come unbidden, attaches words to the wisps of what she recalls.

There are other places to find books. She does not need his books. In the Purified reading circle they are busy with Essie Malan's novel, the story of a girl who pretends to be a servant so that she can spy on the other servants and work out what is wrong with them, why they are like this, these poor white Afrikaners, so shiftless and thick. There are no white servants in Gower. 'Everyone has a coloured,' says Vena Cordier. She directs herself at Adaira: 'But some people, I am sure I don't have to tell you, have a Bantu. In the house.' Enoch does the house and garden at the Therons; Ephraim does the housework at the magistrate's. Two Bantu household servants somehow for

Adaira's account. The other women, who will forgive Henry anything, put this down to his having come from the city, where, it is said, you will get a Native houseboy as easily as a white housemaid, and for less.

The reading circle spends a lot of time on the help, perhaps because it is not a very interesting book, this *Through Borrowed Spectacles* by the sister of the famous Dr DF, leader of the opposition, stoker of grievance, hope of the nation. You can tell from early on in *Through Borrowed Spectacles* that the girl pretending to be a poor white is going to be discovered as a proper Afrikaner lady, and it will have been all right for the mistress's brother to have been in love with her all along.

At last they are released from discussing the book by news of the Trek. It has been three weeks since the twelve-span of yoked oxen were led down Cape Town's main street on a cleared lane between motor cars and trolleybuses, pulling a replica of a nineteenth-century covered wagon past ecstatic crowds as it set out to travel the length of the country and claim its history. The cicada din of excitement about the trek has mounted as the first wagon and then another and another have entered the interior. No one can remember its like, and the newspapers are full of it, their story.

Centenary Trek fever in Gower mainly takes the form of dressing up. The men have their new beards. The women and girls flock to Ira Gevint's haberdashery for pale cotton cloth and lace, and work on the simple long dresses of the Voortrekker era, and copy the Federation's pattern for hooded bonnets. They tell one another over again, a discovery made each time, how flattering these are.

Adaira watches the ladies talk and tries to picture bringing *Turning Wheels* into the circle. Ladies don't do so well in *Turning Wheels*. If she brought in the magistrate's copy, Adaira wonders, would Gower's Voortrekker champions want to burn it on Church Street, to keep up with the readers' circle in Cape Town?

She is irritable and hot. The neckline of her blouse feels too high. What is she doing here, in these matronly clothes, among the settled women of Gower?

All of the committee members are in the reading circle, but it is not a committee thing. They do not mention their Happy Valley work here. The circle is strictly a Party set-up; Party women are forbidden to do charity work in the name of the Party and they know they must not mention it here. Only three things are expected of a Nationalist woman: to educate herself with a readers' circle, to make propaganda for the Party, to raise money for the work the Party men do.

Later this week Mrs Cordier and most of the others will take off their Party hats and put on their Federation hats for the business of food parcels. Right now, Vena is bursting to talk about the midwife that her Federation self has found for Gower. The town lost its midwife more than a year ago; Vena has found a new one and persuaded her to move here. Federation Vena wrote the letter to the midwife (which Adaira typed), but in truth it was her Party self that had looked so urgently; Vena is haunted by something Essie Malan's famous brother likes to say, haunted by the 'one hundred thousand we throw away every generation because of ignorance'.

Mrs Cordier quotes Dr Malan: 'We have a huge country

and a small nation, and we lose so many of our people.' Adaira imagines tumbling scores of children washed away, carried off in the way that the rivers steal topsoil from the earth.

Against the bewildering spite of life that takes the soil, takes the cattle in a contagion of silent sterility, takes the children, they know there must be a God, whatever godless Dr Hertzog may say.

And there it is, humming around the circle of women, the thin fear that insists on God's attention, like a child beating on a locked door to be let in.

Death is the nation's political enemy, but fewer of them will go to waste now that the midwife is coming. She is also a registered nurse. She will keep this parcel of the nation alive, and Vena Cordier will haul it to literacy, civilisation, hygiene.

In a week or so a note comes for Adaira. Will she call at his home? He has a proposition to put to her. Adaira is agape at his bravery; she could not have found him again so boldly, but she makes her own courage out of words – 'ought' and 'friend' and 'over with soon' – and goes.

They meet at his front veranda; neither of them has an inclination for niceties, and they barely say a thing beyond their greeting. There is an ache caused by being near one another again; it closes their throats.

He stays standing, and nor does she sit, and soon with a stiff movement he shows her through the front door, and then guides her past the study, past the kitchen, to a bedroom along the passageway, along from the public rooms and locked. She follows with a sort of trusting horror; whatever it is he has in mind, at least it will move them on …

The magistrate is holding himself carefully. There is slow ceremony in his movements. At the bedroom door he works the key, twists the handle, and at last it gives and they are in a room from which the afternoon light is blocked by dark curtains; when he presses the switch the lights come on, not overhead in the centre of the room but in three lamps, two in corners and one standing on a table among shelves.

On most of the shelves – the room is all shelves, lining the walls and some standing alone to make a small lane of shelves – speckled black-and-grey file boxes take up the lower levels; the topmost levels hold a bristling something, like a parapet of huge insect wings or sticks or small farm machinery. Henry Vos draws back one half of the curtain and the room grows light enough for Adaira to see that these are toys – or not exactly toys, but toylike small carved creatures, or tin snipped in the shape of an animal, a kudu bull it looks like – and an ebony walking stick with a hoof carved where the knob would go; rickety coats of arms of the Zuid-Afrikaansche Republiek and the Republic of the Free State; Queen Wilhelmina's head and bosom in tin, wire, wood, painted on plaited brittle palm blades and sewn from quilted mealie sacks. And in these materials – plus cast metal rubbed to brightness at his pig's-knuckle nose and left to darken at the lion's-tears lines under his eyes – a forest of Krugers.

Most of the speckled boxes are stuffed with letters. Special boxes, only a dozen or so, are empty except for a book or loose sheaf in each one. The special boxes hold the diaries, the magistrate says, and he pats one of them.

'Will you help me?' he says. 'Will you work with me? Read these letters, sort them, type them out?'

Adaira is nonplussed to realise that she is being offered a job of work, and almost at the same moment is eager for this.

She will work in the museum, at his desk, and he moves his hand to indicate the room, then stops himself, clears his throat, says, 'Well, not museum, obviously. The start of a collection. A beginning.'

His plan is to work with two carbons, and keep one copy here and send one to his bank. She is not to correct the writers' spelling or grammar, and when she has to guess at a word she is to type her guess between square brackets.

On the table is a parcel that arrived this week. He lays his hand on it and says, 'From the rectory at Machadodorp. Every so often my notice in the *Kerkbode* brings me a nice fat parcel. I'm amazed at what they send me. People don't know what to do with the things from the war. You can't let yourself throw away such things or leave them to the white ants. So they send them here.'

While he speaks he slips a penknife from his pocket and cuts the string on the parcel. He folds back brown paper, then another layer, then muslin – whoever wrapped this to send to a stranger wanted to keep it safe. He slides the letters he finds in the parcel into a half-full box and places it back on a shelf.

Tomorrow, after the committee, Adaira will begin her work in Henry's museum. Now she has two jobs: secretary to the Women's Federation of Gower, and transcriber and archivist for Henry Vos's great project, the project Anna mentioned but seemed to want to leave at that. Adaira cannot ask him about this without talking about her, so she does not. She guesses the reason: it must have embarrassed Anna; she would have been all too aware that they no longer claim Boer as their marker, not when they are on the way to becoming this better nation.

Adaira will record the living history of the town in her brown exercise books, and at the magistrate's house she will make a record of these snatches of stories of the war before she was born; the work suits her in both cases – being privy to the slicing up of human matters by Vena Cordier, and doing a sort of service of honour to the boys and women, the men and the parents of the war, beyond the parts of it that have been told over and over until they are the only truth, and far from a record.

Possibly there is even mild subversion here. History does not come from people, not like this, welling up among their family papers: history is sifted, combed for orthodoxy, handed down. Yet here it is.

The next day he seats her at a table with a typewriter in the room lit by lamps. He looks back from the door to watch her for a moment, slim as a hare among the many lines of the shelves and the forest of angles above.

There is fresh paper and carbon rolled against the platen and the ribbon is new. To one side on the desk, a letter from a young man to his mother. 'Dear Mother,' it begins, and goes on, with simple-minded single-mindedness, to ask after several animals and siblings and servants, as though after each query he hears his mother answer him.

Many of the letters will be this dull. She will learn to make herself switch from the letter's words to her own thoughts in passages such as these; she suspects already that there is something to be learned even in these sorts of letters, and that the price for that one true sentence or even a few good words is to press through the things that can have meaning only for the two people named and saluted at the top and bottom of the page.

Besides, you do it for all of them or for none; that is the point of Henry's great project: get it all down, bring it all to safety, build a record. Later they will make stories of it. In the meantime, he tells her, these histories will pile up to sandbag what really happened from that which is travelling towards them, the invented history advancing at the pace of modern oxen yoked to a replica wagon.

The rebellion of helping to build a truer history than she is supposed to know suits her, or will change her, she begins to think, to suit it – will breed her as an amanuensis for its needs. His needs.

13

A FTER SPRING, BEFORE THE FIRST good rains: that's when the Agricultural Show comes to the district. You can get anything you need at the Jamestown Show, from bull seed to the Bible in Afrikaans. The Therons and Adaira visit it on a Saturday, a day off from Mr Theron's court work, Adaira's crowded acquaintance of commandants and boy fighters, Nantie's school. They move between the show's attractions as a group, taking turns to see what the others want to see – Mr Theron's elaborate chickens in the poultry and pigeon tent, Nantie's funfair, Mrs Theron's flower-seed booths and handicrafts.

Adaira leads them to the far edge of the showground where, on either side of a path laid between hay bales and fence panels, the livestock shifts in small pens. First come the rams with their horns pressed into fleece as fat as proving dough, sliding their narrow jaws, but she herds the Therons past these: she is here for the cattle. The cattle in this part of the country tend to be red Bonsmara but these days they are bringing in all sorts. Today there is a creamy Charolais, a half-dozen feminine Guernseys and among them, like an expensive toy, a glossy Angus standing with his back to the bigger breeds. She moves close to the packed, muscled bulls, finds one that tolerates her standing quietly at his shoulder and hears the passage of the breath inside him, in his pink echoing nostrils.

After the bulls they run from an early rain shower into a tent holding a mixture of things that belong nowhere else – small Italian tractors, kitchen gadgets, a Dicks Sweets table, and a counter raised on a platform where a salesman's demonstration is about to start. The early rain has put everyone in a good mood and the crowd, heated up and steaming, is ready to have fun with the salesman. To begin with, his product is ridiculous: two artificial sponges glued to small boards, these joined to one another with a cord and apparently hiding magnets. The idea is that they will, when you put them on either side of a pane of glass, move together so that, as you clean the inside of the window, your sponge brings along the slave sponge and takes care of the outside. But he hasn't wet the sponge enough, and the demonstration window is badly mounted and wobbles and tips as he drags at it, and the salesman swears under his breath and gets rough with the sponge and breaks the magnets' field, and the outer sponge tumbles. The people looking up at him – where he sweats and curses through a horrible grin as he tries to right himself, and jostles his bowl of soapy water and splashes his trouser front – treat each new mistake as though it is part of a high-wire act in a circus, and make ooh and aah sounds of appreciation.

The problem is that, even if it works, it is a foolish piece of big-city nonsense, and possibly a poor reflection on them, a clue to how gullible he considers them. Then again, although the salesman may be a big-city sort of fellow who considers them Plaas Japie's kin, he is certainly trying to flatter them – or is doling out the cheap flattery he thinks is good enough for them – to get them to buy his magnetised sponges, many of which are stacked in a pyramid on the dusty ground behind him.

His efforts give a false note to his patter – 'Missus, you look like a forward-looking sort of lady,' directed at whatever woman does not look away in time. Mr Theron watches him with a closed-down face. At his side, Nantie says in a bioscope American accent, 'Phoney baloney.'

The Therons and Adaira drift away. In the next line of stalls one stands out, among the improved mealie huskers and the rest, for not selling anything or even giving much away (the Pepsodent stall is handing out tiny tubes of toothpaste; at the Coca-Cola stand you can get a bottle of real Coke smaller than your thumb. Nantie has a Tyson's Feed bag crammed with these and with literature on mattresses, tractors, semen). At this standout stall a banner announces Onse Erfenis, and in smaller letters below this, Our Heritage. At either side a wagon wheel leans against a bale of hay; a table and easel cluster at the centre. It does not have enough to fill its square of balding grass, this stand.

The easel holds a map of the Union with three thick lines marked on it, one red, one blue, one black. A drop of cloth at the rear of the stand is painted to show a line of covered wagons trekking into the setting sun. The back of the nearest wagon is open and a woman is seated there. She has a baby on her lap and her face is entirely hidden by the white bonnet she wears. The rays of the sun reach to the furthest corners of the painting.

At the table a man nudges a tin collecting box to square it with the table edge, picks up a stack of pamphlets and knocks them into a uniform pile, sets this square to the tin, does the same with the next. He gives the impression of doing this without pause, squaring his table again and again. Nantie and Mr Theron head for the map and trace their fingers on it to find Gower, or Jamestown if Gower is too small to show. The red, black and blue lines start out together at one end of the country and converge again at the centre of the upper bulge, and between start and finish they take off on their own, one tracking west, one vaguely north-east, one due north until it, too, turns east. This, the black line, comes nearest to Jamestown/Gower, but seems not to pass over its dot.

Nantie loses interest and slumps against Mrs Theron, who is resting on one of the bales, a hand on a spoke of the iron-bound wheel. The axle hub is the size of her head. The pamphlet man blinks hard at her using the bale as a seat. He might say something, but before he can find the nerve, Mr Theron asks: 'The Second Trek?'

'The Centenary Trek, yes.'

'Centenary? How did they choose a date, I wonder? And tell me this: who ever heard of a Voortrekker going first to Cape Town? It was bloody Cape Town they were trying to get away from, man.'

The man stops fussing with his table. He stands upright, though his eyes shift quickly to one side of the stand, quickly to the other.

'On the eighth day of August, eighteen thirty-eight, the farmer and landowner Johannes Petrus—'

'Ag, come on, man!' Mr Theron interrupts the man, speaking lightly, but with an edge. Nantie, who has been slumped on her mother's lap, sits up at her father's tone. Mr Theron makes a joking reference in a hard, light voice to 'a bunch of cattle thieves' – a joke that pains the pamphlet man. Beneath the joking, Mr Theron is upset. Their little group leaves Onse Erfenis before their exchange can come to anything. Adaira wonders, as she follows them out of the tent, if there is a difference, a hierarchy, between heritage and history. Perhaps you can make of one what you will, but must accept the other as a verdict? She will have to ask the magistrate.

They will hear later that, after they left, Vena Cordier and the magistrate wound up in Onse Erfenis at the same time, and the pamphlet man could only watch and steady his card table as his cause was argued by the lady and attacked by the gentleman. She was all about 'a mighty people awakening' and 'our pilgrimage of martyrdom'. God was there: God's people, God's work, God ordering the flight of the bullets and ordaining this, the second coming of His nation, by ox wagon and destiny and His own hand; the magistrate's corner was no less than the wrongedness of the whole enterprise.

Mr Theron says, when he has done telling his family at supper in the food tent about the words between Mrs Cordier and the magistrate, that Mrs Cordier might want to go softly if she goes down that path. He is still angry in his quiet way when he says, 'Grandfathers who had daughters with their own daughters are there for her to meet down that road, and worse.

Good men too, of course, but when you say that merely being there is the thing that counts, you put the violator of his own children up on the wagon next to the purest old father Abraham. And you give them turns at the whip.'

Nantie is afraid of him like this. Tears come; she sniffs them back. Mr Theron breathes deeply and looks about him, comes back to the supper table, to his family. He gets up and goes to Nantie, stands behind her bench and touches her head. 'Not your grandfathers, my girl.'

He and Nantie leave to find toffee apples. Mrs Theron tells Adaira that Mr Theron had a great-grandfather who travelled with one of the treks as a boy and told terrible stories about a certain family in his trek party. Mr Theron had loved him and the idea of him, a quiet, humorous man who collected and studied baboons and liked them better than people and named them Maritz and Potgieter and Tregart. Now, in the lore of that time, he is to be harnessed to Burggraaff's progenitor who, as a boy of fourteen on that trek, acquired a taste for whipping black men, and as a man beat them so long he made himself drunk with it and the sjamboks were stiff with blood, so stiff with it you could peel it away from the plaited stock like a scab. And today this Burggraaff is someone to celebrate as a stern patriarch, although his grown son famously wet his trousers when he had to report to him that he had returned from the post depot without the old bastard's new pipe from Holland.

The magistrate is as agitated as Mr Theron, though he had no grandfather in the first trek. In his study on the morning after the Jamestown Show he tells Adaira: This ossewatrek, this fable, 'it is presented as a choice, as a fork in the road, but it is only theatre. We are deciding something important about our-selves in a moment when we are out of our minds, crying and shouting and cheering for oxen. I love the oxen too; but loving oxen is not a philosophy.

'I love even the madness of those trekkers, setting off to-gether for God knows where, blinded by faith, yes, but also knowing that they could rely on one another – but what we have made it, that I cannot love. It takes the story of depending on those who are with you and makes it into a commandment about fearing and mistrusting everyone else.'

And above all, he says, worst of all, the story of it we are told today discounts human courage and choice by claiming God's destiny for it. This is false history, he says. And false history does not just sit alongside the true story: it drives it away. Let me tell you, Adaira, the real story is always more interesting. It's like the difference between how the world came to be and what the Old Testament says about it. The story of the world is enough to choke you with wonder, but we suffocate our curiosity under this blanket of predestination. Stick to the facts! Tell what happened!

She asks him, addressing as much what Mr Theron had said as the magistrate's objections: 'But we can't make all of history separate stories, surely? Don't there have to be movements, theories, patterns, ways to agree about what happened?'

He answers immediately: 'We can say, many people moved over a period of almost ten years; some for these reasons, some for those. Among them were knaves, murderers, good men and brave women. Say it was fed by fear, by fear of change, and say it was fed by courage, and that when they were tested, many rose in bravery.

'Tell it by the light of its time. Tell it in all of its colours, not the way they tell it, like a story for scared children, as though it is part of the Bible.

'And do not for God's sake bend it to meet today's ambitions.'

She had thought her question was unanswerable.

He stops, breathing audibly. He says, 'Actually, in the end, the joke of it is that this is an excellent symbol for the new nation – we knew how to make a circle for safety then, and now we know how to make a wall to keep the fear here, right with us.'

Adaira thinks he sounds almost frightened himself.

He snorts: 'And for a political philosophy, sortes sanctorum,' and laughs hotly, and mimes stabbing a finger at random into a book to augur God's policy.

The man in the Onse Erfenis tent leaves Vena with a collecting box. She goes shop to shop, house to house. On a Saturday night she comes with her tin to Church Street and its early bioscope crowd. She holds her tin and a board with a petition: come to Gower, it reads. When the wagons roll by here on their way to Pretoria, detour to this town. Many are signing. Many drop coins through the slot in the tin. It is thrilling, the thought that the wagons, one of the wagons, might come here.

Henry would prefer to feel as his neighbours do about the Trek, but he flinches from it as though at the cut of the long whip. He could never say to them what he has said to Adaira, but he tries to share a milder version of his thoughts. His remarks about 'history as a novelty act' and his sour puns are met only with smiles – he pleases his neighbours by mentioning the great enterprise; they are not tuned to receiving criticism of it, not in his arch and obscure terms, at any rate. They listen politely, attentively, even, to the magistrate on the Trek because this is how they meet him, always: he has the right of a magistrate to pronouncements; he is not bound to make sense.

It is almost summer now, and on Church Street children in cotton nightdresses and pyjamas chase one another among the adults, who welcome the warm blue night against their cheeks. About halfway down the street the magistrate is speaking quietly to Mr Theron, watching Mrs Cordier rattle her collecting box.

And here it comes, a rough shriek. A shriek, a screech, a scream:

'Tim! You bloody bastard! Tim! I will bloody smash you!'

It is Mrs Poley, out of breath and in a terrible dress. She is trying to run and at the same time has one of her bosoms in her left hand to push it back behind the bib of her apron as she comes around a corner into the bright light of Church Street. She stops dead at the sight of them, a street of people playing Statues and all of them looking at her. For a long second she does not move either – her hand on her breast in its loose dress as though she is holding a spanspek high on her chest, breathing like a running dog, and a boy's stupid giggle the only other sound.

She folds her arms across her bosom. She starts to smile

a sorry-boss smile, then changes her mind, lifts her chin and scowls at them.

Somewhere among the stock-still people on the street the dog Tim is still running, and as he comes into the light they can see that he has in his jaws a long leguaan, dead, its monkeylike black claws moving as he runs, as though they are reaching for something and falling back, reaching and falling. Its tail hangs almost to the ground and the dog has to hold its head high to keep it from dragging on the tar. Now the town dogs are streaking up the street to attack, and although men shout at them and try to block them, there is no chance that these dogs will not go after something that is, rolled into one, an intruder and limping and carrying a trophy.

In a second they have it from him.

The dog Tim trots a few steps away from them and looks back, as a jackal would, but the town dogs, curiously enough, just stop where they are, as though they are waiting for orders.

Mrs Poley, meanwhile, is on the move towards her dog, her face dark with risen blood. Mr Theron says, 'No, man,' in Afrikaans, softly, and as Mrs Poley passes Vena Cordier, Adaira notices, Vena lifts the fingers of one gloved hand to her nose, an extra unkindness.

Before the woman can reach her dog Tim, Mr Villiers from the bank steps up and speaks the name of his dog – it is a ridiculous town name, Monroe – in a voice that does not shout but still carries all the way down the street. The big yellow dog with the leguaan in its mouth comes to its master at once and stands at his feet. Mr Villiers waits a moment and then says, in the same actor's tenor: 'Sit. Sit. Drop it. Drop it.'

Monroe obeys to the letter and Mr Villiers takes out his handkerchief and picks up the great lizard, holds it away from him with both hands, a strangler's grip, and steps into the sanitation lane left over from when Gower was on buckets. They hear the dustbin lid lifting and being jammed tight again, then Mr Villiers is back in the light, wiping his hands on the same hanky. He gives Mrs Poley a schoolmaster's look with a tight mouth and a little nod of his head. She, breathless with anger, tries to catch sight of her dog among the people on the street, calling 'Tim! Tim!', but something in her voice scares him worse than the town dogs and he takes off, splashing urine on his paws. The giggling boy laughs like a bark. Mr Theron says again, under his breath, 'Ag, no, man.'

The magistrate steps out from among the townsfolk and walks quickly across the street to where the big woman stands alone among the proper Gower people. He takes her elbow and turns her, and all the time he has his head down near her face, talking to her, pointing with his free hand; it seems that he is saying something about the dog, making her feel better about it. He has found a way to stop this thing and let the evening go on. As soon as he has turned her, and both of them have their backs to the full street, people start to move, and chatter. In this way he brings her away from the staring Gower people and back to her corner, and there he takes leave of her with a tip of his hat.

Henry, returning to Theron's side, is already regretting his actions. Why had he, alone among the men on the street, stepped forward to rescue her? He is unsettled by the woman with the dog. He knows her, or knows of her: although he used the correct form, and kept it anonymous, 'mevrouw', he knows she is the Mrs Poley of Adaira's stories, mother and grandmother to a nest of bad-to-the-bone Poleys, head of the first family of Happy Valley. He knows he stepped forward out of pity for her, not out of concern that his fellow burghers should be spared her untidy interruption. Yet how had it appeared to her? He had felt the heat and agitation of the woman's outrage when he held her arm and brought her away from the lit street to the threshold of the darker part of Gower. He regretted doing so, regretted doing anything at all. She had hated him, was humiliated, he thought, had furiously strained against a world where cunning and strength and the essential art of veld foraging to feed a family (if that was the intended fate of the leguaan) must bend the knee to the bland ambitions of respectability, to this ascendancy of herd animals.

The dogs have returned to sit at their masters' feet.

Mr Theron says, softly, 'Heritage, also.'

14

A DAIRA IS AT THE MAGISTRATE'S house every afternoon, sometimes to type in the museum and sometimes, later in the day, just to visit. With her daily entrances and exits she recovers her ease with his home, and soon, too, with him. On a good evening for wireless there might be wireless and their own small talk amid the wool prices and cold Benguela current, or the mild clarinet and friendly tenor of Josef Marais and 'When the Jackal Keeps a Howling', for which Henry and Adaira will suspend all else; if the atmospherics are bad, and they are often bad, there is conversation – true conversation. In this way they regather the habits of friendship about themselves and stand gravely back from anything that might bring them to the neighbourhood of wrongful kisses.

One of the things she does is bring reports of Gower to the magistrate. Henry calls her his good scout and she takes boyish pride in it as though, somewhere among the uncertainty about who she is, she is at least partly soldierly, a resource, a squire – aimed and obedient and of use.

They meet on the veranda when he is back from court and her work in the museum is done, at the end of long afternoons when the shadows of trees stretch almost the length of the garden. He is in shirtsleeves and old khakis. 'Good scout,' he says, and puts down his book. She sits on the steps at the foot of his chair and accepts into her lap the heavy head of the dog Tertius, who has brought her out of the house.

When she first came to the house by herself, Tertius blocked her at the front gate, not with a growl exactly, but intending to stop her there. Henry made a ceremony of introducing her to the dog, letting him sniff around her, letting him know she was a friend, and now Tertius escorts her in and out and lets her rest her hand on his head as they walk.

The magistrate has righted himself since his upset at the loss of his sister-companion. He seems weighted, ballasted. While Adaira has tea, he drinks brandy, like a man dosing a beast against field parasites, pressing past his reluctance to swallow, medicining himself.

Tertius leaves her to drop next to his master's chair and Adaira, in her mind, cracks open her brown exercise books. He knows about the yellow jersey, listened closely when she told it so that she began to see it as important, to forget about telling herself it was only a dismal small thing.

Now she tells him about yesterday's committee meeting, the scratchy unease of it. She brings him the minister's wife: Mrs Dominee Ysel at the committee table, who sets her jaw, sucks the flesh of her mouth to her teeth and glares. It is only how she looks when she is thinking, says Adaira. When she catches herself with this tight hard look on her face she gives a little start, and drops her jaw quickly to soften her mouth, tries to open her face, slides the skin of her scalp so quickly back that her ears move. But she'll forget in a moment and look away from the other women at the table and be back in her thoughts – blameless thoughts, going by the way she is, in mime, either pricking out seedlings or pulling pilled wool from a jersey or perhaps just moving her hand to music she hears in her head – and she is concentrating again and frowning, again.

Henry says of the dominee's wife: 'Marry a young theology student for love, and look where you end up, ex officio.'

Adaira likes the magistrate's game of making up stories – theories – for everyone, but she has mixed feelings when it comes to the official but somehow less honourable discipline that fills most of her committee days: she feels both pride and shame about the exercise books in which she notes the Federation judgements. Pride in finding the strong phrase, the right word, and shame at writing down such unkindnesses as a note on how the scab on Evangelina K's lip is healing, or not healing, or that one of their number smelled dagga at the shack of this family, and brandy at another, and the number of times, so often as to make a pattern, that she has written this word on a new line with a question mark: Lice?

It is not a small thing to watch one's fellows and keep notes on them, no small thing when it is a cooperative matter, a matter of seven women at tables in a church hall, with one of them reading out where they were last week on the problem of the Collier daughter, and noting that it was almost a certainty that she was pregnant, and trying to guess her age – twelve, surely to God above not younger than twelve?

It gets to be as if no one has a chance to ever begin again, to be ready to make friends with the world that day, not when there is a record, written down somewhere, of how often in the weeks before that good day they met the world unwashed, drunk and lost among their snotted-up children.

She brings Henry the story of the lice:

These several months into her work with the committee she is, at Vena Cordier's dictation, asking the lice question after every entry. Just writing it down makes her own scalp itch, and on food-delivery days in Happy Valley the ladies have taken to putting down the parcels and stepping back, where before they would have handed them over. After leaving her parcels at this or that door, Mrs Harry Venter walks back to the Drukker motor with her arms held almost at shoulder level to keep her hands from the heads of the children among whom she is a favourite for her habit of hugging them and remembering their names. Naturally, they press closer at this and it is all she can do not to break into a run. These are their people – at least one of the committee has distant cousins living in Happy Valley – but it is becoming hard to see themselves in them. And now they are infested with vermin.

Miss Mostert from the school, chairman of hygiene, is invited to a social welfare meeting. By the time she sits at the pushed-together tables to plan a course of action, they have taken to speaking about 'the infestation' and 'the problem' as though it is rinderpest or heartwater and these are beasts that have wandered into town.

And although Vena does not call it a cattle dip, that day when they wash the heads of the children of Happy Valley, the fact is that they line them up and move them along the tables in strict order, and poke back into line those littler ones or wilder ones that try to escape.

'We must get them all,' Vena can be heard saying. 'It will just start up again if we don't get them all,' and by 'all', says Adaira, you may choose between the parasites and the children.

Most of the children don't seem to mind. They like that something is happening, and they are at the centre of it, and their mothers are nearby, watching from the edge of the corridor formed by two rows of trestle tables, each manned by a woman from the respectable town, some with copies of *The Advertiser* spread open and fine-tooth combs in hand, some with basins of water and carbolic soap, and paraffin in bottles.

But no mother can ignore the insult when another woman judges her child in need of washing. The mothers of Happy Valley have, most of them, long since ceded their authority to the shod, fed and energetic likes of Vena, but there are mutters of annoyance even from these tired women who have brought their sons and daughters at Vena's command and stayed to watch.

A boy yelps. Marie Venter has him by the ear, with his head bent over an enamel bowl, scooping and dousing with the jug in her free hand. His mother calls out from beyond the double row of tables, 'No my son, just be brave, I'm sure the aunty doesn't mean to hurt you.' She stresses 'mean' and the charge is clear.

Mrs Venter, prickly with late spring heat, half-drenched and raw with the mewling and crying of children under her hands and itching all over with the idea of lice, closes her eyes and sets her face in patient fury at this. When she opens them it is to see more of the mothers tentatively nodding their heads in grievance – tentative because the women scrubbing their children also control the family's food supply. Their faces are as tense and mobile as those of dogs who growl but are afraid to bark. It is a sort of cringing defiance and it is already dying down when the boy, no doubt encouraged by his mother's words and feeling those pinching fingers slacken on his ear for a moment, bolts from the corralled children and is gone in a flash and in a flash Vena is on the mother, saying, 'Missus, you go get him back! He will end up infecting the others all over again!' by which she means that, untreated, he will incubate a fresh lot of lice, but which is taken by the mother to mean that her son was the source of the vermin in the first place – and by which she is singled out, cornered. Defiance drains from her and she can only protest that it wasn't her family, it wasn't them who brought this to the camp.

'Yes, well,' says Vena, herself seeming surprised by the effect of her warning. The smaller kids are crawling under the tables and out past the legs of the committee; all of them have stopped to watch Vena and the mother.

'Yes, well,' says Vena again, 'someone did.'

And having delivered her coward's smack, she turns away with the air of a woman too busy for this conversation, bends down and gets hold of the ankle of a child and pulls her out from under a table.

The mother of the running boy is left alone among the women, telling them, 'But that's not true. We didn't bring it. All of them have got it, man.' She is not helped in this; the women around her seem to like the idea that this is something visited upon them rather than something else in which they are culpable.

Then, from the back of the group of women, someone says loudly, 'Are you mad, Vena Cordier?' It is Mrs Poley. The women hunch into themselves to let her through to the front. They look half afraid and half ready to be indignant to back her up, and are waiting to see what she means by 'Are you mad?' The committee ladies, and Adaira, are waiting too, with soapy hands and backs aching for a pause in their work.

It turns out she does not really mean anything – she has, they are disappointed to realise, nothing to add to this, nothing of substance, and only wants to pull Vena up short, stop her picking on the boy's mother. Mrs Poley's whole strength in battle lies in her being prepared to be fiercer than anyone else, Adaira says. But she has no absolute charge to lay on Vena, and as Adaira relates this to the magistrate it occurs to her that they all, the Happy Valley women and, in particular, the committee and the extra volunteers that day, held their breath to hear this because they, too, had the dawning idea that Vena Cordier was mad.

Mrs Poley orders the women and children this way and that and makes the committee make space for two of the blikkies-dorp mothers at the table; with some of their own on the boss end of things, the mothers move the lines of children along. Vena does not countermand this, but retreats behind the tables, flushed red and white and breathing hard. Her glass-blue eyes have the unstable glare of a poultry goose.

Mrs Poley watches for a while, legs braced and arms folded, then says to the dog at her feet, 'Come, Tim,' and he turns with her and they leave the place. Adaira hears one of the Happy

Valley women hiss at the committee woman at the basin next to hers, 'We are white, you know. Just like you.'

In the telling of it, Adaira, who had thought she was presenting Mrs Poley as her villain, knows she is discovering Vena Cordier. But at this, her disloyalty, a thought troubles her: Is she, in telling the magistrate this story, somehow betraying the women? There is a world in which they exercise and submit to one another's power, where they play out matters such as this, and that world ought never be laid bare to the scorn of men for fear of what will come back to them, and likely come, moreover, in the animal and awful words – bitch, cow, sow, shrew.

Henry is quiet. He fondles Tertius's ears.

He says, 'I knew a girl once, a young woman I suppose … she could have been the child of Mrs Cordier and Mrs Poley if they had mated.'

At the thought of Mrs Cordier and Mrs Poley mating Adaira gives a snort of disbelief, but at least now the magistrate is smiling.

The name of this monstrous baby, he tells her, was Cyella Oofit, a horrible name. He tells her nothing more than the name but, as Adaira bends to mutter to Tertius, she opens a speckled box file for the magistrate, and puts into it this Cyella.

And as for Henry –

Adaira has gathered her things and left for supper at her Theron home. Henry sits on alone and, as light fades from the day, makes himself recognise the facts of his life. Anna has gone. In a room in his house his project is at last getting under way. His crisis of drunkenness and flailing is over. If this is to be his life, he has to wake to what it will be.

At Craigievar for the wedding there had been joking about babies; he had thought, ridiculous, she is middle-aged. The realisation that she was not, that Anna was years away from the age he found himself, jolted him – he had thought all along that he had the credible architecture of a home, but it had been, for her, more in the nature of an anteroom. She is thinking about a family. Henry does not allow himself to imagine sons.

The great project will be his legacy, as dangerous as it is for him to approach that time, the war. Already Adaira, holding a silver medal from one of the parcels, has asked about his commando, about Ceylon. He had cut her off with a smile: 'You know the rules of history: you will only know my story when I am dead and gone.'

And for the rest? He could return to his regimen of distractions, although the thought of it irritates him wildly. Jasmine, red tractors, the folly of kissing a girl who if she could be anything to him could be a daughter … but no. No daughters, either.

He thinks that he has been in many of his human dealings an illusionist, a magician. He can see that there may be pleasure for the audience in the swerve to the impossible or, in the case of the women on whom he has practised his tricks, the swerve to romance, and there had been pleasure for him in their own legerdemain when, instead of shouting 'Stop, thief!' or worse, the women, the generous women, had applauded him, invited him to continue. But no matter the pleasure to be taken from seeing both sides of the illusion, there has been dishonour, unkindness, in his dealings with the world, and he knows disgust at it is rising in him.

He cannot continue to sit alone each night, after Adaira leaves, and drink and wait out his body's stubborn breathing, waking, sleeping, or rely on something as empty as political anger to crank out the mechanics of feeling.

Henry holds the bottle upside down over his glass. Not a drop is left.

Then, lying to himself about there being no full bottle in the pantry where he saw it this evening, he climbs into his jacket, lifts his hat from the peg in the hallway and, facing the mirror, looks himself full in the eye, testing his resistance for a last moment against the pull he feels.

And then he is gone.

15

AS SPRING TOUGHENS UP TO meet the hot months, Gower remembers that it has a Jew, in fact any day now might have a whole family of them. Or let it be said, has not ever forgotten what it had here – so it is really more that Gower has always been aware of having a Jew in Ira Gevint, but is now made aware in a different way.

Without the news from Europe they might have left matters at the level of noticing his otherness and telling themselves that this awareness was not particular to them but was just the way the world was arranged. For example, it is only obvious that he cannot take part in church things with the rest of Gower. The bazaar, for instance, the church bazaar some weeks after he came here: he had donated scraps for making things to sell and then been somewhat bullied into giving a full bolt of gingham to cover the tables, but at the bazaar itself there had been no question but that Ira Gevint was a client; he was welcome to buy jam and so on, of course – in the way that people who motored over from Jamestown were welcome to do this. Somewhere to one side of where Gower proper looks out he is to be found, looking out himself, but also looked upon.

Without the news from Europe, the permission from Europe, they might not have given Ira another thought. But now they are allowed to be cruel, and so, on the pavement, they make way for him an eternal split second later than is polite. At the grocer's he is served the roughest flour and is dared to make something of it, is given dented tins with no word of apology.

Ira barely notices; he has tried to see the overengineered and almost ridiculous Burggraaff sortie when he first arrived as not a great deal more sinister than the playing-out of this place's obsession with 'overseas', a junior attempt at the actual menace he had known at home. It was the lack of uniforms that made the difference here, or perhaps it was the language: if English delivered its pain in paper cuts and Afrikaans in slow cudgel blows, then German, his German in the mouths of the new men, was a scream from a deep cave, the atavistically horrifying sound of immense wings brushing by in the dark, and nothing this place could imagine came close to it.

Next, in Gower, they take to jostling him. They shove the odd shove, actually block his way on the pavement. Who does this? Who are 'They'? They are just the everyday them but more so, some essence of them that is leaching, pooling, becoming a thing on its own. He is somehow being defined by another thing that is happening in their lives, the thing that has them sewing long dresses for their daughters (he has had to order extra lawn, poplin, light duck, bolts of the stuff), the thing that has put on every mantle in Gower a bowl, or set of bowls, of ivory china etched in the brown of dried blood with a wagon and eight.

They have no message for the haberdasher, nothing to impart beyond that he is who he is:

'You're a Jew,' Wyville Burggraaff, back with reinforcements, tells him, loud and red-faced from the pavement outside Ira's shop. His rigid right hand beats the air as though he is capping an argument with the word 'Jew'.

And today Ira Gevint makes a mistake. He knows that the code calls for eyes down and retreat, for a noise of irritation at worst. But, heady with fear at confronting it again, at having it said to his face, here, at last, and remembering when he bested Wyville in his shop before, Ira answers back.

He stands in the doorway of his shop and takes his spectacles from where he keeps them on his head when he does not need to read something. He sets about polishing a lens on his tie, which keeps his trembling hands moving, and while he does this he says, in an impression of a reasonable voice, 'You know, it is not true what they are saying about you, Burggraaff.'

And Wyville narrows his eyes and demands: 'What? What's that you say?'

'No, please, no need to worry. I am certain it is not true, in the event,' says Ira in airy, almost-perfect English, if in tones somewhat higher than his usual voice, and turns his back to invite into his shop, incredibly enough, one of the Burggraaff aunts who at that moment reaches the pavement from the chemist's next door. He follows her inside to hide his hands among the rayon and crêpe.

Burggraaff and his boys, red at their shaven necks, red into the hairline, kick the kerb and leave, but with the fall of evening they are back, and as Ira turns from locking the door of his shop they move in and they block his way, shove and jostle and pluck at him. Ira tries to stand his ground, but it is not possible to hold on to dignity when a man is sent stumbling between five young giants, all kicking feet and chests and knees, and his hat goes flying, and hands grab at his lapels.

Today, however, Wyville Burggraaff and his lot, his brother Wikus and the rest of the pack, have made a bad bet. There are plenty of people on Church Street, people who would be astonished if you said they might choose to look the other way when wild boys roughed up a white man in the open like that, and now a whistle shrieks, and Sergeant Meter does his skipping walk and most of the boys take off down the street, making loud laughing sounds to cover the fact that they are running away.

When Meter reaches them it is in time to let Burggraaff give Ira one last shove and take off himself. Then the policeman clamps his hand on the upper arm of the slowest boy, a Poley grandson, one Doep.

Doep Poley will sleep in the cells at the back of the police station that night. Sergeant Meter sends his boy to Mrs Poley to say that her grandson has been arrested. She says, 'Keep him, the rubbish,' and turns away, then tells the sergeant's boy to wait a minute – what is it for? When he tells her it is for shoving the Jew Gevint, she seems unable to understand, and he tells her again – affray, insult: Doep pushed the Jew Gevint. Eventually she nods, still not seeming to know quite what is meant, but allows him to leave without stating the matter a third time.

Mrs Poley is in court the next day, in time to hear Magistrate Vos give quite as much weight as she had to the aberration at the heart of the matter: that Doep Poley stood to gain nothing by his actions. This in her eyes makes Doep even more of a useless, but those few people in the court can see that it particularly angers the magistrate.

He is colder with the boy in the dock than is warranted by pushing and shoving another man on the street; the evidence part of the case is over in minutes, but his summation takes twice as long again. He presses the point. Nothing was stolen, but to hear the magistrate tell it, this made Doep Poley's crime more serious, not less. Henry adopts a blank ignorance of what really was going on when they pushed Ira Gevint, and asks, What did he gain by attacking Mr Gevint outside his fabric shop on a Friday evening? All present ignored the cashbox, the cloth and so forth, he says. Well then, a grudge: was this revenge for some past injury, or part of a sequence of injuries?

The magistrate at last lets go of the pretence. He says: To attack a man with no motive of gain or revenge, but only from a sort of national spite, made of Doep Poley something worse than a common criminal, worse than a robber. The magistrate says he will not allow this to go unchecked in Gower at least.

Mrs Poley begins to breathe loudly a few sentences into the magistrate's summation. By the end of it she is openly shaking her head, and shifts about in dumb protest as the magistrate reaches 'accordingly it is the sentence of this court ...' and sends Doep off to chokey, as Mr Theron puts it when he tells his family about the case that night.

———

Give it a week or so more. The people of Gower had not stopped to think before telling those rough boys – that Wyville Burggraaff, that boy from Happy Valley – to stop that! To shout, Hey! Stop that, and tug on the arm of Sergeant Meter, and make as if they were about to cross the road themselves to pull them away from Gevint. But give it a week or so, and now they are slower to say something, or something more than, Oh, my. Where once they were almost prepared to cross the street, now they fold their arms and shake their heads.

The wolfish boys with their keen instinct for what the town will bear have not been slowed for an instant by Doep's punishment.

It's not right, Gower seems to say. It's not right, but … One of them says it out loud. Tractor salesman Van der Berg's wife, Etta, says: 'Why does he keep coming outside like that if he knows those boys are only going to make trouble with him?'

Behind her on the stoep Van der Berg says, 'Who?'

And she says, 'That Gevint. The Jew.'

And he turns the page of his newspaper and says, 'Oh, him.'

And it is the case that Ira Gevint does not send the boy from his house or even the boy who works in the back of the shop to deal with the slops that cover the left side of the shop window with a film and soft pieces of something, but is there in his shirtsleeves and apron, and it is he who balances on the wooden steps, clumsy with a cloth and a bucket of water, and he who holds his breath and lunges to pick up and tip into the dustbin a stinking shredding paper bag left on the shop's front step, just as he, at the start of this, made a point of moving towards the sneering boys when they came for him.

Do the good people of Gower say something? Does any-one say more than, You! Wikus Burggraaff! You rubbish!? Not more than that, no. The Therons avoid the subject, and when they stop on Church Street to greet the haberdasher, it is in tones between neutrality and condolence – somewhat con-soling, but somewhat cold.

But Adaira becomes unable to leave him alone. She attaches herself to his side, haunts his shop and demands to share in his persecution. To own part of it. Some afternoons she stands behind the pin wheels in the window of the Haberdashers on Church Street, daring a Burggraaff to come near, hoping one will present himself for her to repel.

Her squire's impulse to rescue, his needing all his strength for himself – Adaira and Ira move at different speeds. She cannot keep away from him, though, and there is something in him that allows her near, and so they are together often, in a miserable huddle against Gower, and at times she, with her vehemence and endless interrogation of the latest insult, is a separate part of his torment.

On a Sunday afternoon, she brings him to the magistrate's home for tea, for show, and when they are done with speaking about everything except anything to do with Gower's skirmish-ing with its haberdasher, Ira and Adaira walk back to Church Street together. Gevint holds himself behind a closed face, carrying dignity before himself when usually he is an eager-faced man pressing forward into what next the world will bring. There is a sudden panic in her to crack this crust of reserve he wears, to reach in and draw him out, but she has nothing on hand with which to do so – no philosophy, no armoury bristling with the right words.

They reach Church Street and she follows him into the Sunday-still air of the empty shop, where the brown of the long counter dominates the room until the coloured bolts, the brass cash machine, the draped cloth, everything else, seems to be just another shade of that brown. There is a sense of time in suspension, of waiting. It is as private as thought, this place, and the thick air slows them down and lays a hand on her so that she makes herself hold still, feeling him willing her to go but wrapped in her compulsion to stay.

She leans now with the small of her back against the counter top, awkward, one hand hanging loose, one laid along the wood, and finds the courage to wait in this assumed pose of femininity, perhaps ungainly but gathering in her skin and hair the mild light of the room. Her body faces him, but she keeps her eyes cast down. She would be ashamed to see him look. At the edge of her vision her breasts rise and fall under the pleats and tucks of her blue dress. Stillness is doing its work here: excitement hums in her like a wakened swarm. She raises a hand to loop her hair behind an ear and her hand stays there, fingertips on her neck, and at that invitation he at last makes the crossing to join her.

Ira is intent on her clothing, on each button and strap, drawing the dress and other pieces deliberately over her hips, over her head, from around her waist, as though he is polishing her skin with the cloth as it leaves her. At last he has her breasts free among the everyday shapes of the shop. He stops, steps quickly to a shelf and tugs out a folded length of something red. This will be their bed. At his gesture, as he cracks it so that the cloth billows out, pleasure, gladness even, joins them in the sombre shop, and their bodies grow rosier – hers, lying back on the red ground, his, peeled open from his shirt and trousers, above her.

He is committed to this, as though, were she to try to interrupt him, he would not stop, as though his name would have to be called more than once before he looked up. Adaira suddenly knows she is not equal to it, the thing she has invited, not its equal at all, but she is more afraid to pull away. The safe place to be is close to him, holding on. At one point the thought comes to her that she has duties in this matter, obligations apart from those met so easily by the mere fact of her body, and that it is up to her to manage matters to preserve the momentum and maintain some elegance, some grace, in the movement of her limbs, his limbs, the sounds she makes to meet those coming from him. There is pain and a flash of irritation – worse: an impulse to defend herself from him. This passes, melts into an ache and a thickened lassitude, as though time has slowed. She notices, far within her, like the echo of an imagined sound, a sense as elusive and maddening as an itch she cannot reach; she thinks that by noticing and naming it she has doomed the feeling never to be felt again, and yet it has, at the same time, taken up permanence in her body, but so far away, so far away, as though she is fathoms deep. At last, propelled by something very like the energy of a shout, Ira strains back.

He walks her home, as far as the corner of the Theron block, and although they hurry and by instinct keep away from the street lights, she is suffused with exceptional, weary clarity. She is aware, for instance, that her senses have begun the work of laying down the moment beyond the reach of language. There is no point in wishing for white linen or scented wine. Whatever it is that will summon this, that is the thing that will: in her case, floor dust, furniture polish, the acrid dye of the German Print, some spicy scent in his hair. And now the cooling tarmac and the road dust.

She is shyly, grimly proud to notice in the indoors bathroom at her Theron home that she bled, like, she thinks in confusion, Joan of Arc. Someone young and brave, this is what she means.

Lying awake that night, tapping into the thoughts it has brought her, this new eye on the world, there is another thought she has about what they have done: she wishes they came from happy, confident peoples, people without doubts. They had brought to the act some tinge of sadness and shame. She brought the ancestral shame, and Ira the sadness. Nevertheless, how subtle is a kiss. How subtle the change from her skin to his, the coming together of their heads with nothing to whisper, no viewpoint to share, but giving their faces, seeing only one another if they see at all, and pressing gently to open their sealed bodies.

Schoolgirls and -boys are dancing in the hall where the committee women are due to hold a meeting. The boys stand stiffly, one arm crooked behind them at the elbow and held in the small of their backs. The girls mime holding out long skirts, and approach the boys haltingly, at a tilt, step-together, step-together, as Mrs Bertus Wyngaard at the piano crashes her way through 'Jan Pierewiet'. Child and man, Gower is practising to be Voortrekkers.

Adaira, waiting with Mrs Ysel for the dancing to end and the rest of the committee to arrive, thinks that she has sensed since girlhood that no one will give a straight answer about the reasons for the first trek, the real one. The English say the end of slavery, the Afrikaners say the English, the historians go this way, that way. And this Second Trek? What is its aim? Because no one would say it was simply to commemorate the past. There is far more about the future in it, although also a sense of something being fled, if not outrun. She knows the magistrate would say they are trekking away from themselves, and following a false star moreover.

Adaira stays outside the hall to talk to Vena Cordier about the Burggraaff boys but when she does she learns that Mrs Cordier does not care about Ira Gevint beyond regretting that Hamer's Haberdashers is no longer owned by one of 'the nation', as she speaks about people. She doesn't mind Jews, she says; she doesn't like them, of course, but she doesn't really mind them. There is only one part of the pushing and shoving and the arrest of Doep that rouses her, as Adaira discovers when they enter the hall.

Already seated, patting their hair, their hats, lining up their chairs to face the long tables, settling handbags at their feet and waiting for their chairman, they are as usual Mrs Ysel the dominee's wife, Mrs Co-op Drukker, Mrs Flip Human the hotelier's wife, Mrs Harry Venter and Mrs Bertus Wyngaard.

They have made themselves ready for their chairman, and here she comes, following Adaira into the hall, passing along the back of them and seeming to hesitate, with a low sound of irritation, behind the chair of Mrs Human.

Vena Cordier has a copy of *The Advertiser* in her hand. There is an article on its front page about the arrest and conviction in Gower of DuPlessis Poley.

Surely, when Doep Poley gets out of jail in a day or so, no one in Gower will clutch their children to their skirts as he goes by. Not for shoving the haberdasher. But his misdeed matters to *The Advertiser* where the real crimes in Gower, stock theft or poultry theft, do not, and Mrs Cordier knows who to blame for the fact that the newspaper even knows about it. There is no reporter in town; Philipus 'Hotel' Human sends through the rainfall figures and he is the one who called up the newspaper the time that farmer made the record fleece, and again when Magriet's sister Hester was crowned at the show. It must have been him who told on Gower to the outside world.

Mrs Cordier has reached her place at the head of the table and set her handbag upon it; she keeps hold of the newspaper, which she unfolds and spreads and leans over to read from, out loud. *The Advertiser* is given to paired judgements delivered in wordplay – 'Field Marshal or Field Mouse?' – and tart idioms. It diffuses its views by expressing them as questions. Today, in the edition Mrs Cordier is sharing with them, it asks: 'Has Hitlerism infected the sleepy town of Gower?'

Of the two newspapers that reach them, each has its own Germany – a place full of vigour and pride, or one where rumblings are dark and about which Whitehall is anxious. *The*

Advertiser is of the dark-rumblings school – dark infectious rumblings. Although the people of Gower love to see their town's name in print – pass copies around and talk about it for days – this is different; in today's paper Gower is spoken of not as a town in which such and such has happened, or from which so and so hails, but as a thing on its own, a type of place. It is astonishing to think of, and a bit irritating, not least because they are taken as a type for the very sin of attacking someone as a type. Are they really this one thing?

Mrs Human says over and over that Human did not telephone *The Advertiser*, that he would never. But Vena Cordier likes blame far too much to back down and Human stays guilty, a placeholder while she looks around for who in her town has betrayed it, who made of the haberdasher's misfortune a matter for the outside world to judge Gower by.

The meeting opens at last and Adaira bends to her notes.

Nantie hurries in one day with news from the Therons' boy – for Adaira alone, not Mrs Theron or Mr Theron – that their good magistrate has been seen almost every night at the Hole in the Wall.

People doing their business, their drinking and fighting, carry on not just inside the Hole, which is as small as its name suggests, but on the pavement outside, which makes it a risky business for the Location men who wait there to find a willing white man or child to take their money into the bar and buy them a half-jack. Often enough – so often that Mr Theron, reporting to his female folk at the supper table about what went on in court that day, lays out the situation for Adaira and

Nantie – often enough, the drunk town men and the Location men waiting outside will come to blows. Usually when this happens the Location men know to flee the scene as soon as they can get free of their attackers, but sometimes they themselves are drunk, or new to the town, and they fight back, and that brings the constable or even the sergeant if it is a warm evening, and earns them a night in the cells under the court with the unwashed and moaning fierce country Natives who are in for stock theft – a punishment, says Mr Theron, with a laugh, in itself.

It interests Adaira, plumped out with her own secret, to think that in the town there is this energy, twisting against itself like something you wind tight to wring out, a contained tight coiling of men and bold women, and she thinks she understands when Nantie comes wide-eyed from the garden with her news that their magistrate slips from the sleeping streets of the upper town down to the Hole, and does so every night.

Enoch says he does not enter the place, but waits across the road like a Native until someone from the bar comes to take his order and his shillings. Every night, Nantie says Enoch says, and in the morning, in his court, the magistrate surely risks being recognised by the sorry men looking up at him from the dock as being their companion in sin from the night before.

In the early evening she meets the magistrate on the veranda and they talk over the working of minds, the business of words, until night falls and Ephraim comes around the house and up the steps, a lit oil lamp in his hand. He sets this on the table near Henry and murmurs something about supper. The magistrate nods to him and Adaira gets up to leave.

For a moment Henry holds her there, one hand raised as he counts off:

– Electric light bulb
– Paraffin lamp
– A twist of husk in a coconut shell, in a pool of oil
– Similar, in a pinched clay lamp

'Candle,' she says.

'Candle,' he says. 'Yes, good.'

The two of them match smiles. Affection passes between them, felt by each as clearly as the thump of a pulse.

She has learned from the magistrate this habit of lists. She has learned the art of making a day, and a pattern of days. Perhaps it is from him that she is learning to include in that pattern a repeating point of particular brilliance, or dark contrast: something secret.

– Committee work
– Museum work
– Mornings
– Afternoons
– (Nights)

16

BY OCTOBER A HAPPY VALLEY boy has taken to
hanging around the magistrate. Adaira knows him from
her committee work, and is astonished to see him at Henry's
home.

The first time she meets this Johnny Hartshorn at the house,
she is there before him and answers the door to him. She is
wary – the magistrate jails his sort, after all, and she is one
of the committee: they are on opposite sides of a divide – the
mechanics' road, perhaps – and on opposing sides. His presence is an incursion from another place; she holds the door
only half open. She looks at him for a while, and then she says,
'Yes?' Does he not know that people like him are expected to
go around the back, to knock at the kitchen door?

He looks her up and down, something male and confident
in his eyes. He is surprised to see her there, it is clear, but he
is careful as a cat, and that's what the looking up and down is
about, she thinks: being bold to make himself harder to attack.

The magistrate comes out of his study and sees them, and he
lights up and throws out his arms, and says loudly, 'You came!
Well!' and he is at the door and has taken Johnny Hartshorn's

hand and pulled him forward, so that Adaira must step back to allow them both into the hall.

'Adaira van Brugge, Johnny Hartshorn, Johnny, Adaira,' he says, but offers no detail about him nor any reason for his presence and seems in a hurry to usher him into his study. She hesitates, then nods and makes a quick excuse about her work and leaves them for the museum room, startling herself at just going like that. But she did not ask for this, so why should she have to stay and make conversation with him? She has opinions about this Hartshorn, whom she does not know: brown-book committee opinions. She thinks that Johnny seems always just about to say something cutting, or look up from his lot and complain that he has less than you, less than he was promised. He does not say anything of the sort out loud – or much of anything at all.

He is in his twenties, she guesses. He has green-black eyes and lightly pitted skin and hair as light as road dust. He has a way of walking that puts his shoulders some way back from his hips. Does the magistrate know about Johnny Hartshorn's evil clan? Is the boy's presence here something to do with his kindness to Mrs Poley the other night?

At first she hears cup-and-saucer sounds and talking, then she is deep into a letter to a father from a commandant in the field, an educated man who is not hopeful about the passage of the war and who has a good way with analogy, and she forgets about the visitor.

It has grown dark outside by the time Adaira covers the machine and slides the letters into their file boxes. She stops at the study door to find Johnny still there, in the easy chair, and with enough empty plates on the table to have held a proper meal. He looks up when Henry greets her, gives her a low-watt version of Mrs Poley's dead-eyed look, and she feels sorry about abandoning Henry to him. Equally, though, she cannot bear the thought of being made to walk home with him as, it comes to her, might be the next thing he or the magistrate will suggest.

Is there some way to remind Henry that Johnny is so often at the Hole in the Wall as to be a sort of casual employee of the place? Does he know this already and not care? She is out of the door – no Tertius on the veranda to walk her to the gate today, but she does not stop to wonder about this – and off home.

When she joins them on the veranda the next afternoon he is there before her, sitting on the front steps, almost at the feet of the magistrate. Rather than share Johnny's steps, Adaira takes a chair, and she and Henry sit like a mother and father over this, their pale-haired boy. She burns at this; she is the one with permission to sit easily at the feet of the magistrate, with Tertius by her. Where is Tertius?

'Where's Tertius?' she interrupts Henry to ask.

'He's in the back. Johnny is' – the magistrate searches for a word, perhaps a kinder word than first comes to mind – 'is not fond of big dogs.'

Adaira arranges her face to show Johnny Hartshorn what she thinks of this, but his eyes are closed. He is leaning back on his elbows. He even lies like a cat, and although Adaira knows what sort of person he is, she can see that there is something about him that invites stroking, in the way that one's hand will reach to run along the back of a cat whose fur has trapped heat from the sun.

The magistrate's body is stretched almost horizontal in his chair; the two of them are long and low, and she is upright and tight-shouldered beside them. The magistrate is saying something about the leiwater battles on his street. Hartshorn keeps his eyes almost closed and, at the pauses when the magistrate laughs softly, the boy twitches his mouth in the slightest of smiles. He has not looked once at Adaira, in fact invented some rudeness to do with rolling the cuffs of his shirt as she came among them, and did not look up.

She tells herself she feels bad about leaving Henry to deal with him, and she makes herself stay. She is saved from having to speak by Henry's easy talk, and can look over Johnny Hartshorn lying almost at her feet, can see into his ear and the cupping of grime there, and look along his body. He has washed his clothes, and she feels a tightening of pity at this, and is ashamed of the effort it will have taken to clean and dry his dun cast-offs before coming here. That is as far as he has gone, though. His hair is felted into a single mass, and the skin of his neck and cheeks, and his collarbones and chest, is the reddish-brown powdery skin of the poor who are exposed to all weather, skin that lies on muscle with no gentle fat to cushion it – no slim smooth layer of fat. No fat or too much of it – and, when too much, scooped and dimpled and stiff as tallow – is another sign of poverty among the people of Happy Valley. It is this more than their clothes or broken shoes that Adaira has noticed. Their different skin.

Noticing his skin allows her to push away the pity and see him again as just a rude Happy Valley boy with the cheek to laze like this on the veranda of the magistrate of Gower. Any other man on this street would have him off the property with a flourish of one of those town sjamboks the men cut from old rubber tyres.

Some days later, on a Saturday afternoon, Johnny Hartshorn is damp, and he is clean. His clothes have begun to soften with dirt in the days since they were washed, but his skin shines with the blood under its surface, and his hair is darker and flat against his skull. Before she wonders how he managed the matter of a bath in Happy Valley, and what the incidence of this is – weekly, monthly, annual – Adaira has the equally ungenerous thought that he would do better to coordinate his clothes and body washing, get them to line up and be, for once, properly clean.

Of course, no one remarks on the simple fact of Johnny, bathed.

Adaira sits, the magistrate and she talk, Johnny seems to doze in the sun. In the time it takes for her to drink a cup of tea, his hair dries. Clear blond, it shines softly. He runs his fingertips over it from time to time, stroking himself.

When Adaira stands to put her cup and saucer on the tray before going in to start her work, she can smell him, and almost says something but does not. Instead, she moves quietly past the museum, deeper into the house, to the bathroom. It, too, is damp and clean, with the milky chill of a bathroom lately filled with steam and emptied. The air here is wearing the same scent she picked up on Johnny – the smell of the magistrate himself. There is a ring of grime in the bath, and in Adaira the sudden awful sensation of being flooded with thin toxins, as though what she guesses has snapped the neck off a slim ampoule that has lain buried in her.

Jealousy is to be ashamed of, but outrage she may treat as noble, as being justified and on behalf of the magistrate ... she adds protective feelings, maternal or perhaps daughterly, to the mix of the love she has for him. Johnny Hartshorn is not worthy of being the friend of Henry Vos: this is the unquestioned heart of it. Anna betrayed him, and now this, coupling himself again to someone with no honour.

She has resources of her own. She can wait out whatever this is, this kindness gone mad, this adoption of the ridiculous weasel boy from Happy Valley, this unsayable, unthinkable something else that she half fears might be a myth she has created from the hints dropped in books – the fear resting in her half-belief that it is she who may be at fault for even imagining such a thing about the magistrate.

She blocks the thought of it, listing Johnny's faults to distract herself. She suspects, for example, that Johnny Hartshorn cannot even read.

When he does not sleep between sheets in the bed of the magistrate of Gower, Johnny lies on sacks in a ragged tent tethered to a tin shack. Therefore, the first order of business upon his arrival at the magistrate's house is indeed to bathe. At Henry's suggestion he takes to arriving later, well into the evening, and the night-time baths are something Henry likes to be part of. He runs the water, sets towels on a chair, helps Johnny undress. Tonight the boy asks him to soap his back, and Henry is on his knees beside the bathtub, his sleeves rolled to his upper arms, washing the boy from his toes to his hair, easing him down into the water and slipping his hands about his body. The two are mind-fogged with desire when Johnny stands up from the water and comes, warm and clean, to Henry's bed.

The tenderness of the bath – the swipe of the washcloth across Johnny's shoulders, behind his ears – these stay with them when their pleasures are done and they lie in their ebb. Henry has arranged his bottle and Johnny's ashtray, and he and the boy lie against the pillows, sipping on cigarettes and brandy. Beside him Johnny stretches his legs under the bed-clothes, taps out his cigarette, lifts the magistrate's arm and fits his neck into its curve. He is asleep in a moment. Henry lies awake. He adjusts his hold on the boy, pulls him closer. He looks down at Johnny's face, what he can see of it – the dark brows and his nose, then the clean bright hair that picks up the lamplight, the angle of his shoulder. There is a mark there, a human mark of parallel, unfocused scratches. Did he do that? Moving carefully so as not to wake the boy, Henry kisses the crown of his head, noticing that the hair is cool and slides against Johnny's head as his lips touch it, that it is something between his lips and the boy's skin.

Henry watches himself do these things with detachment. This is what he has wanted for so long, but it feels as though there is an element that ought not to be in it, perhaps revenge? Revenge against some part of himself, among others, or the refusal to acknowledge the authority of another over him, the very insistence on this an acknowledgement of its own.

At last he, too, sleeps.

———

Henry wakes alone. The smell of cigarette smoke is so strong that he looks for the ashtray on his night table, but it is gone, as are his glass and the bottle. As he moves through his morning habits he finds signs of Johnny having cleaned up in the bathroom, too. These proprietary or propitiatory acts make Henry smile as he hurries to dress and swallows the coffee and porridge that Ephraim has ready for him. He swings down the steps and out into Gower, his secret – the fact that he has a secret almost as much as the nature of it – alive in him. He will try, once he is in his robes or even just in his office, to erect baffles against the thought of Johnny; for one thing, it is dangerous to do as he is doing, and he needs to be alert against anything that might give him away. Henry imagines there might be signs of lovemaking on his face, on his hands, perhaps a scent he gives off, Johnny's scent.

As summer begins to warm the earth, the magistrate appears to Gower to be happy. Swifter with his smiles, smiles that are swift to arrive and not there for long, but another coming soon. He stands upright, breathes to the bottom of his lungs, pats his ribs with satisfaction. Women who had been prepared to nurse him over the loss of Anna narrow their eyes at these signs of ease, and hate Adaira for being the cause of this, although all she ever does at his house now is tell him goodbye as she ends her afternoon with the letters and the diaries and heads home.

Some days he hardly seems to notice her, only waves her through.

Some days he leaps to take her hands and swing her around

in a rough dance, flinging her about as though she is someone his size, his strength.

In her committee work she is supposed to look down on the people of Happy Valley; here she is supposed to be a friend to one. Adaira says to herself, as though someone is listening, as though she is recounting her days to an audience, that it would be a great relief to have one thing that was not an absolute choice between the world according to the magistrate and the world according to Vena Cordier. She locks her suspicions, her fears about Johnny and the magistrate, into this binary of Mrs Cordier and Henry Vos. This is a last indulgence of childhood, this concreteness in her thinking, this self-deception, and it cannot engage her for long – but for this thought that she thinks and then slips past: what is she, that both Vena and the magistrate count her as loyal to their cause?

Adaira's archive grows. A Boer writes:

> I confess to you, wife, that I cannot keep straight in my mind who has died and who is alive. Make a list and let me have it. I have given it much thought and I think that this lack in me of keeping straight the dead and the living is because you are all as real to me as when I was home, but also all already gone from me.

> Wife, list all of our children and mark them as being alive or ahead of us in Paradise. Also the servants and the horses – taken, run away or dead, and those still on Draaibos. There was mention of Matteus in a letter

passed around from Mrs Dominee. I am certain she wrote with news of Matteus and his commando, but I cannot keep in my mind why she would set down his name.

I cannot keep this matter straight. I know you will not neglect to list him among our children, and mark his state. Mark if his state has changed, for my mind will not recall it.

There is this:

I will never ask forgiveness for these sins of mine. Why be penitent when this is immutable, this state of sin, this permanent crime?

And this:

There were nineteen of us. We found three wagons and all their carts and stuff and a small band of Khakis on their way to Bulwer's lot. First action for most of our boys. I never was so awash in the sick of others since the time we hit that storm on the way home from Utrecht.

After we made 'dead' certain of the Khakis that were only hurt and trying to crawl off, we set out right away to get the stuff hidden but the smell of sick followed us [for] miles. Tell the girls I have Tommy chocolate for them.

Adaira spends time, while she is doing things that do not use her mind – transcribing, eating, typing up a dull boy's letter – counting back from what happened to what must have happened to make possible the story she can glimpse in the faded ink.

Both of these things come from the same boy, eight months apart:

Soon after joining the commando he writes to his sister:

The food is kak and the camp is rotten (rock veld) and
the rain is rotten and the commandant is kakkest of all.
If they find this by you Papa will beat me and maybe
you and if they find it here they will beat me worse so
WATCH OUT yr affec. broth. Jack Trenneman

Then this, the smallest scrap of a letter begun but not ended:

Building a schanze into the night, talking with the
Gogelin boys—

It is sent under cover of a letter from the Gogelin father, having been found among the things his sons' friend Trenneman left behind. She puts the pieces together and feels, in completing the short arc of Trenneman's life, that she has performed a female service to him, something in the way of visiting his grave or another small remembrance.

A man writes:

An entrenchment blasted with serial charges breaks like
a wave. In the way that a wave disturbs water, the charge

raises the earth up and aside; I do not hear the blast while this breaking opens the ground, then all four of us in the line are knocked down by the sound.

Adaira's work in the magistrate's museum also gives her a taste for detecting, among what is said, that which is revealed. In the way that she reads things twice until the meaning seeps from them to her, she learns a new way of listening.

The magistrate was in this war, as a boy, and on Ceylon even. She has grown used to his dropping hints about it then deflecting the meaning, quickly capping the well whenever she makes out the glitter of a story there. She will get it from him, although he dances around her questions, just out of reach. She cannot quite make out whether he wants her to pursue his story or not, but she knows that she will.

In October, Anna Leibbrandt as she now is makes a party at her new home for the magistrate and the Therons, and Nantie and Adaira are invited too. This is surely the start of a new way for brother and sister to know one another; a crowd will be helpful today.

The Therons have no motor car. They and Adaira fit into the magistrate's on a Sunday morning after church and set off for Anna's farm, as they think of it. Mr Theron is in good spirits, and turns in his seat from time to time and asks with a grin, 'Eh, girls?' Adaira, made amenable to every daytime plan by her night secrets, watches the farms slide by.

Anna has got fancy since her wedding, they think when they see her and her new husband on the veranda. She is smartly dressed in closed shoes, stockings, a frock with a lot of buttons. Leibbrandt comes from the shadows of the veranda in a suit and tie.

Henry and Anna greet with a kiss, and the rest of them cluster on the veranda to shake hands. They can hear voices from inside the house and the sound of a glass being set down on a table: more guests? Anna has really got very fancy. She is stiff as a bride as she moves them into her home, to the wide door to the sitting room, where there are two people already seated, a woman and a man.

At the sight of the new guests the woman, who is in an armchair facing the door, carries her glass to her lips, sips, and sets it down, and only after this lifts her eyes to admit that they are almost in the room, the crowd of them. The man has his back to them. His hair is brown and oiled above his packed red neck; he stops speaking when he hears them, but does not get up or turn around for what feels like a long time. It does not occur to anyone in the Theron party that he is being impolite; in this sort of setting they have not come across bad manners before.

Leibbrandt hurries into the room and they follow more slowly; he is beginning the introductions in the formal 'may I present' way, and it is the magistrate who is being presented to the new man. At least this man is looking at them, and now he shifts his weight forward bit by bit in the chair and gets to his feet to shake Henry's hand.

Leibbrandt presents his brother-in-law as Magistrate Henry Vos, and the fat man says, as he holds on to his hand, 'Ah yes, Magistrate Vos,' as though he is finding the name on a list and drawing a line through it. When it comes to shaking

Mr Theron's hand he again repeats his name, but this time in the way of someone storing it for use. Adaira pulls into herself to give him less to look at in the way he is doing. She lifts her eyes no higher than the powder-horn badge on the fat man's lapel.

His wife – this is the woman in the armchair – does not stand up, or even look for more than a moment at any of them, but offers her hand to the magistrate and nods at his 'Pleased to meet you' and goes back to fussing with her glass, centring it on a tiny doily and sliding this to another spot on the table.

Henry looks about for Anna, but she is gone from the room to welcome her neighbour and new tenant, the widow whose farm Johan Leibbrandt bought. As she enters the room the widow turns her face to Henry with a ready look, a prepared look, and he gathers himself and notices her.

Johan begins, 'Mr … ah … was just telling us …' and trails off, embarrassed at forgetting his guest's name, and the stranger flaps a hand in absolution, backs into his chair and begins to talk. They settle into their chairs, take sips from glasses of ginger beer, all the while listening, polite country people that they are.

They have arranged their bodies to face him as an audience might a performer, and by his cadence and somewhat drifting attention it is clear that he is speaking from a memorised text.

He patently thinks he is better than any man in the room, yet he is labouring to be liked by them – or perhaps not liked; there is something about him that tickles Adaira's brain and then it comes to her that this man is like the window-washing salesman at the Jamestown Agricultural Show. As she watches

Mr Theron in the sitting room of Johan and Anna Leibbrandt she sees his face close down in just the way it did that day at the show.

There is no novelty in what the man is selling – you cannot start a conversation on the street these days without it coming around to this new people that they are all signing on to be. His pitch is made all the time these days, an unvarying pitch – the hope of the white man, the future of the nation. It is, in lots of ways, to do with what they are not. At least, it takes shape, grows muscle, by pushing against what they are not: not the English schoolmaster, or Gevint, and particularly not the Natives plentiful as brown heads of sorghum, sorghum in a field you must fence lest the immature plants poison the livestock, in the metaphor of the man now speaking.

The visitor has the skipping, distracting, bluff patter of a man who intends not to pay his share when the bill comes. As he gets going with his pitch, his wife grows alert, prompting him with sharp sounds of agreement or warning. The men do not meet her very bright eyes as she looks at them, one at a time.

When Anna calls them to the table for the meal, the Party couple stab at the food and swallow fast. They finish before anyone else, even Nantie, and only slow down when they are well into their second helpings. The man is sitting next to Adaira, who can see when he undoes his top trouser buttons and takes a full breath.

Over pudding he tries to sell the magistrate and Mr Theron policies. It seems he is a traveller for the Suid-Afrikaanse Nasionale Lewens Assuransie Maatskappij as well.

Anna's careful hair, Johan's suit and tie, the respect country people will give to people from the city, seem like proof of their not being as clever as the couple, of being easily fooled, and for a moment it seems that Mr Theron or the magistrate might ask questions about a policy just to be polite, but they settle for silence. Anna is seated across from her brother. Henry catches her eye and gives her a look that asks, What are you up to here?

At last the visitors leave, after coffee on the veranda and hints about stopping over for the night. The grown-ups settle into easy chairs, not saying much. Anna tells Mrs Theron that the man wrote ahead on Party stationery. Johan says, Yes, well, he did not think much of his manners, but he supposed the fellow made a lot of sense after all.

On the way home the magistrate pushes the motor to the point of swaying. Mr Theron reaches his hand over the back of the seat to hold the hand of Mrs Theron.

Henry has to brake hard after the level crossing outside Gower: coming towards them, on the other side of the tracks, spread across three quarters of the road's width, boys and men walk abreast and in rows. They are moving together and in formation, almost marching.

'Drilling for what?' Mr Theron mutters. No one in the motor has the energy to answer him. Besides, such a sight is not that remarkable in Gower these days. Dressing in uniform and walking in step with other men, it seems, is another way to be a Voortrekker.

To get by them the magistrate must drive with one wheel off the road, slowly. Those in the motor are lit by the low day's-end sun. The faces of the ranked men are not easy to see.

Those in the motor think they see their neighbours there but they are not sure. They don't call out when they think they recognise someone; this is not a moment for greeting. The motor passes the men at last.

Weary and silent, the party returns to Gower. The magistrate delivers the Therons and Adaira to their home, then turns for his street. He lets the motor roll to a stop in its place under the pepper tree in his garden.

It is an endless imposition, he thinks, to live in a country that is in the process of inventing itself, as his has been since he was a child in the Oranje-Vrijstaat. About him – beneath his feet, that was the feeling – the country heaved with change, settled, changed again. First the Oranje-Vrijstaat, then a prickly, shamed agglomeration under the despised and despicable Milner, then Union, Rebellion … now the Party talk is unceasing, coming to a pitch, and his neighbours drilling for an honour guard for this new version of themselves that is on its way. It is the only place he knows well, but it has never felt quite real, when he tries to imagine the country as something beyond his close surrounds.

And all of it, every so-called national question, is just so many scraps of dull paper compared with – and here he stops. Then he makes himself continue, makes himself think of the boy who will slip from the shadows tonight. That is one real thing: a room whose curtains close in a world, one lamp lit, two in a bed, the way the criminality of this secret thing forces his mind to patrol a short boundary, and contain itself in the small here and the brief now.

The engine contracts as it recovers from his angry driving.

Henry continues to sit in his motor car, within the drapery of the pepper tree, enjoying the way the ticking of the metal intensifies the silence on this silent evening. He has Johnny only because Anna left. In choosing the expected path for herself, she uncoupled him from it. He recognises, in a lazy way, the fever in whose grip he is these days. He wonders, without urgency, whether he will settle again some day. Or is contentment the forfeit of this life condemned by the law to consist, at one and the same time, of secrecy but no privacy? Perhaps, in his state of rebellion, the rebellion alone is what matters.

Night has not quite fallen, and in the gloaming he thinks he sees movement at a corner of the veranda. Aware of the foolish grin stretching his face, he leaves the motor and crosses to the house, and calls softly as he mounts the steps, 'You're early. That's a nice surprise!'

But a female voice answers, saying his words back to him, the sarcasm insultingly exact: 'That's a nice surprise.'

Mrs Poley is on his veranda, is coming towards him from the shadow of the syringa.

In Henry's mind the great puzzle of her being there on a Sunday evening and the menace in her voice when she mocks him, these things are, as it were, held behind thick glass while he scrambles to think how he can prevent her from seeing Johnny when he arrives, as he might do at any moment. Light and noise, he thinks. Light and noise to warn him to wait until she has gone, and so, his mind no longer lazy, no longer adrift, he ignores the several irregularities in her address and greets her as though it is Sunday morning on Church Street. He pushes open his front door, lights the hall, lights the sitting room, invites her to sit, and would she care for tea? By the look she shoots him, she would not. He ignores this, opens the kitchen door to greet Tertius, shuts him in again and returns to the sitting room.

She has chosen a low, ladder-backed chair. Being a large woman, she hides it completely and gives the impression of squatting in her fusty dust-coloured clothes. Now he thinks it was a mistake to have brought her into the house. If it were not that he expected Johnny, he could settle matters right away, whatever it is that she has come about – her grandson Doep, could it be to do with him? Or some expectation on her part after his rescue the other night? He could send her on her way if only he was sure she would not come across Johnny in the garden as she left. He ought not to have brought her into his home.

Mrs Poley, meanwhile, has been settling herself as though for conversation. Now she takes a deep breath and says: 'My Johnny is your special friend, I think.'

Your Johnny? Your Johnny? Henry's mind rattles a handful of titles—

'He is my grandson. My Soela's boy. He lives by us.'

She stops and regards him, and he suddenly sees, in the way her intake of breath happens in quick steps, that she is afraid. Still, he does not speak. Let it unfold, he thinks, while the words 'special friend' lie on his brain, a distinct thing.

'You didn't know he was mine,' she says, and nods to herself, tucking away some piece of information about the world, or Johnny, or Henry.

'So you and me, Magistrate, we are like family now.'

Still Henry says nothing.

She has a bully's timing, the measured doling out of words that says matters will move at her pace, and yet she is also, Henry thinks, reluctant to come to the heart of her purpose.

She licks her lower lip and says, 'Family stands by family,' and sinks her chin into her neck to punctuate this.

Henry lets out a huff of incredulous laughter – the Socratic method of blackmail, he thinks: she wants me to offer before she has to say it. He fights down his chittering dread and crosses the room to take a chair opposite her.

He says: 'Family, mevrouw?'

'A sort of family. A sort of bond,' she says. 'Something to keep in the family,' and the sharp edges of a threat show briefly.

Henry is growing calmer by the minute. He has reached a state of pleasant removal that he imagines is very like the settled sense he has noticed in certain of the men in his dock; they stand square on their feet, spending no energy and losing no pride in resisting.

When she sees him settle and wait she is suddenly impatient with him, impatient about what she wants, and in the end it is only money. Henry is so thankful for this – that she has set a price he can meet – that he immediately starts to find reasons to meet it, reasons beyond the fear of exposure to the town as an unnatural man, or his arrest for breaking the law, reasons to make it not only expedient that he should pay her the several shillings a week she names, but right that he should do so. He hoists his thinking to a level away from blackmail, fits out a scenario where he is even flattered by his charity.

With the crux out of the way, she relaxes somewhat and

volunteers her grandson's history: 'Johnny's father left before he was born. His mother is long gone. He's a Poley, but Soela was married to his father, so Johnny has his name.'

And this, as she prepares to heft herself down the front steps: 'Johnny doesn't know about me and you.'

In reflex, Henry offers her his arm. She looks at him as though she might laugh in his face, but only shakes off his hand and leaves without a greeting. As she closes his front gate, Henry thinks he hears her say, 'Tea!' in tones of scorn. She, at least, is clear on the etiquette of what she is about, he thinks as he watches her go. He hears the word she would not say, holds it steadily in his mind to make it seem more real.

Mrs Poley, he realises, had not shown any disgust or even disapproval about his and Johnny's 'special friendship'. Or seemed to be interested in it as anything more than coin.

Henry does not believe, as is sometimes popular to pretend to believe, that the poor are more tolerant than buttoned-up proper citizens. His work in the courts has taught him that the blankest self-righteousness is usually the public face of the Happy Valley mothers and fathers who come before him, aggrieved at any slight on their probity and Your Honouring him into next Tuesday. No, when Mrs Poley came tonight to offer her silence, and her grandson, it was not any special understanding she brought: just a realist's lack of disgust. Just a stronger stomach than most. He sees that, however she did it – whenever she suspected and spied out or beat from her grandson the story of him and the magistrate – Mrs Poley surely had, in the same instant that she saw it as a miscreation, a two-tailed snake, recognised it as something good for the pot.

———

When Johnny lets himself into the house at the kitchen door and slips through to the front rooms, Henry is in the sitting room, reading, a glass by his side. He barely looks up when the boy bends to kiss his cheek. Johnny says, 'How was it at the farm? How are they?' And Henry, newly aware of how far into his life he has brought the boy, closes off this line with a few words, then says something about the book on his lap, about finishing the chapter, and Johnny settles himself on the couch. He does not take up a book, or even fix himself a drink, but merely sits, looking now at Henry, now at one or other wall of the room. Henry thinks, he is a stupid boy. An ignorant boy. But he feels, too, a new and strange loyalty to him. He and Johnny and, he supposes, the grandmother, are together within, and the rest of the town – the doctor, the lawyers, the chemist and the dominee, Anna and Johan and the Therons and Adaira – are, as ever, without. The thought brings an instinctive tenderness, and at last he puts down his book, unbends his body from the chair and holds out his hand to Mrs Poley's grandson, the son of her daughter and a sometime husband, this scrap of a boy.

'Come on,' says the magistrate, and Johnny smiles up at him, rises and follows him down the passageway to bath, and bed.

- Connection with a dead woman
- Sexual congress with an animal
- Sexual union between male and male

These are Venus Monstrosa (vide Matthaeus). This is the law.

17

IT IS HIGH SUMMER, ADAIRA'S first experience of the season away from the station. Father will get the men to divert the stream to Martie's Pool one of these days, if he remembers, and it will fill in a day and a night to be ready, cool as the dawn, for when a body needs to be out of the baking air for even one half-hour. When she was a girl they swam together, Mother, Father and Adaira, but for some years before she left it had been hers alone in the afternoons and his when the day was almost done. The pool is in a small defile about ten minutes' walk from the house, shallow where a bather enters the water at the split in the rocks and deep and cold at the far end where she can hang over the edge and see down the path. This makes it completely private, and she could have swum naked with modesty but did not; she wonders at herself for having changed into a dark old housedress for the swim and having peeled it from her to get back into her underthings and day dress when it was over – wonders how she could have failed so utterly to see that the silvery shock of the water would have been intensified by throwing her clothes off her body and diving in.

If I were her again, Adaira thinks, I would be naked for every swim.

In Gower the women meet summer by swapping shoes for sandals, leaving off their stockings, shucking their hats of felt or knitted wool for straw with ribbons and cellophane fruit.

Do people have more money in summer, or is it the case that summer suits them better? They are not good with winter and hunch against it, hunch in their houses and shanties or, if in the street, into their own bodies. Summer they meet with chests held out, and their voices dip an octave and slow down.

At the station Adaira's father will have slipped a new cartridge into the seltzer bottle to mix cordials for her and a long brandy drink for himself; in Gower as a special treat you buy bottles of Coca-Cola that fit your hand. And there is a flock of Poley kids passing a bottle between them, followed in train by more Happy Valley girls and boys, calling out without conviction for a taste, there more to celebrate the fact of the Coke for some of their number than in hope of sharing it.

On another summer's day there are more bottles to go around the Poleys, and no one on Church Street misses the fact that these children, who have been fed from food parcels all winter, now have money for American cooldrinks. Then there is money for meat – meat bought with shillings from the butcher, not trapped in the veld; beef scents the air in Happy Valley – and someone has a word with Sergeant Meter. More than one person, it must be, because when Mrs Cordier raises the matter with him he says in a burst, 'I know Mrs Poley has money and should not have money but no one has reported any money missing so there is nothing I can do about it,' and

Mrs Cordier can only narrow her eyes and note this, and absorb another report on Poley spending, a sighting of a trio of them carrying paraffin in richly sloshing tins, they who had grubbed for wood and picked up coal on the railway tracks the winter long.

One warm evening Adaira passes Mrs Poley on the street. She has a hand in her apron pocket and as Adaira draws near she moves it to make a rich jingle as though this is something she wants to tell her.

Even Ira Gevint has found some of the season's lightness. His father-in-law has come to Gower and, far from inflaming the angry boys, his arrival seems to have caught them off guard. For a few weeks now the shopfront has been as clean in the morning as Ira's boy leaves it at night. The old man is seen a few times, seated in a chair outside the shop, or standing, looking down the street and nodding, as though sizing up the town. Ira had conducted a small ceremony of introducing Adaira to him, a ceremony of careful English, careful omissions. The older man, weary, had not even looked at Adaira after a glance of greeting.

Ira laughs at a memory, and tells Adaira about the magistrate coming into his shop to buy a pair of red trouser braces that really were suited to a much younger or jauntier man.

Everyone is going mad for summer.

He makes sure to be home and ready on Saturday nights. It becomes a superstition with him, with more ritual in it than mere habit. He has the stack of shillings ready on the table near the front door so that they leave him cool and separate, not warm from his pocket. He has had them since he visited the bank on Friday – every Friday now; this, too, is part of his ritual. On Saturday evenings he holds himself ready, and at the slam of the leiwater gate he leaves his chair, shuts a door on Tertius, and, taking up the coins as he passes the table, is through the door and at the edge of the veranda, the edge of it that is shadowed and concealed from the street by a black-leafed tree.

He begins again to hate the thought of meeting a Poley child coming onto his land. He leaves the money on the veranda's low wall and turns quickly back into the house, deep into it, switching off the outside light as he goes. Their hands never touch, and they do not catch sight of one another as he and the Poley grandson or -daughter close the deal, with another grandson, the blameless Johnny, due later, and his neighbour on the other side of the dividing hedge keeping pace with the water along his system of mud gates.

The matter of the shillings and the sluice-gate noise, the dog confined and the breath-long wait for a Poley to walk the garden path from the street to the veranda – he does not think about these things during the week, in his office or in his court. And it is the case that he finds wrong in it only if he makes himself pick it apart and lay out the part he can identify as causing harm. This is hardly blackmail. It is more like the payment of an obligation, a tithe for what he is, what the world is. For the most part he allows himself to feel generous and see in it something that, although it is perhaps not entirely unresented, is surely orderly: the sort of arrangement family members might come to. Any motive less neutral than need, the Poleys' need, is given no room to make him feel his hand is being forced and he thereby unmanned. No, the idea of it – in all the hours that are not the hour straddling nine o'clock on a Saturday night – finds a certain acceptance with him.

But what he feels when the hour comes, what he feels as he takes the coins and leaves his front door, is bitterest shame, and he hears the voice of a boy inside him crying out against being robbed of his will, sees five soldiers crowd into a small room in a prison-camp asylum, where not one of them will meet his eye. He wants to make a fist around the money and swing it. Swing it, he taunts himself, and see the other only duck his attack with a smooth sidestep, brushing him off as though he, Henry, were again acting only as they had known he would.

18

T HE DANCE AT THE GOWER HOTEL is in its first, fresh third. Almost everyone is still sober, although punch is being shared and the air is spicy with brandy, too, and with the soap smell and nervous sweat of young farmers anointed with pomade. There are girls collecting in tins at the door for the Art of Dancing, and there's a band, a real band, on the platform at the end of the room. Chairs have been pushed to the walls.

Jamestown has had to come to Gower for this dance. Adaira stays near the Gower lot, the young wives, the girls she knows. They show one another their frocks. Their hands settle on collars, waists. A boy makes a joking stiff bow and clicks his heels to ask Adaira to dance, and he does not stop his acting even when they are face to face and touching. He presents his ear, his jaw, the side of his shallow smile. He is a Jamestown boy, she thinks, fleshier and smoother than the farmers. Every so often he turns his head to face her as though he cannot help himself, makes his face discover her there with delight. Then he drifts into distraction again to wind up for the rediscovery. After a few of these manoeuvres she keeps her own face turned away from him.

She casts about. She will somehow find brandy and have her first taste of it if that will stop her thinking so much. Stop thinking. Feel. Feel! She grabs onto the music, but soon becomes far too aware of its component parts, its snare drum and off-beat bass.

Ira could have come tonight. The wolfish boys are not here; they are at a bloody-knuckle meeting in Jamestown, tracking a new lead, so he would have been safe. But this is something he gives her: waiting in the dark until she has had her fill of being this girl, of putting herself through these paces, of getting her worth from Gower. He is patient with her. He sees easily what she is like, that it matters to her to be seen to be this new person. It suits them both that they are forbidden.

Adaira dances with another boy, watches the girls flick about like skinks, watches them stand against the walls and tuck their hands behind themselves to set out their bodies. She listens to the boy's weird banter. His flattery and need make a small confusion in her mind, blur the clarity there. She withdraws to a seat to nurse her secret, to remind herself that when she has been fulfilled as this person, this public girl, she will go to the unacknowledged him.

On the pale cloth of the table in front of her, a rhombus of light frames the hand of the man beside her, his wrist, and at the sight of this she grows impatient. She waits until a song draws most of the dancers to the floor, then slips out. She has hours before she is expected home.

He has been looking out for her. A block from the hotel he steps out of the shadow of a tree and calls, softly, either her name or the word 'here'. They brush against one another in the street, under the light, amid the scent of their bodies. There is fine, dark hair at the edge of his wrist as he holds her hand at the level of their shoulders in a waltzing embrace. Her head is turned towards their hands, his breath is on her cheek. His other hand is at her back and she is aware of nothing but his wrist, his breath, the scent of his shirt, the scent of him. She loves every aesthetic thing about this, his German words, his warm mouth, her own words describing these to herself as they come to mind.

It has become their pattern, hers and Ira's, to walk together most nights through the sleeping town and when they know by instinct they are safe, to find their way down the lane and to his bed. With the old man living in the house behind the shop they cannot head there, but summer is generous with them. They kiss on banks of grass or pressed into the hedges that overflow gardens. Tonight they make their way past the weeping pepper trees in the church grounds, to the stream where the houses end.

Away from the dance, there is barely a sound – the faraway putter of a motor, a dog begging ark ark ark, ark ark ark, why will no one listen?

He covers her body with his, with the good weight of him. Her eyes are open. The darkness of Gower suits them, the guessed-at greens, the illiquid black-blue above.

The thump of the music reaches them when at last they brush leaves from each other's clothes and re-enter the town. Their bodies part as they gain Church Street. Their hands part. Across the road, a slight way up the block, Ira's shop is glowing.

There isn't a sound. The dog has given up. The motor has left. All there is is the crack of a rifle shot.

Not a rifle.

Glass, cracking, then crashing tunefully to give the flames air as they paint over the sign that reads Gevint's Haberdashers.

Ira is running down the street but Adaira is reluctant to wake and follow him. That which has been travelling towards them has arrived, and she wants to refuse it recognition, refuse to admit it has come. She feels the last of her energy leave her. Something in her turns away like an overtired child, almost peevish amid the shouts of men, the sound of their feet hitting the pavement, the sergeant's whistle.

IV

JUSTICE

19

THREE NEWSPAPERMEN COME TO TOWN for the trial of Doep Poley on charges of arson and worse: two from Johannesburg, joined in Gower by *The Advertiser*'s fellow from Jamestown. One of the Johannesburg men, an Englishman, is said to represent a London newspaper, a development that horrifies Gower. The outsiders put up at the Gower Hotel. They eat their lunch, all three, on the long veranda of the hotel, facing onto the street, in their shirtsleeves and hats. Adaira comes by as they finish their meal. One of them is lighting a cigarette. London, she decides from his accent, age and girth, is asking Jamestown about Gower; Johannesburg is listening, and looking out at the street in the manner of a man searching out something, or deciding something. There is an awareness about all three of them, as though they know that they are observed in the performance of their jobs.

They have met only Gower's most helpful self since they arrived in town. Here is the hotel, there is the court. This is Church Street, with its blackened cavity among the narrow shops. No one knows anything about four or five grown sons sent swiftly out of town to hide on farms; all anyone knows is that the Poley boy was held within the hour – Doep Poley, who is suddenly almost popular in Gower for being so clearly to blame.

Mrs Flip Human herself, Adaira's committee fellow, comes to offer fresh tea to the men on the veranda of her hotel. No? She steps back, signs to the boy to clear the table, stays to watch it done. She catches Adaira's eye and widens her own eyes to signal the need to be on guard.

The three men set off for the court; Adaira is headed there, too, and she has them close behind her all the way.

'Any marches? The watchamacallits, Grey Shirts – are they around?' Johannesburg asks Jamestown. Adaira does not hear his answer before she is at the steps of the court. Ask me! Ask someone who knows, she thinks, although she has not even heard of a Grey Shirt until this moment, does not yet know it is a capital-letter matter to do with men who march against men like the haberdasher and his father-in-law, the nation's own sun-bleached imitation of the Brownshirts and the Black.

The courtroom is filling fast. Gower is avidly ashamed of the several things the room holds – Poleys, Gevints, the fire. The unknown old man, most of all. Feeling culpable itself, Gower wants to see the Poley boy tried for this even though it is not quite sure the court has the measure of the matter. If you take the old man's burned arm as a terrible chance consequence of someone setting a fire to drive out the two Jews – but not harm them, surely? – it is simply a horrible mistake.

But, one way or another, the verdict will reflect well on them. The magistrate, who is their own, will either punish Doep to the extent of the law to prove the nation's grasp of justice, or exonerate him convincingly to prove this thing was never in them. Grave matters, German matters, overseas matters have found them, and they will be equal to them.

Mothers have sent their daughters, and the committee has sent Adaira, to save them places on the public benches.

Mrs Poley is already in court; she has taken her seat in the centre of the front bench of the gallery, behind the dock where her grandson is now being directed to stand. She will face the magistrate across the room; when he looks up, there she will be. The correspondents are at a table in the well of the court; Henry, Magistrate Vos, when he enters, gives them a quick glance. Then he meets Mrs Poley's eye, and gives her a look of fury. He will not be cowed by her, his look says. Her grandson will answer for this, no matter the cost to him, the magistrate, when the case is over. Mrs Poley looks away before he does.

He sits, the gallery sits, and the dozen or so men among the anchored furniture, beneath the clock and a picture of the King high on the wall. Mr Theron, the lawyers, in fact most of the men in the well of the court, are dressed, like the magistrate, in full-sleeved black gowns over sober suits. Doep has found a jacket somewhere, and a tie. He turns once, quickly, to look at his grandmother. He has shaved and his hair is held back with grease. His face is mottled with fear. Now that it has begun, there is a chill of seriousness in the court.

One of the black gowns pushes back his chair, which gives a pterodactyl screech. He gets to his feet and addresses Henry. He says, 'Your Honour, in the matter of the Crown versus Du Plessis Hancock Poley ...' and the case is engaged, as though all in court, even those in the gallery, have at once hooked themselves to a moving chain that will carry them through the numbered stages until this matter is tooled up and tightened, and can be cast off, completed, at the other side.

London's man makes a note; after half a beat Jamestown does, too. Johannesburg holds out and then, as though a new thought has come to him, picks up his pencil and writes something in his small book on the table they share. The other two watch him, and seem poised to write again. Adaira thinks, Nothing has happened yet. Unless they are taking a long time to note Doep's full name, their notes must be the feared 'observations' about Gower, about this thing that Gower now is.

The public entrance door opens and closes and a townswoman hauls herself along the benches to the seat that has been kept for her.

In the court, Doep has pleaded not guilty and Henry is asking if the prosecutor, the man who stood to start them off, is ready to proceed to trial, and he says he is.

'Very well,' says Henry. He has so far used his everyday voice, and the prosecutor has used his normal voice back to him, and those in the gallery can only just hear them. Now the lawyer clears his throat, raises his head, fills his lungs.

He says, 'If it please the court,' and sets out the case against Doep, with all its 'night of's and 'accused's. The language, more than the black robes and the immovable furniture, brings home how grave this is. Adaira almost can grasp what the magistrate means when he speaks about The Law as though it is a real thing, a realm.

The prosecutor says, 'The Crown calls Sergeant Hannes Meter.' Gower's senior policeman enters through a door near the witness box with his leather-covered stick and a folder of papers under his arms.

The sergeant casts white-eyed glances at the correspondents each time they take up their pencils to note something he says. There does not seem to be much of a pattern to what is worth noting and what not. Adaira clears her mind and concentrates on what Sergeant Meter is saying. What might she write down about this?

He is saying that he was called from home at ten minutes after nine o'clock and the fire was raging and the water cart on its way. All were at Gevint's Haberdashers by half past nine, and the burned man, burned. They had not known who it was' – had thought it might even be the arsonist until Mr Gevint arrived and knelt beside the injured man and from there made his name known to the sergeant.

He says that he had 'acted on a tip-off' and sought out Doep Poley at his grandmother's domicile within the hour, that the accused was wearing trousers reeking of paraffin and would not explain this, nor say where he had been that night. A search of his tent turned up an expensive pair of trouser braces in a box hidden under a mattress; these would be identified by Mr Ira Gevint as being of a type kept in his shop and likely evidence of theft before the fire – 'Charge three, Your Honour,' the lawyer tells Henry in an aside.

He says that he had thought it best to question the accused away from his family members, away from … he falters … away from where his questions were answered by those family members, and he loses the struggle to keep his eyes on the prosecutor, and looks at Mrs Poley.

Adaira thinks of the thoughts Sergeant Meter must have, the things he must know, about the people he lives among. Does he know about her and Ira? Her feelings about the fire, about all that she has learned of Gower and herself, have unbalanced her so that she sees herself, and the town, from a low angle that causes its public faces – the committee, the policeman, the magistrate – to loom vertiginously.

Now Doep Poley is at the police station, being questioned, and sleeping in a cell and waking to be asked again, and he will not say where he was at the time in question. Will not, cannot. He has, says Sergeant Meter, no alibi.

What he does have is a record of criminal insult against the son-in-law of the injured man. And here they all are.

The lawyers have planned only so much, and it is not enough business to fill the afternoon. The court will rise and sit again tomorrow. The gowned men and Henry leave through their several doors, Doep goes down to the cells, the newspapermen and Gower's gallery come into the sunny afternoon, the world outside. They, the reporters, speak not about Doep Poley or the case at all, but about Henry Vos.

'Capable chap,' says London.

'Yes,' says Johannesburg. 'Yes, he's managing pretty well.'

Jamestown stays silent. Perhaps he, like Adaira, is trying to work out what they can mean – what conversation or shared opinion precedes this exchange and makes sense of it.

Johannesburg, ever ready to serve London as an interpreter, says, 'They are all over the place these days, of course. They mostly get the job in the first place because of the quota.'

'Oh yes?'

'Yes, something about a percentage of the civil service being able to speak Die Taal. Most of us don't speak it beyond a pretty basic level, so they've had to hire more of them. Overall, though, I'd say it's honoured more in the breach.'

Oh. That.

The court-goers have arrived in a calm, warm afternoon. Ahead, some way up Church Street, a farm cart is backing up to the wide double doors of the seed store, the cart low on its springs with fat sacks. In the traces, two feathery-hoofed horses step backwards, one careful step at a time, their heads tucked to their chests in dislike of what they are about. Men lead them backwards, step by step. Now the back of the cart is on the pavement, almost across it and in the store, but the front wheels lurch over the kerb and one of the sacks slips from the bed, falls heavily on the ground, cracks a seam. Adaira has left the reporters at the hotel; she has been walking towards the store up Church Street, and now she is close enough, and still far enough away, to see a smooth spill of shiny brown seeds, and above this, around the stilled cart and the hatless men scratching their heads and the horses nodding as if vindicated, a halo, a holy light of seed dust filtering the low sun. Her hands lift towards it to be part of it, this picture with something of the magical light of the day and something of the usual works of men.

Further up the street a Native child has an arm looped around the hollow metal pole of a street light. In his other hand is a stick; he hits the pole again and again, beating out a rhythm that carries far down the street. I am here, it says.

They will begin again tomorrow.

Today, Ira is in Jamestown to see about his lease on the ruined shop. The father-in-law, Gower's ghost, will leave town on the Wednesday train, his arm in a sling. Ira will follow him as soon as he is released from his court duties.

'And then I will try Johannesburg,' he tells Adaira that night, on the back streets of Gower, not taking her arm. 'Or Jewhannesburg, I should say. I have learned this from Burggraaff, this stupid boy.'

He almost smiles.

'It would be in my interests for this to be so. To find more like me. Here, we are only two, and this makes me for my comfort too much jüdisch.'

There is no talk or hint that she might go with him to pursue a life in the outside world. It only occurs to her later, when she is thinking through the day, that this has not been mentioned. It would have surprised her if it had been. To follow Ira, to know him outside Gower, would be like following a figure from a dream – like travelling to Jamestown or Johannesburg in the hope of meeting a man she dreamed was there. Does this suggest she has failed at her first attempt at love? She thinks she has, in several ways. This was a thin business, in the end, one that seemed to have left her untouched in a way that such matters ought not to. Although she has felt his weight on her, felt her body meet his, she has never looked properly at him, has never, she thinks now, met her human duty of seeing him.

That night she takes paper from the drawer of the table in her Theron bedroom, following an impulse to write out the brief story of them, to find in it or force from it its meaning, and as she describes the forbidden pair of them to herself, she realises with shamed surprise how thoroughly she has pressed Ira, the idea of Ira, into the mould of what she required, that which was required, to fulfil an essential step in her Gower apprenticeship. To do so (and *in* doing so, for it was a cycle with its own generative force, this blind way of seeing) she had kept him at an awkward, fictional distance, far enough away that she was not made to see him as he was, in all his defiance, loss, energy – and far enough away that she never saw how he regarded her.

She will not be enlightened for years about why she had done this. When she does at last grasp that the exercise in scripting Ira as she had – exotic, besieged, unknowable – had been to corkscrew out of the real man the materials for a sort of moral permission for herself, she will think back to the day she put down on paper what she knew of what had happened, seated at the little table in her lockable bedroom in the Theron house on one of Gower's more modest streets: that night, she will remember, she had noticed a curious thing – noticed it through nothing more profound than a tic of her penmanship that snagged her eye as she read over what she had written: Adaira could find his name in hers, she saw, hidden when she said it but plain as the sign on a shop window when she came to write it down.

Doep Poley's defence gets its turn with Sergeant Meter when the court day begins the next morning, and learns nothing new from him. It is already a bit dull, this: everyone can see that, as Mr Theron reported at breakfast, Doep did it, Doep with his history and without his alibi – perhaps not Doep alone, but Doep and someone – and the rest of this is surely just the work of filing papers.

But the papers must be filed and so the first lawyer calls Hotel Human's cousin, who was on the door that Saturday night at the dance, selling tickets and keeping kids and Happy Valley types out.

Doep Poley was there that night. The cousin had noticed that the accused was a bit shabby when he presented himself at the hotel soon after the doors opened for the dance, but his shirt was new at least, so he had sold him a ticket and let him in. He kept a bit of an eye on him, he says. The accused had stayed mainly with the other boys. The cousin had not seen him dance. In the dock, Doep's head jerks as if to challenge this or perhaps object to it being said.

He did not have his eye on the time, the man continues. Later, he was at the door, smoking a cigarette and keeping a lookout, when he saw the accused leave the hotel and head down Church Street. He thought there was another man just ahead of 'the accused Poley', as he calls him, a man looking at his pocket watch under the street light and also, says the hotel cousin, behaving like a man in a hurry.

The cousin hitches up his trousers and says both of them looked like men hurrying to something, and not just leaving the dance early.

The second lawyer makes a sound of objection.

The magistrate stirs to say, 'Upheld,' with the evenly stressed syllables of someone saying one thing while thinking hard about another.

After a pause during which no one speaks, or moves, the magistrate seems to wake. He turns towards the witness box to tell the cousin that he must say only what he remembers seeing, not what he thinks was on another man's mind.

The second lawyer stands up to claim his turn with the cousin, asking only, if he saw two men hurrying, how does he know it was not the other man who was on his way to Gevint's Haberdashers?

'I don't know that,' says the cousin, and continues, with heavy stress on the last three words, 'I only know what I saw.'

The magistrate is leaning forward in his chair. There is tension in his neck that suggests he is about to speak. In the gallery, there is a lick of interest at the possibility that he is angry with the man in the witness box. But it is to the first lawyer that the magistrate addresses himself when he asks, in almost his everyday voice, if this 'other man' will be called.

The lawyer picks up a slim sheaf from the desk in front of him and turns a page.

He says, 'Witness number four, Your Honour. A Mr Meurs?'

The correspondents lift their heads. They have the look of spectators, jaws loose and eyes flicking about. Adaira has no idea what has happened but, like the correspondents, she thinks that something has. Several of the men in the well of the court are holding themselves unnaturally still, weekend hunters who have seen their buck.

Mrs Poley stretches her spine, settles her shoulders and breathes what sounds like a sigh, with a nasal grunt of satisfaction.

From his elevated seat, Henry's thoughts lope out, ranging

for a scent, falling in at Poley's heels to track Meurs, Henry's upright, Trek-bearded, heedful neighbour.

In the dock, Doep Poley has tilted his head back as far as it will go, in the manner of a man pleading with or cursing God. The first lawyer, picking up the new strain of tension in the court, rises to cross-examine the hotel cousin. He slows his questions to pick apart the cousin's answers, unwilling to let him go. It is close, the thing the court is after, and he chases it, circling the small matter of Doep leaving the dance, but question by question the trail grows colder and at last the hotel cousin is allowed to leave.

The court adjourns for tea. A tea-girl knocks at the magistrate's door to bring in his tray. She finds the office empty. She sets down the tray and leaves the room, closing the door behind her. She does not notice that his gown is hanging from a wooden peg on the back of the door.

Henry is moving, fast, along a street behind the courthouse, headed for where the railway line cuts off the road. There is a sketchy fence between him and the tracks, and he leans into this like a man breasting the tape in a race, letting the top strand of wire tense against his outspread arms. He looks one way down the tracks, and then the other, noticing the thickness of the steel lines, their air of consequence. A dull glint near the tracks catches his eye and he ducks between the strands of the fence and crosses to the gravel bed supporting the tracks, where he picks up the piece of iron pyrites that had drawn him, and another piece, one of plain stone; this he flings down the line, putting a small conclave of sparrows to flight. He had not seen them there; he holds up an apologetic hand. Every movement he makes proves to him that time can be stretched.

The railway line marks this edge of Gower, or used to. To his right he can see a few homes that have spread beyond the tracks and relaxed into a sprawl of orchards and stands of mealies, almost smallholdings, and nearer than these and still contained by the tracks, beyond a stretch of back walls, he catches sight of a knot of scrap metal and jutting shapes that he realises is the back of the Hole in the Wall. He gazes at the puzzle of shapes without really seeing what he is looking at, until there is a shift in the silhouette and a shape resolves into a man, leaning, half-seated on what looks like the cylinder of a boiler, and Henry sees that it is Engel. Of course it is.

Henry hefts the glittering rock, the piece of fool's gold, in his hand, turns to look down the tracks in the other direction, plays with the idea of kneeling to press his ear to the hot steel to listen for a train, but the sense of danger in merely standing where he is standing, inside the railway reserve, straddling the left rail, with his back to the old man, is enough for him.

As he turns to retrace his steps he sees that Engel has moved beyond the Hole's backyard, taken a step or more than a few steps in Henry's direction. He has the eager forward-leaning gait and lifted hand of a man calling to a neighbour with news. Henry fears the evil old man with his scabbard of secrets, or perhaps his offer of silence, of partisanship against respectable Gower. But he dreads what is waiting for him in the court, too, and for a moment he stands suspended between the two.

The moving chain has its own momentum, however, and as Engel continues to come towards him, loud enough to hear now – he is definitely trying to speak to the magistrate – he ducks back under the fence and hurries away. He moves at an awkward clip, his need to flee clashing with his refusal to run, until his walk is a stilted rush and he despises himself for this and for every tight breath he hears himself take.

That afternoon they call Albertus Meurs, bring him into the room: Henry's neighbour, the first man, the man Hotel Human's cousin saw leaving that night ahead of the accused Poley. In a few businesslike answers Meurs tells the court that he was indeed looking at his watch, was heading home to make the last sluice opening of the week, the run of water into his miraculous miniature farm, leaving Mrs Meurs and one of the Misses Meurs at the dance with a promise to return.

And what can Henry do but stay as still as he can, inhabit the rhythmless, uncoupled drone of answers and questions, as though the lawyers and the hotel cousin, and Mrs Poley, and these scraps of consciousness who fill out the rest of the gallery, are just parts of his mind, just fleshed-out thoughts demonstrating an essential proof.

'You left the dance?'

'Yes.'

'To take care of your garden.'

'Yes. The leiwater. Yes.'

'This is a regular occurrence?'

'—'

'It happens at the same time every week? Every Saturday night?'

'That's right, every Saturday.'

'At what time does it happen?'

'At nine o'clock. From nine o'clock to nine thirty, that is my turn.'

'At nine p.m.!' The lawyer turns in triumph to the magistrate, but Henry is there before him, has been there since before tea.

Because of course Doep Poley has no pocket watch. If he has been the Poley grandson sent on his grandmother's errand to the magistrate's house every Saturday night – and Henry knows that he must have been – how else has he arranged to be there at the moment Henry kills the light on the veranda?

In six weeks of Saturdays Doep Poley would have learned, as any clever animal would learn, that the leiwater gate rattles in its channel at or about the time that the punctual darkness invites him to take the money.

Doep would have made himself clocks all around town, Henry guesses – the station clock, a watch held by the man at the Hole in the Wall, and Mr Meurs, a clock in himself. As long as he kept one of them in sight, he would have been in time to scoop up the coins in safety at the home of the careful Vos at an hour when the streets were empty and the dog gone from the garden.

Adaira, later, will find herself unable to separate what she knew then from what she would in time plot out and tease into a narrative with logic and guesswork. Years later, or in this moment, watching from the gallery, perhaps at the prompt of a growl from Mrs Poley, she sorts through memories of Johnny Hartshorn wearing the magistrate's soap smell, wearing the red braces the magistrate bought from Ira Gevint, of Mrs

Poley's jingling pocket, of the time on Church Street less than a month ago that she saw her pretend with a ridiculously turned head that she did not know the magistrate.

Adaira will one day see that it is Henry who, determined not to be swayed by what Mrs Poley knows about him, determined not to be cowed into corruption, has been braced to break Doep Poley on the law, to jail him for the attack on Ira Gevint's shop no matter what his grandmother knows about him, the magistrate.

And she will see that Mrs Poley is there to protect not her grandson but the magistrate, to see that Doep goes down for this rather than risk the stipend.

It had helped Henry Vos that Doep Poley was so clearly guilty – until he was not. That Doep was in fact in possession of an alibi was the one thing Mrs Poley must keep him from sharing with the court – but the magistrate knows it already.

Adaira will recognise at last that what had seemed to be Mrs Poley's pleased stretching of her spine, the settling of her shoulders, her happy sigh, was none of these things: this was a woman pulling herself upright, bracing her shoulders, stoking her courage for the trek to the next fruitful field, the next place that could feed this many-peopled Poley animal that she had undertaken to keep alive.

The magistrate, Mrs Poley would have known before he knew it, was spent.

In court, all that is said is that Mr Meurs left the dance before nine, and was followed by Doep Poley. Here is Sergeant Meter's proof, putting Doep outside the dance, heading towards Gevint's home and shop at exactly the right time. Only the magistrate, among all the court men, knows he must not have detoured to Gevint's but followed Mr Meurs almost all the way home to collect what his family was owed. Does not know with certainty, but knows nonetheless that that is where he was at nine o'clock on Saturday night when Ira Gevint's father-in-law woke in his bed at the back of the store on Church Street to the dreamlike pulsing light of flames.

The magistrate will not meet Mrs Poley's eye, and after a while she looks down at her lap, and concentrates on holding her grandson to his silence. And it is the case that Doep does not betray the magistrate by claiming his criminal alibi, and perhaps has even been resigned to allowing his conviction (and prison is no terrible thing, he would know, when freedom is Happy Valley), but his silence has no meaning; it was never going to be up to a Poley to stop this trial. Mrs Poley has Doep on her rein, but she cannot hold back the magistrate with his idiot luxury of honour.

A lawyer is speaking. The magistrate brings up a hand to silence him and asks both lawyers to meet him in his office. He leans over to speak to Mr Theron and after they murmur together for a moment, Mr Theron gets to his feet, coughs once into his hand and tells the room that the court will rise for the day. He does not say when it will sit again, and after an awkward pause he follows the magistrate out of the room. The correspondents' eyes sharpen as though the men know they are being cheated.

At the other end of the room the public gallery begins to shed its many spectators. Adaira is near Mrs Poley as they approach the door and hears her furious, frightened breaths.

20

NANTIE IS IN THE GARDEN when Adaira leaves for
the magistrate's. She is dressing herself in tiny blue
flowers, using their own sticky ends to attach them to her ears,
her hair, her sleeves. She heads Adaira off at the gate and presses a careful fan of them on her dress to make a brooch above
her breast.

For months Adaira had worn the enamelled powder-horn
badge there to earn Vena Cordier's tight glance of approval,
but on a recent morning, without ceremony, before she washed
or dressed or left her room, Adaira laid her coat on the bed
and unpinned the badge from its lapel. With her thumbnail
she worried at the pin holes until they no longer showed on
the cloth, and recalled the day she met Mr Cordier at Vena's
home and he loomed in the doorway, so much larger than
Adaira and Vena Cordier in their low chairs, as though to make
a point about who owned even the air they were breathing in
his front room.

There was no need to hand the badge back. It could be left
in a drawer.

Adaira guesses that the blue flowers are Nantie's way of
giving her support in these days when, just by entering the

magistrate's house, she invites the dreadful susurrus. She has earned the girl's acceptance without knowing how or why; she is aware of a complementary feeling in the somewhat lonely ease within herself.

The magistrate is in disgrace for letting Doep Poley go, on the blunt grounds of insufficient evidence. It had been understood that he would take care of this for Gower, but the case remains open. The weight of it still presses on the town. Things threaten to unsettle further before the outside world will let the matter go. There is talk of bringing in a new magistrate to try Doep all over again. There is talk of the magistrate himself coming before a hearing.

London and Johannesburg have made sure that the embarrassment has deepened. In roundabout allusion they put the matter down to the fact that the magistrate and the accused share a language, an affinity; *The Advertiser*'s editorial cartoonist puts Doep Poley, labelled with his name and with swastikas on his blinkers, in harness with Magistrate Vos, showing them as two donkeys fleeing their runaway hay cart. The hay is on fire.

Worst of all, what the magistrate did was puzzling, and the fact that he has not returned to his court in the days since he let Doep Poley off the hook is puzzling too. There is no easy blame to ascribe. Vena Cordier tries, of course: with her old familiarity with fear, she says Magistrate Vos lacked courage.

In his study in his fine house on Gower's best street, Henry puts down the newspaper that calls him a Nazi fellow traveller. He cannot laugh at it, but nor can he find much anger to spend on it. This equanimity stands in golden contrast to the years of turmoil that he can now so clearly recognise, the years when he was as uneasy as a half-broken horse, startling into anger or laughter at the smallest thing. Henry takes a deep breath and lets the gentle air, warmed by his chest, out again.

He can no longer imagine himself in Gower. He can see as far as a wretched, difficult meeting with his superiors in James-town to recuse himself from the arson case, resign himself from his magistracy, and convince them not to pursue a case against Doep – but beyond that? Will he be able to remember being an attorney? Is there a place in the realm of law for a man with the thoughts he has about what ought not to be subject to that realm?

The day after the case ended, Ira Gevint had stopped by to say farewell. At first he was as formal as a man from the previous century, and Henry realised from this that his visitor was offended, perhaps even hurt, by the way the case had ended, and he rushed to tell him that it had solely and completely to do with new evidence, evidence of a … sensitive … nature, that truly did undercut the Crown case against the Poley boy, and then he risked saying, in tones that matched Gevint's formality, that he could assure him that there had, of course, been no 'national consideration' in the decision. Henry despaired that he now seemed to live in a world that could make such assurances necessary, but this had been what Gevint needed to hear, and he had relaxed, and waved away Henry's somewhat vague apology.

The two men spoke about their plans. Gevint seemed to assume that Henry's would no longer involve Gower. He did not repeat his bitter crack about Jewhannesburg but reached past the conventions of conversation, reached through their shared dignity to meet Henry's eye and say, with seriousness and a note of urgency: 'Cities, Mr Vos, are better places for certain men.'

Henry had known a moment of terror at being seen. Ira covered his words immediately by taking the magistrate's hand and holding on to it after the downward tug of farewell, and offering another reading.

He said, 'There are more of us in the cities,' and Henry caught his breath at the 'us', the gift of it.

Henry has indeed begun to imagine another life. Perhaps the law, perhaps the bountiful garden of Johannesburg, a place casual as a whore's shrug about whatever you had decided to be. What he has decided to be. He has, he realises, begun to see his present circumstances as part of his past. The substance of his Gower life has revealed itself to be as fragile as the ash simulacrum of a branch after a fast, hot fire has been through: one tap and it could drop away to powder.

He looks up at the sound of his gate opening. Adaira.

Henry notices the flowers right away. He says: 'Plumbago.'

He is quiet again after this and Adaira reads his silence as despair and her spirits sink. She leaves him to make tea. Ephraim is ironing in a room off the kitchen. Only the thump of the iron and the shuffle of cloth break the silence, until kettle noises take over. She brings the tray to the study to find Henry gone from his chair at least. He is at the window, not looking out, but reading from a small book by its light. The orange cloth cover lends a flicker of colour to the room.

He looks up again, says, again, 'Plumbago.'

Then: 'The thing about language ... Plumbago is a blue flower that little girls use for earrings. But the flower is named for – you will not guess – lead. From the Latin plumbum. Plumb the depths. Out of plumb.'

He sounds calm. He carries on: 'In Ceylon, they mine it. A plumbago mine is hell on this earth, a dark filthy crack in the world where men scale ladders down and up to bring out chunks of soft black stuff, each one the size of a man's thigh. What we call graphite and they call plumbago. So which is it? Why is one word both?'

He has the beginnings of colour in his cheeks.

He says, as much to the window as to her, 'I worry that it comes down to fear.'

He has moved on from the graphite mine.

Is fear the reason he cannot muster enough hot blood to fight? Why he keeps his counsel and holds tight to his story, and reduces all matters to the tiny aperture of his own con-science – while the loud men of the town, even if they are defining morality for other men, are at least thinking beyond themselves? Have at least adopted a public faith? All he has is good taste and his privacy. His beliefs are too subtle for the light. Can't make a slogan out of such thin stuff, he says with a sad laugh. Try to gather them into a platform, these instincts about goodness, and they harden, their nature changes. His only argument against the new certainty is an inarticulate and mild fellow feeling, a philosophy of carrying on in a way that tends towards a balance of fairness. Much of what he believes is defined by what it is not: it is not Destiny, not directed, not loud. Not, he must admit, terribly effective.

He goes on, a tap running until the water is cool, until the water coming out is from deeper down, further from the place where it meets the air.

And at last he comes to the point ('Punctum, Adaira: a particular point, yes, certainly, and also the name given to the tiny hole in the corner of your eye that allows tears to flow, hah!').

He says, 'I will not let it be about fear.'

He crosses back to his chair, motions her to another, takes a cup of tea.

He swallows some of this and then swallows to prepare his throat.

He says, 'Something happened in Ceylon.'

He says, 'On a tea plantation, a big plantation, there is a building full of rooms they call withering lofts. Deep, long rooms. I don't think we have anything like it here. They lay the fresh tea leaves out on trays, hundreds of trays, and huge windows keep the air moving over them. They do this until the leaves are limp. Limp enough to take a twist, so that they can be rolled without breaking.'

He stops speaking and looks hard at her. Adaira does not truly hear him; her own thumping triumph blocks her attention because, before she quite realised that he had begun to tell his story, he has.

At one point he says, 'I am making it all up, you know.'

'You're making it up? Ceylon? Your, your ... Prem?'

'Oh, the facts are as they are − a boy fighter went to that country and all the rest, but the feeling of it, the experience, is imagined. I cannot truly remember having those feelings, just that I did.

'Of what happened, of love, I have no real recollection. Only that I – the I that I was then – knew it at the time. Now it is as though I am reading it on a page. As though someone else has described it for me.'

At one point she feels she has become a creature of dark greed and prurience, listening fervently to his secrets. She accuses herself of making a safe place for the magistrate and this Prem, this robed boy, of plying them with opportunity and watching through a keyhole or from behind a white-barked tree. She dislikes having this within her, this imperfect understanding that defaults to what she can imagine of wickedness. She hopes this wickedness in her own thinking will be exorcised by listening.

She listens. She forgets to remember that he said she would know his history only when he was gone.

21

ADAIRA COMES TO PACK IT UP, his papers and the Boer fighters' papers, some for her and most of them for Henry's Mr Hamilton in Cape Town, the man in the real museum. Johnny is at the house to collect things he says he was given; Adaira shuts Tertius in the kitchen and the two of them pick over what the magistrate left in the house where no one comes.

Johnny and Adaira do not speak. She cannot forgive Johnny, and Johnny can think only about what he was promised. He does not go so far as to claim the motor car abandoned under the pepper tree, but there is this. And this, and this. She is trying to ignore him although she is burning to find more in him to despise, burning to know where and how Henry Vos found this of all creatures. What is his meaning, this Johnny Hartshorn?

This is not the only question the magistrate left her with when he quit Gower in an impatient fury, thrusting at her the key to his home and a few hurried instructions, on the day he returned from seeing his superiors in Jamestown. Adaira is startled by his story. Ashamed of how little she has seen of what was before her all along. Belonging, ownership, being watched, being seen, being depended on, a hidden emotional life sped through in half a season by the magistrate who had seemed to stand so distinctly apart from the mess of the town. His burst of hidden belonging, as though he truly was a constituent – even a vital – part of the town's rushing bloodstream, its essential plasma: this is what startles her.

After an hour or so of the chest-sinking, awful work of touching Henry's things, and exhausted by the need to rescue his artefacts before Anna arrives – as she is bound to do tomorrow or the next day, to collect Tertius from Adaira's care, and the motor, and whatever else she will claim – Adaira allows herself to sit for a moment, drink a glass of water. Wretched Johnny Hartshorn somehow gets her to fetch him a drink, too, from the kitchen that Tertius will not let him enter.

When she comes out of the kitchen with his glass in her hand, while she is still in the dim hall, she sees Johnny on the edge of the veranda. He has a slingshot in his hand and is firing stones down the garden, aiming for the postbox on its pole next to the gate. He hits it. As she watches, he chooses another stone, fits it into the kettie and stretches his body into an archer's stance again.

There is no one in Gower to tell him to stop, no one apart from Adaira. The town has emptied to its edges to welcome a wagon that, all along, had planned to roll this way, to loop through Gower on its way to Jamestown, whatever the efforts of Vena Cordier to bring it and Henry Vos to keep it away, she with her petitions and collecting and effort, he by steadily despising the enterprise. The town has been allocated the wagon named Vrou en Moeder. It will not outspan here but only pass through. On the edge of town, Vena Cordier in her sinister bonnet and men in beards and unconvincing waistcoats have gathered to welcome it, to see history made or, as the magistrate would have put it, made up.

There are boys, marching boys, ready to outspan the oxen and pull the wagon in on their own shoulders (although after fierce whispers between the men on the wagon and Mrs Cordier, it will be judged that there is no time for this if they are to reach Jamestown tonight) and other boys with cement to set the wagon's tracks for all time. Gower, preoccupied, turned inward and, moving carefully until its own turmoil should settle, will not, as other towns have, bring its brides or babies to be blessed at the wagons, but there will be shouting along Church Street and weeping from some of the old men. As the wagon, having made its ponderous turn at the other end of the main road, passes the courthouse on its way to join the Jamestown road, a girl in a white dress will reach behind a slow rear wheel to scoop out axle grease and, crying to Jesus, smear the stuff across her breasts.

The Therons have gone to see the wagon, too. Standing further back than the believing boys, but they are there.

On the veranda of the magistrate's empty house, Adaira watches Johnny shooting the postbox, sets the picture of him in her mind, trusting that his meaning will, in time, be discovered by her.

22

A LMOST A DECADE AFTER HER year in Gower, Adaira allows herself to visit the rock monument the town raised to the Centenary Trek, next to the crumbling tracks set in cement. It has taken these years away from the town for her to forgive Gower its monument enough to look it over. She has hated it before seeing it; it lives in her thoughts with the memory of the magistrate in flight, shooting gravel from his wheels as he left town ahead of the advancing wagons, his life cut back to what would fit in two panniers on the Indian.

A postcard had followed, Joubert Park looking towards the Art Gallery: 'Made landfall safely. Natives friendly. Letter to follow, Henry Vos'.

A year after Henry left Gower in such haste, war had found a use for Adaira. She assumed the unlovely tag ASWAAS and found herself among SWANS, anchored off Cape Town in late 1939 on what the receiving officers liked to tell recruits they must think of as a static battleship defending the Allied ships, but was really only Robben Island. She was a soldier at last, useful, directed, and even an honorary white man for the duration, or so she heard in the regular reminders that the dozen women doing this job were there to replace men spared for more important work.

Her duties on the island as a member of the Artillery Specialists of the Women's Auxiliary Army Service had been entirely absorbing, so that she grew habituated to absorption. Her daily round – sometimes high above sea level and at other times in a deep bunker – involved the twinned tasks of cross observation and underground plotting. Only rarely did she visit the battery of big guns whose range and bearing she helped set. On another part of the island, sister SWANS sat in silent communion with their headphones, straining for the pings of midget submarines. All of it was entirely unreal and then as ordinary as breakfast, and in the strange half-light of her wartime days she had felt herself fold closed as smoothly as the Cape daisies, the Spaanse Margriet that clung to the island's sandy soil.

A letter from Henry had indeed followed, and found her on the island. Tucked into the envelope was a postcard of gentle Miss Fairfax on her cloud of marble. She was, said Henry, his favourite in the gallery, and reminded him of her, Adaira.

Then he had proceeded to fill two pages. The Highveld climate was superb, he wrote. He told her about the park outside the gallery and described in detail an encounter with a parrot at the zoo. He listed the dishes he had sampled at a fine rich restaurant and the books on his new shelves, in careful, clever words. He ended with an anecdote, apparently intended to amuse, about a miner on payday buying a saddle, all of it in tones that carried the chill of having been written for posterity, or to a stranger.

She made herself read to the end, gleaning only one true thing: the pleasure he took in having found work defending people under the laws he had so lately spent his days judging them by. For the rest, she heard again his repulsing charm, the same hollow charm of their long-ago veranda meeting, when he had succeeded in erecting a barrier of diversion between them, and realised that his true impulse, beyond the good manners and generosity that made him write, was to slip away to his new life with no trace of Gower on him. He had sought escape from them all, and this must, in the end, include her.

A decade since she last saw him, and still she misses him with a stab of petulance when she discovers that the inscription on the Gower monument to the Centenary Trek is carefully worded to hide the fact that no trekker wagon passed this way on the first, great, trek, that no wagon came except that one in the simulation of a commemoration in the year inscribed here, with its flags and hungry marching boys and thin cry to Jesus, a pre-echo of the halting procession that in this monumental year of 1948 has carried the nation all the way back to Pretoria, clutching God's promise.

There is no one left to share the memorial to false history, the acrid joke.

The people of Gower have raised it, their cairn, on what was once the edge of town not far from where, one night, Johnny and Henry met for the first time. She eventually got that much out of the boy as she and Johnny sorted through Henry's things in the house he had shed. When she has seen enough of the cement tracks – she can almost hear Henry on the heavy, heavy mark their people feel they have to leave – she carries on to a certain willow tree to see what more she can find of a truer story, Henry's story.

In the years since she left, Happy Valley's tin town has abated, like a stream that spread beyond its banks for a season and is already back in the channel – a catastrophe that turned out to be the merest rumour of a flood, just enough to concentrate Gower's fear, to feed the tinnitus of dread they had to drown with shouting. The Poleys of that place are sure to be Railways Poleys these days, pulled tight to the bosom of the town, stupefied with dull work and regular shillings, employed chiefly in order that they be kept out of mischief, kept ready.

Adaira comes back from her walk to the willow tree bearing the gift she found there, a last gift from him, to do with the habits of imagining he taught her, the way he showed her how to watch those she was among, to try to see all of what they were, and recognise what she saw.

She was there at the moment the street lights surged and flickered and came on as night fell. The light behind her lit up, and a string of them down the road, but not the one above her. Dark, it is the single note added to her museum of his memories and her imaginings that – after the process of time passing and things that come in dreams, of cross observation and underground plotting – completes the mix, and Henry stands before her, more real than when she knew him in Gower, when he pressed against her, made her laugh, leaned to kiss her on the mouth.

Her car is parked in front of the Gower Hotel, on what has

been known, since that shouting week, as Voortrekker Street. The back seat and boot are crammed with boxes and a pair of suitcases. A smaller case has already been carried upstairs to her room in the hotel. Adaira's night in Gower is a detour on her trip from Cape Town to Johannesburg: she is moving cities, and all she owns is in her car. She has to open more than a few boxes by the light of a street lamp before she roots out what she is looking for, but at last she finds them, the solid stack of dark-green logbooks she had helped herself to on her last day on the island. Since then she has hefted them from barracks to digs to a flat of her own; now she takes one from the stack and packs away the rest. Between the sturdy boards of the cover are cool grey pages, ruled, with a margin.

Adaira dines alone. After dinner she sits on the veranda of the Gower Hotel, smoking and watching the town settle for the night. She recognises the odd face on the street but is not, she thinks, recognised herself. At last she gathers her cigarette case and lighter, steps down from the veranda to the street to breathe in Gower's evening air, and then she goes inside.

There is a table in her room. On it she has laid the green book and a pen. With the broken street light in mind she writes fast, deep into the Gower night, with Ira and Henry watching from the room's darkest corners and her own heedless apprentice self pacing behind her, waiting for her cue.

And after all, this, too, is a beginning:

The first light, or the last light, depending, is a disappointment to the man in charge of the twenty-nine street lights of Gower. It is always out of step with the others. They will burn steadily but this one will suddenly need to be replaced, and in the week when the rest of them blink out, it will burn on, outlast the week, the month, the months. It is a blot on the orderly order book of, a disorder in the store cupboard of, the man in charge. Twenty-eight bulbs in concert and then this otherwise one, this odd man out.

The light stood at what was then almost the edge of town. Nearby, showing as a doorway and a shuttered face during the day, was a place of the sort found somewhere in most towns of this size. It promised, at once, safety and risk, this hole in the wall – the safety and danger one might find in a pack of doglike creatures: domesticated wolves or house dogs who have gone too long without a master.

It was no place for the magistrate of the town; he was perhaps the one person – or he and the dominee – whose presence there was impossible, uncomfortable, to imagine. The station commandant used the place early in the evening, most evenings; the doctor bought his brown bags there when the hotel off-licence was closed. They were tolerated as visitors. The magistrate would not be, he knew.

Nonetheless, miserable and doubting his place among men, casting about for a way to be when all his schemes for inventing himself had failed, the magistrate had set out one night for the greasy tavern. He had come no closer than across the street, where he stopped under a street lamp and waited. At length a boy had crossed the street to him. The deal was quickly done, the magistrate's shillings carried back across the road where, he could see, heads leaned towards one another in the lit room. He had, after all, found a way to visit it, and this became his lonely habit on the nights that followed.

But on this night a different boy appeared with his bottle. He stumbled from the doorway as though he had been pushed, then recovered his balance and walked towards the magistrate, holding the creased paper bag.

When he was a bit more than an arm's length from him, the boy stopped. He stood just within the circle of light cast by the street lamp. He did not speak or hand over the bottle, but only looked at Henry. The magistrate was taken aback, annoyed, but even as he jerked his head to signify this he felt as though he were part of something that had been reset by the boy's odd behaviour. They had been moving on one track – a very slightly fraught, but mindless, exchange of money for brandy, late at night, on the street, illegal, but hardly prosecutable even if he had not been who he was – and the boy had jumped that track. He seemed to be weighing up whether to return to it, or start a new thing.

Henry tilted his head, raised his hands, made a question without speaking. His own palms looked very white and smooth in the light, as though they had been cast in wax. This dreamlike circle of light, the absence of words, the break in the expected order of things, these sharpened his thinking.

He could see, for instance, that the boy had pitted skin on his cheeks, and hooded eyes, silky dark brows that contrasted with his childishly blond hair. He was watching Henry from under those brows.

Henry dropped his hands to his sides. He took a deep breath and looked around. He decided to wait out the boy and say not a word, to be a passenger in whatever was intended.

The boy stepped alarmingly close to Henry, holding up the flat half-jack in its packet. Taking it, Henry felt their hands touch. The boy did not step back, but looked over Henry's face, his beard, his mouth, and it came to Henry with a cool flush of fear that the boy intended to seduce him, if that was even the word for what was afoot here. Henry bit back a laugh, almost spoke, swallowed an impulse to commend the boy on his courage. All he could let himself do was blink at the surprise of it. If that was really what it was: it could be the prelude to a lunge with a knife, or a knee slicing up towards his groin. They were almost the same height; Henry was heavier and, he guessed, stronger.

'Got a smoke?' the boy said. His voice was flat, poor.

Henry croaked the beginnings of an answer, stopped, cleared his throat, managed: 'I don't smoke.'

The boy shrugged and slid a hand into his trouser pocket, drew out a half-pack and a box of matches.

'Then I suppose I won't offer you one,' he said.

Henry frowned. 'No.'

The boy sighed. There was an edge of impatience to it. Afterwards, when Henry went over every word and tried to put a number to the moments when nothing was said, he took the sigh as the starting point: it was his cue to clear his throat again, lick his dry lips, or whatever it took, and so he had – drawing the cork from the bottle, offering it first to the boy, then sucking hard on it himself, and falling into step with him as he turned, not back towards the tavern, but down the road they were on, towards the little spruit that crossed under it.

At the stream, the boy guided Henry, without touching him, to the edge of the culvert, then jumped down to the wide dry bed of the stream and made for a stand of trees, looking back once to see that Henry followed. With both hands, the boy parted the trailing branches of a weeping willow and stepped into the cave they made.

Henry looked about him; there was another street light not too far from where he stood, but it picked up no other person. He eased himself down to sit on the edge of the road, found the next level with his feet and, ducking his head from whoever, whatever, might be watching, made his way to the tree and between the branches.

The boy was barred in light and shadow, and his face was mostly in darkness, pricked by the coal of his cigarette. Then the branches or the boy shifted and Henry could see his face; he had one eye squinted shut against the smoke of his cigarette. The open one was in the unfocused state of a man turning a crank handle or about some other small everyday task. His hands were at his belt, then his trouser buttons, then his sex, which he tugged free of the cloth. He plucked the cigarette from his mouth and dropped it at his feet. His penis bobbed as he stepped on the coal. Henry, who had begun to tremble, did not otherwise move and for an instant, for the first time since he had taken Henry's shilling, the boy looked uncertain. Then Henry stepped to him.

Once they were done with setting down the bottle, and freeing Henry from his trousers, and finding their balance against the wide trunk of the willow, and a sharp pain in Henry's nose as their faces knocked against one another, it was a surprisingly graceful matter. The boy, it turned out, was a bit shorter than Henry. Henry looked past his head at the leaf and light patterns and felt his legs, his chest and arms, grow dense, grow thick with blood, held in an almost immobile, one-armed embrace, a wrestling hold, while their hands took their pleasure.

'You sure?' The boy held out his pack. In the striped light Henry shook his head. He and the boy were seated in the cave of leaves, side by side. The boy struck a match, held it to the end of his cigarette, then did not immediately shake it out. He moved it towards Henry's face, then back towards his own, and said, 'Johnny.'

'Henry,' Henry said, frightening himself, remembering all else that he was. The match burned out.

'I seen you. You the magistrate,' the boy said. Perhaps the boy heard his sudden breath, because he added, 'Ag, don't worry. I'm not like that. I like you, man.' And again, 'I'm not like that.'

He pulled on his cigarette, said softly, as he looked around the cave under the branches, 'I like you.'

The boy brushed a small clearing in the leaf litter by his side and crushed the cigarette into the ground. He yawned, then got to his feet and held out his hand to Henry.

'Come on,' he said.

Henry stood. He felt that if he spoke he would sound feeble-minded, blunted. The only thought he had was to get away – get away and contrive to never see this boy again. What he offered, the release, was not worth this fear, or this shame, or the risk of Engel so close in the dark. He remembered the boy stumbling from the door and he was suddenly certain of Engel's grinning, grimy presence behind him, sending the boy out of the bar for some evil purpose of his own, driving him towards Henry.

Johnny showed no awareness of Henry's chill. He was fonder than he had been before they entered the privacy of the tree, and now he was being sleepily familiar, brushing willow-leaf shards from Henry's jacket, tugging it into line. He picked up the half-jack and slipped it into Henry's pocket, then held aside a curtain of willow branches and gestured for Henry to precede him back to the dry bed of the little stream, back to the road.

It was bright out there, too bright under the street light. The magistrate held back, deeply afraid of being seen with the boy coming from this place, and his fear twisted into a sort of defensive outrage on his own behalf. He was better than this. Who did he think he was, this rough boy? Having felt the agony of thawing as he warmed himself with Johnny's body, he was desperate to retreat back to numbness.

Henry stepped to the edge of the tree's shelter, but would go no further. The boy crossed the ground and sprang from the stream bed onto the road, and looked over his shoulder at the willow. He saw Henry hanging back and smiled at him, his hands on his hips. The yawning boy of a moment before was now capering, playful, and the anger in Henry stuttered at this, but still he could not go to him. He told himself he was untouched by the embrace, the release. He wanted tonight to be done and himself back in his lonely remove.

He did not move from where he stood at the parted curtain of branches.

The boy nodded, then seemed to decide something. He widened his eyes at Henry and called softly across the open ground, 'Wait there. Just a sec,' and Henry saw him stoop over, then pull something from his trouser pocket and step backwards once, twice. He tilted backwards at the waist, holding one arm rigid before him, the other drawn back. Henry heard the whistle of a stone leaving the kettie; it glanced off the metal frame of the light and spun away. The boy grunted, chose another stone and again leaned at the waist to shoot it at the street light. This time the bulb broke with a crack and a pop, and in the swift darkness the boy laughed, congratulating himself.

'It's safe now. Come on, Your Honour,' he said, and stood at the lip of the culvert, his hand out to invite Henry up from the stream bed to the dark road. Henry stood for a moment longer, looking across the open ground towards the dark shape of the boy, and something changed in him.

Only later would he attach a theory to this change: that, having been offered this unlikely small gesture of help, he had in a flood, a subterranean flood of his inner self, begun to understand the world anew. That this understanding took so long after that night to surface in him, and did so only after he had been shown again the impossibility of the world as it related to him – after the court case where he was taken to the lip of the chasm of shame that waited for him – was not the point. The world might withdraw love from him if it knew his true self – it almost certainly would – but that, for him, was not the point either.

The understanding would come later; at the time, that night under the broken street light, he felt his life being held, unmoving, for a long beat. There came to him the idea of the ocean holding itself still, and he being given the privilege of looking, for as long as he needed to, right into a wave.

He got moving, took the boy's hand and gained the road. The boy kept hold of him. They did not kiss again. They stood close, not speaking. It was almost as if they were scenting one another, each breathing the other in.

Sounds – voices, breaking glass – reached them from the direction of the tavern. The two of them moved apart. The boy shepherded Henry onto the road that would take him to the town proper and home, then took his leave with – another small pop of surprise – a handshake.

'Goodnight, sir,' he said, turned on his heel and was off down the street, his hands in his trouser pockets. The magistrate watched him go, then set off himself. His legs, at first so heavy as to feel they were not part of him, gathered pace and lightness as he walked through the sleeping town, and by the time he turned into his own street he was moving smoothly as a boy of seventeen, a boy whose open face was known to all the world.

The man in charge thinks about replacing the bulb in the rogue lamp even when this is not called for, just to get them to line up, Adaira decides. But he cannot waste one like that; he curses number twenty-nine, yet leaves it to burn on until it goes out in the middle of the normal cycle, the cycle of the rest. He will leave the problem to his successor in the municipality, as he had inherited it when the job was created and he was named to it, just before the war of all nations from which he was turned away as not fit to fight.

His unfitness for war and the eccentricity of the twenty-ninth lamp post chafe against one another in his thoughts until he comes to ascribe willed spite to the lamp. Which is one of those odd things you come across from time to time, Adaira thinks as she puts down her pen: he made the lamp post stand for spite, when what really had been witnessed by its rough cast metal and in its lumpy paint, flaking in layers like a contour map where the ornate base had taken a knock, was kindness, the slender thread of kindness between men that in time may thicken, and bear their weight.

NOTES

DETAILS OF THE BOERS' SURRENDER, Diyatalawa Camp and Ragama are taken from *Recollections of a Boer Prisoner-of-war at Ceylon* by J.N. Brink, published by Hollandsch-Afrikaansche Uitgevers-Maatschappij in 1904, although *The Magistrate of Gower* departs from Brink's history in several respects.

Many of the Boer names used here are borrowed from the war graves and Boer War Memorial in the Old Burying Ground in Simon's Town.

The bill quoted on pages 80–81 became the Immorality Act of 1927.

On page 89, the phrase 'The Governor General is the Supreme Chief of all Natives …' is taken from the Native Administration Act of 1927, as amended a dozen times until it was overtaken by apartheid legislation in the 1950s.

Mother Vos's musings on her own obsolescence on pages 97–98 owe much to *Woman and Labour* by Olive Schreiner, first published in 1911.

The judgment quoted at length on pages 104–106 is an edited, but not embellished, version of *Rex* v. *Gough and Narroway*, case number 159 in the Cape Provincial Division, handed down on 15 December 1925 by Mr Justice Gardiner with Justices Searle and Louwrens concurring, followed by gleanings from similar cases from the period.

On pages 146–148, Senator 'Hunter' Halgryn's arguments proving the existence of God belong to Senator Dr W.P. Steenkamp as expressed in his book *I Conclude: Convictions and Experiences of a Free-thinking Doctor and Hunter*, published by Juta & Co in 1947.

The kruithoring or powder horn on an orange field was adopted as a logo by the Purified National Party, soon to be known as the National Party, only in 1939; it appears here on the Party letterhead and various lapels a year early.

The translated (and somewhat truncated version) of the Suid-Afrikaanse Vrouefederasie anthem on page 157 is taken from 'Man-made women: Gender, class and the ideology of the *volksmoeder*' by Elsabe Brink in *Women and Gender in Southern Africa to 1945*, edited by Cherryl Walker, where it reads, in full:

'Tis glorious to carry the name of daughters of South
    Africa
There's work, there's work, my sisters, work for women
    devout,
And free and strong! To serve her nation, honour her
    God,
O Lord, guide her Yourself, the woman, in service of
    her nation,
In honour of her God, guide her Yourself, the woman,
    O Lord!

The phrase 'static battleship' on page 311 and details of the work done by women on Robben Island in World War II come from the South African Military History Society's *Military History Journal* Vol. 13, No 1 (June 2004): 'Robben Island's Role in Coastal Defence, 1931–1960' by Marinda Weideman.

ACKNOWLEDGEMENTS

F ROM THE DEPARTMENT OF JUSTICE to several lit-
ters of siblings, and from Clanwilliam to Colombo, this
book found good friends. Thank you to James Robertson and
Lucy Neal, Julia Sullivan and Helen Sullivan, Anton Ferreira
and Leon Ferreira, and Aubrey Paton. Beth Lindop, Jenefer
Shute and Fourie Botha gave invaluable advice and guidance,
and for this I thank them. Thanks, too, to the Office of the
Registrar of the Western Cape High Court, Cape Town, and
to Gillian Kay at the Department of Justice and Constitu-
tional Development.

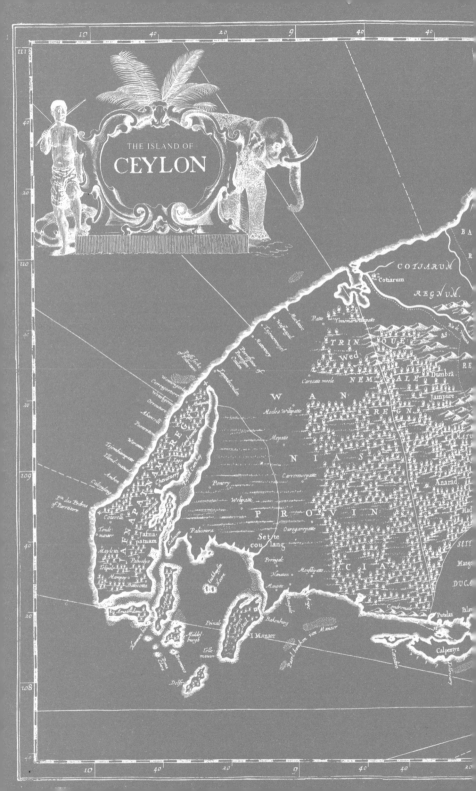

THE ISLAND OF
CEYLON

COTIARUM
REGNUM
Cotiarum

TRIN QUE
Wed
NEM ALE
Dumbra
Jampure

W
A
N
REG.

N
I
A
S
Masles Welipatte
Meyatte
Carronwerpatte
Anarad
Poncry
Welipatte
P R O V I N
Oweginerepatte
Set te
cou lang
C I A
Mango
Perriode
Nanaues
Mostlygatte
DUCA
Minatte
Comdermale
Putela
Palicoura
P.ta das Pedras
of Barribure
Couvele
Toute
manar
Yafnapatnam
Manaer
Calpentyn
Mayleu
Paboothy
Dipola
Manpay
Badecotte
Boxenbaey
Priccla
I Manaer
Middel
burgh
Tollo
manar
Delft